Big Morning Blues

GORDON WILLIAMS

reinkarnation

www.reinkarnationbooks.com

Once you're dead you're made for life

JIMI   HENDRIX

John Smith had been dangling for fifteen minutes on the Tyburn gallows when the apologetic bearer of his reprieve emerged from the huge crowd. The hangman cut John Smith down. He revived. The multitude cheered. That was December 12, 1705.

1

MY STICKY EYES OPEN under a mesh-shielded bulb set in a ceiling far above human reach.

I am horizontal on a brown leather mattress so thin it only underlines the grind of hip-bone on slab planking.

My face is inches away from a wall of dull yellow tiles, their oily surfaces an exquisite filigree of cracked varnish. Lifting my head I see a heavy door with an eye-level hatch.

Above me is a window of thick, opaque panes in a metal frame.

I cannot remember being locked up.

I try to clear my head by screwing my eyelids tightly shut, at the same time contracting vestigial ear muscles.

My head fills with that tiny roar children think is the sea inside a shell. Is it the noise of muscles in movement? Is the whole body loud with sounds we never hear?

Thoughtful of Him not to put our ears too near our arses.

Twisted round my trousered hips is a leprous, mud-coloured item, more holes than blanket. It has a stench that is almost visible. It has obviously been here for a hundred years, a mockery of comfort for generations of frightened nobodies.

Taking care not to let their accursed rag touch my bare hands I jerk my hips until it slithers to the green floor.

I flop back, panting. Fuck them and their stinking blanket. The cell is silent and still. I shudder. The movement of my body against the hard wood under the mattress makes me feel soft and disposable. I would turn on a display of maniacally concentrated violence, just to let them know I am not a disposable nobody, but that would be stupid. You cannot leave your mark on a cell. The skull will fracture, smash and flatten before it could add a single hairline crack to these tiled walls. No boots made for man can dent that door. The leather of the mattress has a texture teeth could not rend.

There is only one way to beat them. Stay cool. Do not give them an inch of satisfaction.

But I am not really a hard man, am I? Not at the core: whenever I am not looking directly at the walls or the door they seem to be moving.

I move my eyes this way and that, fast then slow, trying to analyse this hallucinatory phenomenon.

Staring along the ridges of my nose I see, for the first time, a message printed crudely on the door:

> *Please God*
> *just one*
> *more chance*

Somebody managed to make a mark then.

I hate people who whine.

I lift my wrist high enough above my chest to see my wristwatch. It says 3.55, whether post or ante-meridian only time will tell, if I live that long.

To go to the lavatory I have to stand up, there seems no other way. My heart has become a stable for a small, violent horse. The yellows and greens, the smooth tiles, the gloomy but inescapable lighting, the secondhand oxygen, all make it feel like drowning at the bottom of a fishtank.

The lavatory is behind a tiled baffle-wall. The pan is choked and overflowing. The stink is strong enough to lean on. I switch to mouth-breathing but the taste is worse than the smell. My contribution cascades little breakers over cracked porcelain onto an already wet floor.

"This heavy drinking will be the urination of you," I growl, to cheer myself up. The walls come an inch closer.

Wet footprints mark my route back to the bunk. Clothes rasp on skin. Every time I breathe I have a fearful sensation of falling over a cliff. This cliff seems to be inside my body.

I stretch out on the bunk and tell myself that all the evidence points to the likelihood I was drunk last night.

On past form this is no shock.

Half-Hanged Smith didn't think death was too bad—a commotion of spirits he called it. The most painful part was blood returning to his veins after they cut him down. Hanging was no deterrent in his case for he was soon on trial again for burglary. He was found innocent. Nothing daunted he went back to crime and was caught again. The day before his third trial the prosecutor dropped dead. They abandoned the case. Half-Hanged Smith seemed to have had enough. He disappeared.

2

My real name is Ian Mintlaw McGraw. I was born the only child of Protestant parents in Shettleston, a residential part of Glasgow. My father, a boiler-maker, ran away with a woman from our tenement close when I was eight. Her name was Mrs Norah McCafferty. She left seven ragged-arsed little Papists for her husband to bring up. The biggest of them, Michael, and I fought each other regularly.

My mother frequently paid five shillings to Mrs Ferguson the speywife, whose racket was reading tea-leaves or cards. She said my father was alive but unhappy, exactly what my stupid mother wanted to hear. Even at ten I was too cynical for that peasant superstition crap.

My mother got a job in a hairdressing salon and claimed we were middle-class because I had shoes, even for playing in. Her job meant that I usually always came home from school to an empty house—as we called our one-room flat, a 'single-end' in Scottish parlance. I was supposed to do my homework and then get her tea ready. If I played football in the street or 'got up to' any of my boyish tricks she used to belt me with my father's old razor-strop, at least until I became big enough to hit back.

One of my boyish hobbies was killing cats. Our tenement was crawling with the filthy brutes. I would put a saucer of milk just inside the door and wait till a big scabby one came slinking into the lobby and belt it over the head with a hammer. Then I'd shove it head first down the lavatory and sit on the seat until it was drowned.

I got most of my early culture that way, reading the latest Hank Jansen book while neighbours rattled the door of the shared lavatory and half-drowned cats tried to rip the arse out of my trousers.

I was bright but lazy. The English master said my compositions had originality. The music teacher said I had perfect pitch and wanted me to take singing lessons. He was one of those dopes who have a mission to open new vistas for slum children. Singing lessons!

At fifteen, through the owner of the hairdressing salon, who was big in the Masons, I was fixed up to see the works manager of a local newspaper, a rag which people bought only for the hatches, matches and despatches.

They couldn't take me as a printing apprentice because the union had a strict quota but they wanted a lad to help with the advertising—two pounds a week and five per cent commission. I was keen to be a printer because everybody knew they drank a lot and could tell the bosses to shove it but my mother fancied me in a collar and tie instead of dungarees, us being middle-class.

I had to paste sample ads onto clean sheets and take them round the local shops, telling lies about the circulation to persuade those tight-fisted bastards to buy space. I earned about twenty pounds commission in two years. I was always in dread of the sack, being young and stupid, a weakness I soon cured.

As soon as I knew what time of day it was I started writing away for jobs in England. My first was in Newcastle. I was nineteen. I gave my mother more notice of my leaving than my father did—a whole week. I've never seen her since. She may very well be dead.

It didn't take me long to reach London. I had twelve or thirteen jobs, all in advertising. Once I had a go at something different; an Irish bloke I knew was making good money buying five shilling doorknockers wholesale and selling them door-to-door in dim suburbs like Alperton and High Barnet as genuine brass at two quid a time. Corridan specialised in frustrated housewives but I soon got bored—most of them had varicose veins. I have always been easily bored.

I lived all over the place-Brixton, Kilburn, Earls Court, Wandsworth Common—and Chelsea, briefly. I spent a lot of time in pubs looking for Life. I even started going in for talent night competitions, singing sentimental ballads and often picking up prizes of ten shillings or a pound. A couple of people, especially a queer pianist in a Brixton pub, said I should try to go semi-professional but the way he described it you needed a lot of bullshit to break in.

It never bothered me that I was drifting aimlessly because I always had it in my head I would one day be A Somebody. Maybe I would be discovered as a singer without scratching round for auditions. I used to write bits of songs and the first pages of TV plays. Or maybe I would become a gag-writer for a top comedian. The options were endless and in your twenties you think it's all going to last for ever.

Then I more or less drifted into The Rookery.

I met this girl, Deborah, when I was an advertising rep for a give-away paper in Wandsworth and she wanted to get married. I wasn't daft about her but I was tired of cafe meals and digs. As soon as we were engaged she wanted me to get a better job, with prospects, to make Daddy happy. I wrote to a box number in the *Daily Telegraph*—assistant advertising manager of a new magazine at two thousand a year and ten per cent commission.

I only applied to keep her quiet but you know how it is, the job you don't give a fuck about is the easiest to land.

It turned out to be one of the new sex magazines—the same old tit and bum stuff only they didn't touch out the pubic hair, and yards of spankwank letters. I started to make a lot of money. I also met Neville Thirsk, alias The Beast.

He was a freelance who did occasional articles about bondage whores, flagellation parties, sauna baths. Nobody knew much about him, although when he got drunk they knew about him two streets away. I've always been a drinker but he didn't mess about with small measures.

I was twenty-seven then and he was twenty-nine, although his blond hair and country-boy complexion made him look younger than me. His complete lack of guilt impressed me. Nobody ever got an apology from Neville The Beast. The nearest he'd get to sorry was a smile and a wink:

"That's me, old son, Thirsk by name and thirst by nature."

He had an office in The Rookery, which I'd always avoided under the impression it was only a tourist trap. He introduced me to such exciting dens as The Armpit Club, The Hum Drum and The Amorous Congo. It was a safe bet that any woman you met on that circuit was available and if you didn't pull an amateur there were plenty of whores. I've never been one of these lying bastards who say they've never had to pay for it. A lot of the time I find it's cheaper to pay for it.

I told Debbie we were no longer engaged.

For several weeks she kept phoning me with pleas and threats. She even came to the magazine office one lunchtime but I got out by the fire-escape.

Then the sex magazine collapsed, the owner disappearing with the liquid assets to Spain, leaving us in a pandemonium of bouncing cheques and hysterical creditors—most of them no-hope freelance hacks doing their nuts over a couple of nights' drinking money.

The Beast came into the pub while I was pondering my next move. After a few drinks he suggested I go to work with him. I said I was cheesed with business and fancied doing something creative. He said he'd always had the idea of writing a smash-hit musical about the Duke of Wellington, about whom he had read a book. By the time the pub closed we were a hotter team than Rodgers and Hammerstein.

That night I kipped in his posh flat over the Thames at Battersea. He had married money. His wife was a big blonde, the beauty queen type. She didn't like me from the start but he said she didn't like most of his friends. He always referred to her as The DOM – The Duchess of Moody!

It was his idea that I could change my name and save myself a lot of money; income tax had been deducted at source from my sex magazine salary but not from my commission cheques. I owed tax on about two thousand pounds.

I decided to use the name John Thompson after the Glasgow Celtic goalkeeper who got his neck broken in a Glasgow–Celtic game in the thirties. When I was a boy in Glasgow he was a fenian hero, along with Benny Lynch the boxer. It was a little private joke on all those Masons and Orange bastards I'd been brought up among.

Neville said he would pay me forty pounds a week in cash out of the band agency money until we saw how our various new enterprises turned out.

" Skinning the government is the modern man's last frontier," he said. "My accountant is as bent as an electric golfclub, he'll wash it all away in the books."

I didn't bother to get a self-employed National Insurance card. By changing my name and disappearing into the Rookery I got rid of all obligations and responsibilities. On paper I ceased to exist; I figured in no voting roll, doctor's panel or telephone book. I became immune to all bills, HP instalments, insurance or assurance premiums, superannuation contributions, union dues, bank charges, mortgages and all the rest of that financial haemophilia.

I lived here and there, sometime with stray women, sometimes in a residential club for men at Notting Hill Gate, sometimes with Rookery faces who had spare bedrooms.

I even the dodged the National Census, which the newspapers said was impossible. I was sort of shacked with Katie Coleman by then but I moved out of her flat for a week and slept on the

Dunlopillo mattress The Beast had bought for late-night office-floor seductions.

At times I would have liked a room or flat of my own where I could write songs of TV plays (and keep all the paperbacks I normally flung away) but there is nothing alerts the Inland Revenue bloodhounds quicker than a permanent tenancy.

You could of course say I was only a drunken layabout but to me it felt as if I'd found the secret of staying young for ever.

I knew what life was all about. Getting on with it instead of drearily wondering what life's all about. It couldn't last, could it?

The greatest escaper of them all, Jack Sheppard, was born in Spitalfields, London, in 1702. As a teenage apprentice he drank in the Drury Lane gin-houses. The love of his life was a whore called Edgeworth Bess. Another love was Poll Maggot, who instigated his first burglary. This led him into the Jonathan Wild web. Wild invented organised crime as the western world knows it. He controlled London's villainy and its law simultaneously and they've been trying to separate them ever since.

3

The watch now says 4.06. My, how the carefree hours flit by when we are young and gay. The soles of my feet are clammy and hot. Provided this is the day after, yesterday must have been a day to remember.

A noise jerks me out of a nightmare in which I'm in prison for life. I open my eyes and realise I have not been sleeping. The noise is the double-pulsed jangle of a telephone. It stops but I hear no answering voice.

I shiver, although the cell is overheated

I hear something else, thank God. In the silent tomb you are relieved to hear yourself farting. Dead bodies go on farting agreed, but *they* can't hear it. The new noise is of a man coughing, hacking and racking cough without end. Last night we were all whirling dervishes of laughter and song. Now we are unshaven men slumped on bunks in whole rows of identical tiled traps. Snatched out of life!

I stare at the wall. I could tap out a message in code on a pipe, to maintain sanity through decades of the dungeon's living death, only there are no pipes and I know no codes and have nothing to say anyway. It is 4.26.

The man goes on coughing.

A month or so passes slowly and uneventfully.

To cool the soles of my feet I draw up my knees and drag off my Hush Puppies. As I go to drop the battered suedes on the floor I see something blue. Inside each shoe is a wad of what looks like Treasury paper.

I find myself spreading damp, blue, corrugated fivers across the dark brown mattress. Fourteen of them, seven from each shoe.

I sit up. I touch them. I smell them. I hold them up to see the metal strips. I twist an ear lobe till it hurts.

This is not a dream.

Hearing heavy feet in the corridor I quickly shove them down into my black nylon socks, pulling on my shoes and assuming a face of innocence.

The footsteps pass on. The tomb is silent once more. I get the fivers out.

How the hell did I come into seventy gash pounds?

To emerge from a Rookery piss-up night *minus* your money is a basic law of Nature; that's what The Rookery is for, to rob people.

But to wake up with *more?*

What happened to yesterday anyway?

Four years imprisonment in the Poultry Compter for debt taught Wild about London's underworld. On release he became a thief-taker in partnership with Charles Hitchin, the City Marshal. He organised gangs of thieves to cover each area of London and then acted as intermediary to restore stolen property, its rightful owners paying him a percentage of its value ostensibly to buy it back from the thieves. Wild had his own boat to export excess stolen gear to Belgium. If his puppets misbehaved Wild turned them in for hanging, as he also did innocent people, when his thief-taking reputation needed a boost. He may have sent as many as 120 people to the Tyburn gallows. Each time the government paid him forty pounds.

4

That freezing December day when, by a fluke, I was to meet Ramsay Shand and also to become entangled in The Spoofer's murder really began in the morning with a phone call from my partner The Beast.

I had been smoking too many cigarettes too early in the day and was feeling less than dynamic. The view through our grimy window on the top floor of Nailed Down Chambers, a shabby canyon of higgledy-piggledy rooftops and back walls, had not changed by so much as a single pigeon squirt in the three dreary days I'd been beating my brains out on *A Bed Of Men*, our latest easy money scheme

I had not sat still for so long in my whole life and I was in one of those edgy moods that could only be dissipated by a quick drink.

"What's happened to Wilma now then?" was The Beast's first question, in his adopted cockney voice.

"I've got her whipping a naked property developer, to give it a bit of social conscience. Where the fuck are you? I need a quick drink. This crap—"

"Stick with it, old son. Soon as we deliver forty thousand wank worthy words we collect three hundred sheets and—"

"*We?* When d'you propose writing your end of it?"

"Okay, you're doing the graft—I'll settle for a small commission."

"Handsome of you."

"Got much else on?"

"We're meeting that guy with the funny band at twelve in The Leafless— "

"Ah. Yes. Rentapest Sibley. Look, I'm a bit tied up—you see him. Give him the elbow. A lot of fucking art students in funny hats? By the way, this pools reception tonight—"

"Can't make that, either?" I said, sarcastically.

"I'll try but if I don't get there in time make sure you grab the hundred cash they're paying Pilbeam. Bastard's got more money than he can jump over but he won't settle up with us."

"Arguing about money with Pilbeam is your speciality, matey—"

"You've always wanted an excuse to smash his face in. Try not to spoil his speaking teeth. I'll probably catch up with you later on, down the Congo. I've got good news—I might just have found a mug to buy a slice of the band agency. Walter Just has put me in touch with this party—it's a she. I'm down to meet her up there at 11.30 tomorrow, only I could be late. Give her a bit of chat—"

"No thanks, conning widows out of mites is your end of it, whatever a mite looks like."

"She's loaded, this one. Anyway, you can't con somebody who isn't trying to con somebody else, it's well known."

"Yeah? Really? Like you trying to con me into agriculture?"

"Agriculture? Don't get it."

"I'd say our partnership was fairly agricultural, I'm doing all the ploughing and you're doing all the larking."

"That's not true, old son. We'll talk about it later. See you tonight."

I lit another Silk Cut kingsize (less tar so you live longer, cough cough) and went over to the window, I spat and rubbed a peephole in the oily dust. The sky was the colour of mortuary corpses. The women and girls crowded in the Indian tailor's black hole of dress-cutter across the canyon had their curtains drawn across the cold.

I wondered if they could exist on less oxygen than white folks. Ferns were growing from a broken gutter. They went well with the rackety exterior of The Rookery's smelliest office block, called Nailed Down Chambers by the constantly shifting tenantry because otherwise why had it not been stolen? It was the kind of architectural relic that gives the past a bad name, a decaying Victorian warren that served as training ground for aspirant burglars and business premises for a rancid diversity of commercial incompetence and larceny masquerading as private enterprise.

I went back to the desk. The room smelled of melting bakelite, from the overheating plug of the two-bar electric fire. Neville lived in hope of the plug inducing flame so that he could collect two hundred pounds from a policy on the contents—two collapsing desks, shaky metal shelving, two chairs of archeological potential and the incongruously new swivel chair on which I had been cultivating piles while engaged on hardcore pornography.

(Neville grabbed this swivel job from the apparently deserted offices of the Caribbean Travel and Investment Corporation. "It isn't stealing," he assured me, "Their door was open." That was as near to ethics as he was ever going to get.) I decided to re-type page one hundred and sixty-seven of *A Bed Of Men*. We'd been making up ludicrous titles for hardcore porn to amuse ourselves in The Leafless Tree—next day Neville announced that *A Bed Of Men* was too good to miss. A Surefire Earner. He contacted a legit Surrey printer who ran off hardcore on the side.

Quite apart from the three hundred, I had been excited at the idea of getting down to something creative, at last. I had read that many famous writers started off doing filth under fake names. I also remembered a magazine article in which many successful people said you had to achieve something by thirty or it was probably too late. I was twenty-nine. *A Bed Of Men* would be my first real test.

Easy money?

I couldn't remember working harder. And this hardcore pornography was only supposed to be a sideline. I still had to look after the bent band agency, the one Neville was trying to con somebody into buying a slice of. I had flagrant handouts to write for the joke press agency (sole client—Pilbeam the disc-jockey and 'personality'). I had to ghost Pilbeam's weekly show biz column (bought by five local papers at four guineas a throw and regarded as authoritative, in the Fen country).

Then there was the pen-pal bureau; in my wire basket was a pile of sorry letters from naive teenagers who believed the No Girl Or Your Registration Fee Back guarantee, all requiring evasive answers.

Not forgetting administrative tasks—the carpet needed sweeping, a slippy rectangle, originally red, which to touch with the bare skin rendered advisable a quick tetanus jab. In one corner, waiting my executive attention, was a cardboard crate containing stale newspapers, sticky paper cups, cigarette ends, ash, possibly an old-fashioned french letter or two, all settling nicely until the overflow would force me to lug it down to the rubbish bins behind the block, the freehold of which, incidentally, belonged to the Crown.

I typed the words *towering buttocks* and then looked at my watch. It was 11.05. The Leafless would not be open until 11.30. A quick drink with Rentapest Sibley and I knew I'd feel more like rattling through this titillating crap. My heart wasn't in it but I was determined to prove I could do it. I had a battle of will with my fingers. They were calling out for a quick drink as well but I forced them to replace the leather dog-whip in Wilma's slim, bejewelled hand. We could all have a quick drink in half an hour.

By quick I meant one that didn't take longer than two days.

No! A couple with Sibley and then I'd be back up here, pounding it out. All the successful people in the magazine articles said the same thing—anybody can make it if they're willing to work hard. This drudgery was the price.

I was still on page one hundred and sixty-seven when I saw that it was 11.15. I pulled on my blazer-style jacket, yanked out the overheating plug, told myself I'd be back in an hour, and headed down the stairs.

On the second floor landing two silk-trousered Indian women were hovering outside the padlocked door of the London-Delhi Personal Finance Corporation. They eyed me with all the oriental modesty of peckish timber-wolves. I didn't stop to point out the bailiff's distress notice tacked to the door, fair indication that their life savings weren't merely out for an early lunch. Besides who ever got anywhere with an Indian woman?

Outside it was numbingly cold. The sky was darkening, as if for thunder. I headed for The Leafless. To go with the prematurely dark sky The Rookery was adorned by rubbish. The binmen had been on strike for a week and against the walls of striptease basements and porn shops and betting shops and delicatessens and film offices were growing mounds of waste, some of it sealed in black plastic bags or crammed in cardboard boxes, most of it dumped loose, papers, plastic wrappings, empty wine bottles, cardboard whisky cases, coils of cutting-room film, all of it spreading and creeping along walls and gutters. The Rookery was going to have a rubbish-grey Christmas.

Electric bulbs strung round the market stalls in Pollett Street gave the oranges and bananas that special Christmastime shine. I got caught in a crowd watching a shout-up between two shopkeepers standing aggressively against a fleshy blur of nylon frills and plucked corpses.

The blue-aproned butcher was accusing the shirt-sleeved ladies'-wear man of obscuring his window with mobile racks of bargain nighties.

The dress-shop man, a suntanned Jew with a bald head and thick black pelt on his forearms, refused to pull back his racks. The butcher, a short man in a straw hat, yelled violently. Up and down the lines of stalls the barrow-men bawled gorblimey witticisms.

A woman came out of the dress-shop and handed something to the Jew. Backing at a crouch across the pavement he drew a chalk-line from the wall dividing their plate-glass windows to the gutter. When he stood up he smiled. The chalk line showed that his racks were an inch short of the butcher's territory.

A gold watch gleamed on a hairy wrist as he rolled the racks *nearer* to the upside-down hens and turkeys.

The butcher snarled and dashed into his shop, odds on to fetch a meat-cleaver, I decided, admiring the coolness of the Jew, who stood on the chalk line, hands on narrow hips, amazingly relaxed for a man who would soon have both ears close to the ground.

Nothing happened. The Jew gave us all a smile. We dispersed, disappointed.

In Amblers Court a crippled woman was shrieking abuse at a red-faced man selling dusters from an open suitcase on a folding stool. The woman's right leg was nothing more than red skin round a stick-thin bone. The duster man paced up and down in front of his suitcase, never looking directly at the woman but snarling at her quietly to fuck off out owit.

A half-starved, bespectacled man was shouting sales patter when he was not ballooning his cheeks to blow warmth into his blue hands. He was trying to sell a dozen pairs of well-worn men's shoes, the heels of which were neatly aligned with the granite wall of the kosher restaurant.

Sleeping with his back against the same wall, tattered body in the foetal position, was an old alky, shredded trousers revealing black-grained ankles. No official announcement had been made but it seemed the police had stopped arresting these bums. I got stuck behind a line of middle-aged men in shabby coats or cardigans. I recognised them as a three-card trick team strolling between pitches. The big one with the bald head and the hooked nose had a friendly arm round another's shoulders.

"So wot've you chopped ahta the load then, Chawrlie?" he was saying.

"A monkey, din Oi?"

"A monkey! Good load then, wunnit? Oi'll tell yer, Chawrlie, Oi fakkin regrits gittin' ahta the metal gyme. Oi wus coppin' well at that, wun Oi? It's a lovely fakkin gyme, the metal gyme, innit?"

I was standing at the bar of The Leafless with two early arrivals, Tony Thunderbuttocks Watson, a smalltime comedian and compere, and little Roger Parkes, an A and R man for an independent recording studio, when Sibley showed. He immediately said he would much prefer to do our business at his club.

Sibley was a former art teacher, aged about thirty-five. He had found a band of ex-art students who were trying to do a modernised version of Spike Jones and the City Slickers—novelty numbers, visual gangs and a Dixieland sound. Next year he was going to have ten bands and smoke torpedoes but at the moment he still wore a cheap tweed suit. They called him Rentapest because he was a relentless ear-basher—always on the topic of his own projected success story.

I had a vague idea he was just single-minded enough in a creepy way to become Big. I left The Leafless with him, intending to have a couple of big gins off him and then get back to the regular semi-circle of familiar faces in The Leafless.

Not that I intended to waste all lunchtime.

No, just a few to pep me up and then I'd be racing back to Wilma.

"Yes, I detest pubs," Sibley said as we crossed Colman Hedge Lane, "They're so smelly, just a rough and tumble of shabby nobodies bumping your elbow. You'll find my club much more civilised."

"Not that one, is it?" I said, nodding at the Prado, a basement clip-joint in a tenement whose windows were still sealed with corrugated iron and whose brown brickwork was still charred black from the night some disgruntled patron had chucked a petrol bomb through the window, failing to punish the hostess who'd taken his money for a romantic assignation but burning to death two Chinese waiters sleeping on the top floor of the building.

"Whoever did that did a good job," said Sibley, seriously.

His civilised club turned out to be The Coral Beach, a high-priced clip-joint for well-loaded idiots, the sort of place Yorkshire farmers later brag to each other about spending a fortune in. The decor was neo-Las Vegas and the prices so brazen I would have said that membership was certifiable evidence of insanity.

Still, Sibley was paying.

To make doubly sure of this I made a little performance of patting my hip pocket and saying that we'd left The Leafless before I remembered to cash a cheque.

Sibley said that was no problem.

We stood at a black-topped bar. Sibley asked for gins and tonic. The big barmaid was something special—about six foot tall, brown hair with chestnut glints, suntanned face, big milk teeth, slit maxi-skirt. Farther up the bar three middle-aged businessmen were waiting for her to rejoin their witty Smalltalk.

"And how are you, Mary pet?" said Sibley, trying to look immensely urbane as he gave her two pound notes.

"Very well thank you," she said in a voice as smooth and distant as the Muzak.

As she looked down at her change drawer Sibley gave me a little nod, to encourage my appreciation of all this sexy civilisation. He gave her a fifty pence tip but she still didn't remember his name. I followed him across the wide room. The furniture was low and square, deep purple divans and low, glass tables on which were leaf-shaped glass trays of peanuts, white olives and green gherkins.

Apart from the three men at the bar the only customers were two dark-suited men facing each other across a table covered with leather notebooks and pages of figures, and sitting by himself by the wall, a red-faced man in a hairy suit of brown tweed and shiny brown brogues, no doubt another Yorkshire farmer doing the town.

He glared at us aggressively.

"Best bar in London, didn't I tell you?" said Sibley.

"I suppose you'd need to own a lot of slum property to get a date with the barmaid," I said.

"Mary? Wonderful person, isn't she? And so intelligent!"

He shook his head in marvel at it all. I got stuck into the gherkins. He began to outline his plans. The novelty band was going to be very big, make no mistake about it. Big agencies were phoning him hourly, trying to snatch them up. He could name his own price but he had plans.

He had been told our agency was young enough to grasp his imaginative concepts yet experienced enough to make up for what he frankly and openly admitted was his current lack of practical experience.

As he gabbled on I saw a woman coming into the big room. She was wearing a red, low-cut dress. She sat down about ten yards from the farmer in the tweed suit.

"Have you any idea what it costs to launch a band the way you describe?"

I asked him this for two reasons. One, to find out how much siphonable cash he had. Two, because I didn't know.

The woman in the red dress leaned forward to examine her foot. The red dress fell away to reveal a fair length of leg in black nylon. The farmer stared, as he was meant to.

"I have access to all the capital required," Sibley said. "Of course, I would prefer to do it by ploughing back what the band earns—and already this is not inconsiderable, even in these early days. Care for another drink?"

"Well—I've got to see somebody at 12.30," I said, doubtfully. He looked prematurely relieved. "Okay, just the same again, ta." He went to the bar. I finished the gherkins. Sibley was a dum-dum or he'd never have come to a pair of slags like Neville and me. We didn't know anything about *management,* we were just a couple of piss-artists who'd found a cheap way of screwing living money out of a telephone.

The whole thing was a joke. I'd have this drink and then slide off back to The Leafless.

The woman in the red dress found a reason to grimace and re-examine her ankle. The sight of her knee and a slice of thigh didn't inspire the farmer to rush over and offer her a drink. She left the room. Sibley came back with the drinks. The farmer got up and lumbered to the door.

"Cheers," I said. "Listen, best thing is for Neville and me to discuss this, then we'll give you a ring, maybe—"

The farmer reappeared, his movements jerky enough to catch my eye. He strode towards the bar. I saw that he was wearing motoring gloves and carrying a heavy walking-stick.

"What we have to discuss is projection," said Sibley, nodding wisely. "I'm hoping—"

A violent cracking sound made us turn our heads. The farmer was hitting the bar with his stick. Glass broke. Looking a lot less like a trainee duchess, the big barmaid backed away quickly. He followed her the length of the bar, swinging the stick at her head. She ran in the opposite direction and got to the door, shouting for help.

The farmer came charging across the room at us. The two men with the papers jumped to their feet just before he whacked the stick down where their heads had been.

For a few moments the four of us ran this way and that like sheep before a dog. He lashed out with the stick at tables, divans, even the floor, his face perfectly calm.

A small waiter came running and jumped on his back. The farmer carried him round the room as though he weighed nothing. I felt like a fool, cowering with Sibley and two strangers in the narrow space between a glass table and a purple divan.

The manager came running in, a big chap in a dinner suit and a frilly blue shirt. He put an armlock on the farmer, who proceeded to drag him and the waiter back towards the bar, still lashing out at bottles and soda-siphons with the stick.

The manager tripped him up and got him face down on the carpet, one knee in his back. The farmer went on struggling. Then they managed to drag him out, both arms tight up his back.

For a few moments the rest of us stood in a little shaking group, each contemplating his own reasons for not being a hero. The barmaid returned, looking round the floor for her shoe.

"He's been in here every day this week," she kept saying, eyes blinking rapidly, "he never spoke to anyone, he just sat and stared at me!"

"My God, he went insane!" said Sibley. "Surely he isn't a full member?"

I realised I still had the glass in my hand. I drank the rest of the gin and tonic and said I would have to be making tracks. Irritatingly enough, Sibley came with me.

"One thing about the pub, you don't often get attacked by stick-wielding maniacs," I said chattily as we went down the stairs.

"He was a guest member," Sibley said, indignantly. We saw the farmer as we passed the door of The Coral Beach manager's office. He was sitting with the heavy hand of the bouncer on his collar. His face had gone a dark red and his legs stuck out awkwardly. Sibley stopped on the pavement.

"I'll have a quick one with you in the pub," he said, holding his chest, trying to minimise the shock by exaggerating his reaction.

Rather than spend more time with him I said I had to meet this other person in a restaurant but he said he would go to The

Leafless anyway. I was forced to walk off in the other direction. I found myself in Bishop Henry Street, where the crowds were thicker and slower than ever. I decided I might as well drop into The Maggots and have a quick one with Careless Kate, she of the seven abortions, otherwise known as Everybody's Wife, the girl with whom I was living. She usually spent lunchtime in The Maggots with her arty-smarty friends. I'd give it twenty minutesand then slope back to The Leafless. Sibley would have swallowed it by then. I could tell the rough and tumble slobs what was happening in civilised circles.

But for this incident I would never have gone anywhere near The Maggots at that time of day, if at all.

Jack Sheppard's first escape was as a visitor. Edgeworth Bess was locked up in the St Giles' Parish roundhouse. Jack knocked down the beadle, broke open the door and carried Bess off. This made him a hero of the town doxies.

5

Going along Bishop Henry Street I had to step into the gutter to pass the queue at the bargain wine shop. When I tried to remount the kerb I was blocked by a bunch of French students from the language school. They were enjoying the posters outside the wanking cinema:

This is a programme of body and blood, said the big red letters. *She was forced to grow up in a sexual pigsty. . . the film that shocked the Vatican.*

Normally I would have elbowed my way through, just to remind these unwanted tourists that we aren't all dummy gentlemen on the island, but after the madman with the stick I found myself wary of physical contact with strangers.

Of course I'd always known how many nutters there are walking about behind normal faces but this time it had been very close to.

Inside The Maggots I saw Kate's jet-black hair in her usual place at the end of the bar.' I saw her talking to a twit in a leather hat. I shoved through the gabble of intellectuals and held out a pound note. That was when I saw the man with the cropped head of grey hair.

I knew the face immediately but couldn't put a name to it. This was not unusual — The Maggots attracted unknown stars and anonymous celebrities; men with light-meters strung round their necks to make you think they were film directors; novelists whose stuff was far too *now* for the moronic publishing industry; painters who let spattered jeans vouch for their talents; female poets with north country accents and hysteria on tap; actors whose faces you might just remember from margarine commercials of the year before.

Most of these wankers actually worked in advertising agencies or the like but total honesty makes me admit I was always a bit jealous of The Maggots crowd. Pretence or not, they always made me feel I was being excluded from something. Naturally I reacted by affecting scorn.

Take the guy Kate was with; he wrote reviews and articles in the 'better' Sunday papers but always talked about his poetry. He was wearing a wide-brimmed leather hat and every so often would blow out one of those kids' paper trumpets, the kind that curl up. In broad daylight?

On the other hand, he wasn't writing *A Bed Of Men,* was he?

I bought myself a large brandy, knocked it back, bought another—for that class of poseur is never manly enough to buy a fair share—and went along the bar.

The cropped-headed man was sitting under a fancy mirror between two young fancy dans in suave suits and expensive sheepskin jackets. Katie introduced me to Pally with the paper trumpet. He was friendly enough, if you could ignore the toy and the giggling, but I kept looking at the other man. He was burly and wearing a black leather jacket. Even from five or six yards across the crowded bar I could see slack folds of redundant skin round his neck. Whoever he was I felt sorry for him—it isn't crash dieting that shrinks the neck.

Paper Trumpeter bought a round of drinks, for a wonder, and I bought another and then I said I was off.

"I'm working tonight so I might be late," I said to Kate, knowing full well it would surprise Paper Trumpeter to know I was living with her.

"Give me a ring so I can arrange my evening," she said off-handedly, perhaps not so keen to admit that I was the best she could do. I had never been a classy dresser and she was looking good, high black boots, a purple coat with a black fur collar, red lips and an interestingly white face.

"Yeah," I said.

I went to the lavatory.

He came to the next pissing basin, the burly man in the black leather jacket. Funnily enough, as soon as I sensed he was going to speak I knew it would be in a Scots accent. The possibility of him being a Maggots queer never entered my head—gay as they now say.

"Another few quid up against the pisshouse wall, the story of my life," he said, his voice surprisingly high-pitched but hoarse.

"Aye," I said, arching to give it a shake, "like the snowdrop in the river, there for a moment then gone for ever."

"A jock! One of the Burns Supper culture-lovers!"

I stepped off the ledge, zipping up. His head turned side on to the wall, both hands down at his cock.

"You know this area well, Jock?" he said. "Where could a man get a quiet drink when the pubs close? I used to know all the places there are but—"

Suddenly I knew his name.

Ramsay Shand!

I stared at his great cropped head. Ramsay Shand!

Across the years many things came flooding into my mind. Headlines . . . *The Building Site Playwright. . . Scotland's Answer To Brendan Behan . . . The Pie-Eyed Writer From Dundee.*

I could see and hear my mother reading out a story about him from the *Scottish Daily Express,* the time he was thrown out of a big London premiere for punching that Irish film star.

"Him? He's a disgrace to Scotland," I could still see my mother snorting. "He was just a common navvy! You'd think they'd have better people to put in their papers!"

For a moment I felt totally out of breath, so many years did his face make my memory leapfrog.

"I'm going to a club," I said. "I can get you in."

He stepped off the ledge, clumsily zipping up. He was much shorter than me but he took up a lot of space.

"I've got myself saddled wi' two bloody reporter blokes," he said, obviously roughening his Scots accent for my benefit. "All right if they come?"

"Sure."

"Ach, I'd just as soon fuck off and leave them," he said, coughing and spitting dark catarrh into a wash-basin, "but they're maybe writing me up in the Sunday papers—could do me a lot of good."

I didn't respond to this bait. By not one flicker of an eyelid did I let on I knew his name.

That would have been girlish.

The two smooth journalists found it amusing that another Scot was taking them and Shand to a drinking-club. I ignored them completely. Shand and I walked ahead of them along Bishop Henry Street and into Blue Boy Street.

Shand didn't say much and I was keeping my questions for the right moment—where had he been? Why had he disappeared? Were all those long-ago newspaper stories true, like the time he was supposed to have flown from London to New York half-pissed in his pyjamas?

Just before we reached the dirty entrance that led down into The Hum Drum a hovering striptease tout shot us the usual doorway spiel, twelve lovely girls, continuous show, double acts, no extra charges. Behind I heard the false laughter of the trendy journalists.

Shand seemed withdrawn and depressed.

I went first down the dark, narrow stairway. As we were still in legal hours the steel door was open. Most afternoons you came through that door into a crowd of ravers and liggers re-enacting gold rush night in the Yukon but because the pubs had not yet disgorged the long narrow room was occupied by only six or seven men and Paddy the red-haired Irish barman runt.

"Just a light ale for me," said Shand quickly as I produced some pound notes.

"What, a miserable light ale for Ramsay Shand?" cackled one of the reporters. "Hoots mon, we can't have that. What do you Scots call it, a wee dram and a hoff?"

"Just a light ale," Shand said to me.

The other two wanted gin and tonic, as if you didn't know. I asked for brandy, simply because they were on gin. We sat at the low table used by the evening poker school (as opposed to the lunchtime poker dice school, whose three regular members were busy with the yellow eggcup at the other end of the bar). It didn't take the scribes long to get restless. One went to the bar, the other ponced up to the one-armed bandit. I could have told him it was a bent machine; the pay-out cogwheel notches had been heavily soldered to prevent jackpots and if it ever did let loose a few coins in a moment of mechanical aberration Paddy was under the orders of Gentle Jim Kilgallon, the guv'nor, to throw a towel over the glass front and phone for the mechanic. I didn't tell him because he had not even asked my name.

Shand and I sat in silence. As the only light came from a small fluorescent tube above the bar I couldn't see his face too well. It was so quiet apart from the rattle of dice against plastic and the occasional ping of the cash register, we could hear the continual shuffling of feet in the street above, scuffing over the pavement grille of metal and glass which formed the ceiling of the basement area, onto which the window looked but did not open.

I could have done with some noise to camouflage our lack of conversation.

Suddenly Shand pushed his glass away and started growling in my ear.

"I'm finished with booze. I made quarter a million pounds from my plays, you know that? I've been through the lot—or the tax got what I didn't piss away. My second wife left me as soon as the cash went and my first wife won't even let me see our little girl. Fucking booze—I've been in homes and institutions and sani-bloody-toriums and even fucking gaols because of it. The last doctor I saw—it was a woman, a young bloody thing, too—she said I have fatty heart, degenerated kidneys and my liver is twice the size it should be. She said I had six months left if I went on drinking the way I used to."

"How long ago was that?" I asked, in a neutral voice.

"A while ago."

I was glad the light was dim because he was searching my face for some reaction and I had none I wanted to show him. He had been a big thing in my life, when I was a boy and just old enough to realise that the luck of the evolutionary brantub had put me in a stinking tenement in starving Scotland.

On the other hand, I had always despised neurotic weaklings who couldn't control their lives the way men are supposed to.

"Here you are, me hearties—a real drink for the great Ramsay Shand," said one of the reporters, sliding two glasses of whisky onto the table. He went back to the bar and lifted two pints of draught Guinness.

"No, just a light ale for me," said Shand.

"A wee drappie will make your eyes sparkle," said the young smoothie, going back to his friend at the bandit.

"Are they supposed to be interviewing you?" I said.

"I know their game," muttered Shand, "get me pissed and then write about how the wild man came roaring back from the grave. I don't care, if they do an article about me, could be a big help with this."

He elbowed me secretively. From inside the leather jacket he brought a wad of folded paper, which he waved in my face and then slipped quickly back into his pocket, as if it was the vital formula. "I've almost finished it. Best thing I ever did. Lots of these buggers think I'm actually dead, you know that?"

His hand went out for the light ale, ignoring the other glasses. Before the weak beer reached his mouth he had a desperate cough or two. "I'm only forty-seven, you know that? Just getting my second wind. I was just a clown before—but this new play? I've grown up." He nudged me with his elbow. "You're a Scot, you know what needs saying about Scotland." He tapped his leather jacket. "Well, I'm the boy to be saying it."

His wet eyes searched my face for a reaction.

I managed a cheery nod.

Paddy came across to pull the curtains across the basement window and lock the steel door. Then the other reporter came across from the bar with two more glasses of whisky.

It was not my style to allow myself to be needled but I felt uncomfortably close to Shand in the other man's eyes and I had a need to show I was a big, healthy bastard who should not be patronised.

"Why can't you buy people what they fucking ask for?" I said quietly.

He laughed.

I stared at him unblinkingly.

Somebody hammered on the steel door. Paddy squinted through the peephole.

"It's Jim," he said, excitedly, as if sunshine was coming into his dreary little life.

Gentle Jim Kilgallon, one of those nicknames that mean the opposite, walked into his own club, saw me and said:

"Ah, John—can I have a quick word—in private?"

Knowing that Kilgallon would be struggling to place William Shakespeare I didn't bother to introduce them. Shand had been a front-page celebrity, sure enough, but Kilgallon never got that far forward in a newspaper.

I said to Shand I would be back in a minute.

Kilgallon bought me a brandy, and then told me authoritatively I was a geezer who could be trusted not to speak out of turn.

"All I need to know is—confidentially—purely to save me wasting time—does Neville really have nine grand in cash—I mean, actually in readies?"

"His wife's rich," I said, having no idea what he was talking about. "Yeah well, I can't afford to be buggered about. I want cash down, in my hand, no terms, no instalment, no promises."

I kept a deadpan face and he naturally assumed I knew all about my partner's latest Surefire Project. With half of every pound going across the bar clear profit, owning that gloomy little basement den was as good as an opencast goldmine in your backyard but Kilgallon's quack had told him to get out of the club business before high blood pressure turned him off.

"Bit of a coincidence," he said, "only two days after I've seen the doctor Neville asks me if I'm interested in selling up."

"Yeah, funny, wasn't it?"

Coincidence? Like hell. Neville knew what the quack had told Kilgallon because Mrs Gentle Jim was one of Neville's string of what he called therapeutic dalliances. (So was Mrs Terry Pilbeam. With The Beast for a friend no husband need fear his wife becoming a *lonely* afternoon drinker.)

"I ain't got time to be messed about," he said. "I'm ill, John, really ill."

"Well, you know that they say, none of us is going to come out of this alive," I said, helpfully.

I went back along the bar. Well, well, I was thinking, I wouldn't have learned that little snippet if I'd gone back to the office to write hardcore rubbish. I'd been right to feel aggrieved about Neville's laziness. I was doing all the graft for the joke businesses while that bastard was planning to give me the elbow from the first real money project we'd ever sniffed at?

He'd have to be taught that I wasn't a mug.

Paddy was letting two people through the door as I came up the bar, a villain known as Exquisite in tow with a dark-haired woman in an ankle-length maxi-coat. I gave them the slip and reached the low table in the corner.

I had been away about fifteen minutes.

Shand was tilting a glass of whisky into his throat. He grinned up at me.

"I thought you were off that stuff," I said curtly, seeing that he'd already emptied two of the spare glasses. His manner had changed.

"Ach, I get bored wi' that gnat's piss," he said. "Waht's the point of living if ye cannae have a good bevvy now and then, eh?"

He stood up energetically. He saw I wasn't smiling. He grabbed hold of my lapels. Because of who he was—or had been—I didn't knock his hands away. His eyes were like wet marbles and his breath was unbelievable.

"I'm still number one at anything I do," he proclaimed, right into my face, now holding on to stop himself overbalancing, "don't make any fucking mistake, I'm going to show these bastards. Think I can't handle a few drams? Come on, you big cool Glasgow bastard, drink up, those two overgrown Fauntleroys are paying."

"I don't need to sponge," I said.

He let go of my jacket. He dropped his eyes. He licked his lips, evaded my eyes, said "The hell wi' it", threw over another whisky and began to sing Habbie Simpson as he flailed past me.

I picked up my brandy glass and went back along the bar to where Kilgallon was buying drinks for Exquisite and the woman.

I heard Shand and the journalists laughing and joking. Then Shand was bawling that he knew a club with some life about it. He didn't say goodbye to me and I didn't look round. Paddy locked the door.

"Glad your friend's gone, I'd've had to ask him to swallow the singing," Kilgallon said to me.

Then he looked at the woman. "No music licence, you see." He laughed, letting his hand touch her knee. It was a fat hand. One gold ring. Thick nails that had been cut short with a chain saw.

"No fakkin licence of any bleedin' kind," said Exquisite.

I was the only one who didn't laugh or wink or touch the woman's knees. Kilgallon lifted his glass—Malvern water, the tipple that was going to prolong his life—tapped ash off his long, cheap cigar with delicate blows of a fat index finger. He had a red nose and open pores and a big gut.

I sat there seeing talking faces looming out of the gloom.

"If you've got two small green balls in the palm of yer hand, wot've you got? I'll tell yer. The undivided attention of a leprechaun!"

"Like it, like it."

"You hear John the Baptist's losing his GLC wrestling venues? People've been complaining about the big stars who gets on his posters but never show on the night."

"Still up to that old caper, was he? Surprised he got away wiv it so long."

"Losing the venues wouldn't be so bad only his star attraction's died on him, hasn't he? The Hunchback of the Himalayas. He's a decrepit Sikh waiter from Manchester but it was a good act, he had his Sikh hair over his mush and they led him into the ring snarling like a wild animal. Always tried to strangle the ref. Died of cancer. Real blow to JTB, he's been having a run of bad luck I'm glad to say."

"You makes, your own bleedin' luck in this game I always say."

"How come The Beast and JTB has got the needle so bad for each other?"

"Some deal went wrong,"

"Yeah—one of JTB's clever strokes—they were going to cop a few grand flogging metal badges of some pop star. Only the temporary typist puts in an extra nothing and they wake up one morning with geezers carting in boxes of fucking badges—crates of 'em! Quarter a bleeding million of 'em! And JTB knows fuck all about pop—he's picked some kid who never had another hit. And they're left with quarter a million fucking metal badges! JTB had to bankrupt a company and The Beast wouldn't chip in for the expenses."

"You hear JTB's latest? He's hiring semi-pro singers to do an

LP of Wehrmacht marching songs—"

"Nah?" "Straight up! Nazi fucking marching songs. It's for the nostalgia market, he says."

"Nostalgia for the bleeding SS?"

"I'm bloody bored," the woman announced.

"Shut your mouth then," said Exquisite pleasantly, his right with the blue heart, tattoo giving her bare knee a merciless tweak. "You hear wot's happened to old Den-Den now then?"

Seemingly reassured by Exquisite's brutal attentions the woman subsided. I'd seen Exquisite touching her for money to buy drinks. Poncing off women was his other talent. She was a common enough case in The Rookery, a refugee from the plastic gnome belt, a heavy and embarrassing drinker now she was on the slide. Having escaped from the TV set in Thistle Dome or Tain Towers she was now desperately wallowing in the glamour of Exquisite's cheerful brutality ("I can git twenny men on the street in arf an hour") but the day was not far off when she would be accidentally sober just long enough to see her face in a daytime mirror and curse her luck for abandoning the frozen food rep.

"Yeah, Den-Den's landed this part in a Eytie movie, four weeks steady, a ton a week—first gainful he's had since flamin' June."

"He's taught me one thing, Dennis—them scientists are wrong, you can make solid objects invisible, just lend them money."

"So our Den-Den gets tanked up on the Rome flight," Exquisite went on, tattooed hand now stroking the woman's bare white thigh.

"He's hit Rome about twelve, he's dived into the first grogshop pronto and gits stuck into the old vino. So naturally he turns up at the studio an hour late, well pissed. 'I'm finin' you a day's wages,' says the Eytie director. Den-Den goes spare! 'Don't you oily-skinned war heroes know how to address a British officer?' he shouts— and then he's clobbered the geezer, bang, in the mush. They've bunged him on the first plane back to London. So there he is, that same fuckin' night, back in the Leafless, sinkin' a few pints. All in the same fuckin' day!"

"He *was* an officer, you know that? Day it came over the wireless the war's finished he gits the lads out of the tank-that's what he was, a tank commander, all through Normandy—he gits them outa the tank, pours in a jerrican of petrol and lobs in a match. Burned the fuckin' tank to a cinder!"

"Is this all you do—talk?" moaned the woman, voice beginning to rise.

"Don't git stroppy or I'll give you a funny face, darlin'," said Exquisite, raising the tattooed hand to her chin. She laughed. The tattooed hand went back to her thigh. "Bren's the artistic dancer I was tellin' you about, Jim, ain't yer sweetheart?"

She closed her eyes and swayed on the stool, clicking her fingers. Suddenly it seemed we were all waiting for something. Nobody told me what it was. It was too late now for me to go back to the office, even if the thought of writing *A Bed Of Men* hadn't been so boring.

Maybe that wasn't the whole reason I stayed on the stool in The Hum Drum. That maniac with the stick had shown me I wasn't quite so hard as I liked to think. Then Shand. That hopeless wreck had once been a hero of mine! Not that I cared a hoot about Scotland but wasn't it typical, another boyhood Scottish idol who turned out to be a drunken waster?

I wasn't disillusioned, for only kids and dumbos have illusions, but I did feel a bit wary. Especially with Neville's sneaky little treachery on top of everything else.

Kilgallon kept looking up the bar at the only strangers present, four hooray squares from an advertising agency or a film company. They were having pre-Chrissie drinkies, smoking cheroots, trying to look suave between bouts of girlish laughter.

The three regulars of the poker dice school left for their office desks. Then the advertising men seemed to sense a change in the atmosphere, maybe from the heavy eye Exquisite started giving them. They left with a lot of jolly cheerioing. As soon as the door was locked Kilgallon told Paddy not to let anyone else into the club. Exquisite was muttering something at the woman's ear.

"Not if there's any strangers," she said shrilly.

"Only friends here, darlin'."

They had to buy her another drink. Then Exquisite nodded at Paddy, who reached a pebbly-biceped arm up to the top shelf and brought down a dark liqueur bottle with a round body and a slender neck.

Exquisite helped her climb onto the bar. I sipped my latest brandy and watched, deadpan, not moving even when she almost fell back on top of me. In the ghostly light from the fluorescent tube Kilgallon's face was a waxy blur in the mirror. The poker dice lay silent in the yellow eggcup. She threw down the maxi-coat.

Despite the weather she was wearing only nylon panties and bra, both red. Exquisite's tattooed hand gave my thigh a knowing slap. She put both heavy arms up behind her head to pull the comb out of her chignon. Dark hair fell free, hiding all of her face but the tip of her nose. She was humming. She wriggled goose-pimpled hips, leg muscles flexing as she dropped off her shoes. Her reddened toes arched and flattened against formica.

Clicking her fingers and shaking her hair she began to sway to the music. Nina Simone. The tendons of her long feet tightened into fine fan shapes a few inches from my face. Then she slid down her red panties, kicking them at Exquisite's face. He let us see him sniffing at them, for a laugh. Her hips were marked by tiny treadmarks, as though she had been run over by baby tractors. Her big buttocks were white. She began to crouch over the bottle. I heard a knee-joint crack.

You know Nina Simone? You don't know what it's like? Very sad, especially if you're killing time watching an amateur flesh show in a locked room under a dirty street. Killing time—as if it wasn't dying fast enough without our help.

I had a dreamlike premonition of an explosion lifting the rackety building off our heads and exposing our shabby little games to the winds and rain. We were the anonymous people who don't get into the history books and this was why.

"Cor!" moaned little Paddy, "all the fookin way!"

Just for a moment I felt trapped. The infantile pleasure on their brutish faces revolted me. I refused to let my eyes take in the woman's pathetic flouncings.

I briefly thought of hurrying back up to the office to do a few more pages of *A Bed Of Men* but I had a distasteful vision of myself rushing crudely through the streets and panting up the stairs.

Self-control, that was the secret.

Then people started hammering on the steel door and Bren short for Brenda had to get down off the bar counter.

As new, excited faces came into that gloomy little den I told myself sharply that it was time I stopped looking like one of these nobody bastards who had nothing more to do with their lives than scurry eagerly towards another pointless, tawdry night in The Hum Drum. Even Shand was better than them, for he had some magic to remember.

For the first time I felt *tortured* by a desire to be Somebody.

One of Jonathan Wild's puppets, a villain known as Hell and Fury Sykes, turned Jagck Sheppard in while he was drinking in St Giles. Jack got out of the parish roundhouse through the roof. Shortly afterwards Jack and his mate Blueskin Blake were caught trying to pick a gentleman's pocket in Leicester Fields. Jack was taken to the New Prison. Edgeworth Bess visited Jack and was immediately locked up with him as an accomplice.

6

"The sooner they bung us the fucking bread the quicker we can swallow this drag scene and sniff out a bit of grumble down the Congo," said Pilbeam in a low snarl, going off to pose for more pictures.

Teepee, who was not, of course, as young or inane or pleasant as his infantile radio chat led the millions to believe, had been hired through our agency to give this tired sideshow, this social candyfloss (starves the belly, rots the teeth) a bit of cut-price glamour, the statutory celebrity who would hand over a cheque for one hundred and ninety-three thousand to a Lincolnshire farm labourer who, unable to read or write, had stuck a pin against eight lucky football matches.

As I was merely present as the celebrity's companion, it being axiomatic that the famous must never travel alone, I was able to stand back and view this crummy huckstering carnival with all the detachment of a man who had long been cured of the common provincial delusion that anywhere in London is where the glamour is, who was actually present to filch the star's money, and who had been drinking gin and brandy all afternoon.

In those inflationary times, a mere one hundred and ninety-three thousand wasn't going to make the front pages; those Fleet

Street eagles were in fact only dogsbodies poised not for scoops but to drink the free bar dry; the TV camera was only shooting for the local East Anglia channel; the celebrity was a last-minute substitute; and the way Heath was cutting prices at a stroke the lucky yokel was going to be fortunate if his tax-free fortune would stretch to buying him a slightly bigger hovel.

He was brown-faced, sitting awkwardly on a high stool on a low band platform. Behind him was his own photograph blown up to wall-size, a grinning sod-basher in working clobber, forking organic dung onto a trailer against a background of mud.

They had hurriedly fitted him into a new blue suit and white shirt. He blinked rapidly against the TV lights as the press asked him enough stock questions to justify the amounts they intended to drink.

As the TV cameramen were posing him and Pilbeam again the pools company man murmured in my ear and we slipped out into a corridor. He gave me a hundred pounds—ten brown tenners. I signed two sheets of paper. We winked at each other. When we went back into the banqueting hall Pilbeam was posing with his arm round the yokel's shoulders. Then he came off the platform.

"Got the loot?" he asked.

"Yeah, you want to swallow this scene?"

"Must have a drink or two. It's expected of us big fucking stars."

He slipped on his friend-of-the-people smile and headed for the bar. I was just going to follow when I heard the voice from behind.

Forgotten by the crowd, dwarfed by his own grinning photograph, the wealthy ex-labourer was still perched awkwardly on his high stool. Not hearing what he was mumbling about I walked towards him.

"Is it all right if I gets down now then?" he asked, obediently. I made some crack but he was too naive for mockery. He latched onto us. He kept saying he had always been a 'genuine admirer' of Pilbeam on the radio. He showed us a creased snapshot of his fat wife and underfed children looking over a stone wall at what he said, proudly, was his master's prize saddleback boar. When I said he was probably now richer than his fucking master he giggled with embarrassment.

"I'm glad I met you two," said Mangel-Wurzel, "I'm going to tell that pools chap I'm going with you two for a proper drink-up. It's too important here for a simple chap like me."

He went off.

"Come on, I'm not getting lumbered by a fucking *fan*," growled Pilbeam, fan being the lowest human category he knew. "You got to watch them dung artists-shifty and brutal by turns."

"He's lonely, Teepee," I said, mockingly.

"Wait till he buys his Sunningdale mansion and finds the hooray neighbours won't speak to him, then he'll find out what loneliness really means. Let's go."

We went in Pilbeam's Lotus Europa to The Rookery. He drove in sharp, murderous bursts. The seating was slung low to inspire a jet pilot fantasy but in me it only inspired fear of having the skin rubbed off my arse.

In Colman Hedge Lane a big saloon was only a few yards ahead, preparing to reverse into the only parking space.

Pilbeam swung the Europa in nose first. The saloon driver, a middle-aged man in a dinner jacket, got out of his car, shouting. We opened our doors and climbed to the perpendicular. When he saw two of us he got into his car and shouted violently as he roared off, a spew of white vapour obscuring his red tail lights.

"You were in the wrong there," I said to Pilbeam.

"Yeah but I got the parking space, didn't I?" he said, smiling evilly. We went down the carpeted stairs to the door that led into the reception foyer of The Amorous Congo. The duty manager, a big German bouncer known as Martin Doorman, told us that Neville had just left. He didn't know where to.

I decided I would not demean myself in a petty argument over money with Pilbeam.

We sat down at a table in the corner of the main drinking room, which was still fairly quiet.

"Okay, let's have the bread," Pilbeam snapped, holding out an aggressive palm and clicking middle finger and thumb.

"Neville wants me to hang onto it," I said, in a neutral voice. "He says you owe the agency a bit."

He snapped his fingers again.

"Fuck Neville, he's screwed me for plenty."

I raised my hand to attract a waitress, making Pilbeam realise I could not be rushed.

"Tell you what," he said, with a little upwards jerk of his chin, "we'll come to an arrangement, you gimme the loot and I won't break your arm."

I stared at him without blinking.

"Don't come the heavy with me," I said. "Wait till you're as big as Frank Sinatra and can afford bodyguards to thump people."

We stared at each other. With that amount of drink in me I could have lasted an hour without blinking but suddenly it all seemed childish. I brought out a thin wad of brown tenners.

"Here's ninety," I said, sliding notes across the table, keeping one in my left hand, "This is the agency's ten per cent, right? I'll leave you and Neville to squabble over the petty book-keeping."

"As long as we remember who makes the money," he snarled, shoving the notes into the waistband pocket of his flared blue velvets. Then he shook his head and laughed, falsely. "Fuck the petty book-keeping, let's get a bloody drink."

He told a half-naked, mesh-legged waitress to bring a magnum of champagne. Then he spread his arms along the back of the seat. "Maybe I'm not up there with Sinatra and the chaps," he said, "so what kind of future are you planning?"

I refused to react to this sneer, telling myself he was only a lout who proved you didn't need talent to be A Somebody. If I had the obsessional drives that come from an inadequate personality.

41

I could be a bigger star than him—I was wittier, better-looking, I had read a book, I could even sing.

Shand was a good example of the kind of childish neurotic who became a success. I was happy the way I was.

Then the woman came to ask for his autograph.

She was in her forties, silver-tinted hair, green fingernails, white trousers that started just below her exposed navel. She came across the half-empty room and shoved a menu at Pilbeam. I watched him scribble his signature.

Looking over his head at me she said:

"You aren't famous, too, are you, luv?"

Quick as a flash Pilbeam said cheerily:

"No, he's with me."

I looked away contemptuously.

"Here, I'll put down my private number," said Pilbeam, squinting up at her knockers. "Call me any time I'm free."

I made a little grimace at her to show that mature, intelligent people could afford to smile at his adolescent loutishness.

Putting a heavily-ringed hand on his shoulder she said:

"You're awful but I like you."

Her thinly-caged buttocks jugged away from our table, our lasers searing her white slacks with invisible scorch marks.

"I could very well be giving her a right seeing-to this very night," he said, winking at me.

Before I could be provoked I got up to go to the lavatory, or crab ranch as regulars called it. A voice called at me from a wall-side table. It was John The Baptist, real name J. Talbot Baxter.

"Come and have a drink, John," he shouted.

JTB, as we all called him to his face, was dapper. I don't know what it means but it suited him. Dapper and daft. He made money but in every other way was an idiot.

He wore his brown hair in one stiff, cemented sweep from forehead to shirt collar, without a parting. He still wore suits with padded shoulders, narrowed at the waist to give him a corseted look.

He was about five feet seven; narrow trousers and pointed shoes (black, leather, with laces) and a tendency to walk on his toes made his every movement seem preparatory to a pirouette. He had a bunchy face, with that kind of translucent complexion that makes you wonder if its wearer has ever seen the outdoors.

The years had passed but for J. Talbot Baxter it was all still happening back there on the band platforms of the thirties. He'd never done me any harm. He was sitting with some hairy young buggers. He was well pissed and they were taking the mickey out of him. Behind his buttocks, stretched out on the wall-seat was No Chance Cheesewright, one of JTB's agency bookers, a red-haired lush from the Isle of Man. Cheesewright got drunk every night starting at 1.00 p.m. in the afternoon.

His lifestyle was practically celestial—an inert object hurtling through black space. One time I was in The Armpit trying to chat up some gorgeous lovely for a quick workout on the office floor and she said I was drunk and I said I was as sober as the next man and when I looked over my shoulder just to see who this next man was that everybody kept mentioning I found Cheesewright slumped against the bar, his face lying in a large, overcrowded ashtray. When he breathed out a cloud of cigarette ash mushroomed over his face and when he breathed in it scurried back into his nostrils.

A great booker, though. As JTB said, No Chance could promote more action in the two hours before the pubs opened in the morning than six sober Salvationists at a sex orgy.

As I sat down at his table JTB, looking like an egg with legs, was having an argument with the hairy lads about music. They were in some kind of folk-rock group. JTB had played saxophone in pre-war dancehalls.

"Is that all you've got to boast about, your years?" he said thickly, pointing a fat finger at each in turn. "Go on, brag about how young you are, I don't give a fuck. Ten years from now some teenager will be sneering at your pot bellies and then you'll know."

He banged the table. "Being young isn't a talent, you twats, it's water dribbling through your fingers!"

"Hang about, Dad, they might give you a spot on *All Our Yesterdays*," one of them said. They left good-naturedly—surprisingly so, considering he'd started out that evening to sign them up.

"Fuck 'em." he said. "So what's with you, John? You're a good nut, John, I don't mind telling you. Why don't you come and graft for me instead of that wanker Thirsk? I need a bloke like you around me, 'stead of this dead body." He looked down at the snoring Cheesewright. "I knew him when he was full of promise," he said. He gave him a smack on the cheek. Cheesewright didn't stir. "Meet my executive staff! So why don't you, John?"

"Make me an offer I can't refuse."

"You bring me the right ideas I'll make you so much money, John—ah, here's my fucking minicab."

The driver was a young West Indian in a white fisherman's sweater. JTB told me once again I was a good nut. I was glad he had Cheesewright for that night's alibi—JTB always needed somebody to go home with him to prove to his wife that he hadn't been with women.

They made a jolly chorus-girl trio of linked arms as they lurched towards the door, Cheesewright hanging from the middle. I didn't imagine JTB would remember any of this the next day. I found him likeable but stupid. I went back to our table. It was around pub closing time and the Congo was getting steam up. The guvnor, Henry Spinks, otherwise known as The Black Whoremaster—but not to his face unless you were tired of teeth—stopped to shake hands and offer us a drink. Spinks had his sidekick in tow, Mickey Coyne, but Coyne didn't stop to socialise. One night we'd been sitting in there and Ireland had come up and I said the IRA lost my vote when they shot those three teenage Scots soldiers in the back of the head, in a ditch, after getting them drunk and inviting them to a party.

Coyne said the IRA man who pulled the trigger was a hero because didn't the TV recruiting commercials keep telling us British soldiers were now The Professionals?

I had the water-jug off the table and swinging towards his skull when Spinks smothered my arm. He said if he ever heard us talking Irish politics again he'd get Martin Doorman to break our arms. Every time I saw Coyne I wondered if the water-jug would have killed him. And if I would now be in gaol. And if this kind of violence was deep inside me all the time, needing only drink to open the doors.

While Spinks was talking to us I noticed that Pilbeam was staring at a pair of flashily be-furred black whores, the house speciality.

When Spinks moved on, he said: "Nip over and ask those two jungle bunnies if they fancy a drink."

I said: "Smalltime stars have to do their own pimping."

His eyes narrowed but just then a loud argument broke out at the bar. Two men on adjacent stools were waving fists at each other. They calmed down at the appearance of Martin Doorman.

Pilbeam turned back towards me. The publicity image we had devised for him was little short of being the Dr Schweitzer of disc jockeys (he often made appeals for more playing fields) but he was an erratic bastard in drink, powerful, too.

Time, as they say, stood still. He started to speak.

At that moment, above the flattering noise of the Congo's resident trio, we heard a woman's scream. Heads turned.

Two blonde women were grappling frantically beside a table occupied by five shaven-headed heavies from the Maltese striptease syndicate. This gentry laughed boisterously as the two women, known lesbians, tore and kicked at each other. Martin Doorman stepped heavily between tables.

I caught the eye of one of the black brasses, a big-breasted mama in a tigerskin coat and chestnut ringlets. She rubbed her stomach with the flat of her brown hand and winked a false eyelash at me. The fighting lesbians fell to the floor, hitting an adjacent table and sending a cascade of glasses, drinks, lumps of ice and an ashtray into the laps of instantly galvanised patrons. The big black woman crossed her legs and saw me gazing at her heavy brown thigh. She stretched her arm and pretended to scratch her ankle.

"Your pal the yokel would have dug all this," Pilbeam said sarcastically.

I took my time about jerking a cigarette out of my packet. The black whores who used the Congo charged ten pounds for the night, plus taxi fare and around four quid for a room in one of the no-luggage hotels near Paddington station. I was carrying a miserable ten pounds.

"Were you a big-headed cunt to start with?" I said. "You haven't had enough fame to turn your head."

Pilbeam didn't have time to react. Back at the bar of that popular lounge the two disputatious members had resumed their tiff. The one wearing black suede shoes grabbed the other's brown hair with his left hand while his right hand screwed and jabbed a broken half-pint glass into cheek and temple. The other man's face was quickly curtained with blood. In that lighting it was not so much the redness I noticed as the *wetness*.

A waitress yelled for Doorman, who was busy cuffing the two lesbians. The broken glass merchant walked calmly to the exit and disappeared into The Rookery night.

Out of the general hubbub a man approached our table, grinning. I had seen him around, an elderly Flash Harry, in his fifties, silver hair that was almost blue, bushy sideburns hiding his ears.

His spectacles had thin gold frames. He wore a light blue blazer of sporting cut and a young man's floral shirt and matching tie.

In his fifties but a real goer, the kind of oldish geezer who goes to gyms and likes to challenge people to thump him in the belly, just to show off his stomach muscles. Just a hint of danger, too, particularly round the aggressive eyes.

"Ain't that a terrible thing?" he said. "So how's it going, Tel me old mate? Ain't seen you since Nosher's morry. You and your friend have a drink with me?"

"We're on champagne, dad," said Pilbeam.

"Big bottles I see. Tell you what—fancy a bit of sport? I'll spoof you for who buys the bubbly."

"I like your style," jeered Pilbeam, "you offer me a drink but I end up betting against myself to buy you champagne? Clever fucker are you?"

He grinned down at us. There was an electricity about him I didn't like. Then the waitress came over.

"What was that all about?" I asked her, nodding towards the geezer with the wet-look face.

"I think they were arguing about football," she said, a homely, tired sort of girl—in black mesh tights and stiff satin.

"Nah, that was probably one of the Bentley mob," said this oldish bloke with the sideburns. Did I say Flash Harry? His bloody name *was* Harry.

"Word is they're moving in on this scene—new protection team from up Islington way. You pay 'em a pension or they carve up your punters. The guvnor better jump on 'em quick or they'll move in and take over."

"Did you want an order?" said the girl. Pilbeam stared up at Harry, who held out his hand and juggled some coins.

I got up and headed for the crab ranch. In a locked closet a man was laughing quietly. I ran off about five quid's worth of brandy, gin and champagne, splashed my face with cold water and washed my hands. Dirty water streaked the basin, the grime of all this glamour. In the mirror I saw that my hair had gone greasy. Black hair shows it more. I needed a new jacket. My eyes were tired. They stared back at me, puzzled at the injustice of it all. Pilbeam's fame I mean.

When I got back Flash Harry had gone and Exquisite was slipping into my seat.

I didn't remonstrate.

Exquisite was a paid heavy, when he could find anyone to pay him, a sloping-shouldered, round-eyed, boyish-cheeked, curly-haired *menace*.

I swung a chair over from the next table. Pilbeam offered Exquisite a drink. It's an old show biz custom, fans you despise, gangsters you flatter.

"I could do wiv one but I won't, Tel, fair dos," said Exquisite, "I can't buy you one back cos I'm boracic."

"Have a bloody drink," Pilbeam insisted.

Exquisite poured himself a none-too-reticent ration of non-vintage. "What happened to Brenda the artistic dancer?" I said.

He looked at me steadily. We both knew I was insulting him for sponging off her. Luckily he was in a passive mood. (I felt sober enough but I obviously wasn't. Insult Exquisite? No, I must have been a long way from sober by then.)

"She passed out on me, not long after you shoved off from The Armpit," he said. "She's one of them educated slags. Fancy her, did yer?"

"No and I don't fancy being here when Old Bill shows and wants witnesses for that caper with the bottle."

"Let's get up the Abortion Clinic, Tel," said Exquisite. "There's an ice-cream I'm wantin' to see, owes me a few bob."

"Plenty of grumble up there, is there?"

"Crawlin' wiv it!"

As we turned out of the alley cop cars were stampeding into John Carpenter Street. I walked a pace ahead of Pilbeam and Exquisite listening to their chat about ice-cream freezers geezers, grumble and grunt cunt, Vera Lynn gin, boracic lint skint, Newington Butts guts. I suppose I must have been drunker than I imagined at the time for it's around there my memory went on the blink. One minute we were in the cold street, the next in a jam-packed joint full of whores and queers with a few heteros in between.

One thing I do remember; there was a barney going on between a taxi-driver and a car-driver. They were examining their interlocked bumpers and we stood for a moment to see if they'd turn physical. Traffic was blocked all the way down Colman Hedge Lane. Just where we were standing on the pavement there was a stationary avalanche of paper rubbish against a corner in the wall. My eye caught a movement among the rubbish and thinking it was a rat I nudged Pilbeam and Exquisite.

As we looked down at the slope of paper trash it moved again and a man's bleary face stared out at us, the skin red and blue with bruising.

"Good digs, is it?" Exquisite said. The blotchy face didn't move. "It's one of them bums from the square."

I do remember that.

No sooner were we in the Abortion Clinic than Exquisite, who was now insisting we show him respect by calling him Stan, although he wouldn't stop calling me Jock, ducked and dived into the crowd to see if he could tap an old mate for a fiver, an off-duty detective-sergeant or so he claimed.

I hoped he'd stay away. Pilbeam, like so many on the scene, thought he was colourful but I knew he was moronic. He had done time in Dartmoor for attempted murder with a breadknife, his wife being the victim. He didn't think he should've been found guilty, on the grounds that the Old Bill never found the knife. He'd pulled it out of her guts, unscrewed the cap on the waste-pipe under the sink, shoved the knife up the pipe, screwed the back back on, mopped up the flood of greasy water on the floor, all with his wife bleeding equally messily a few feet away, and then gone out to phone for an ambulance. As she survived to give evidence you wouldn't have thought he had much to complain about but he had some mystical belief that somewhere a lawbook said a man could not be convicted unless the weapon was produced in court.

It was remembering this that stopped me from telling him that I thought he was a moron. Pilbeam and I went to the bar.

Up came Harry with the gold frames. This time he said he was insisting on buying his old mate Tel a drink. He got us to move to a table by a curtained window. A half-naked waitress brought us two large brandies and a large scotch on a tray. Harry gave her a five-pound note.

While she was digging in her change-sporran Harry shoved his liver-spotted hand up between her arms and onto her knockers. She slapped it away without indignation.

"I don't care," said Harry, "when you've seen one you've seen them both."

The girl gave him three pounds.

"Hear about the two IRA men who broke into the Ford factory at Dagenham with a bomb during a strike meeting?" he said, holding onto her hand. "They both voted for a walk-out and they're still on the picket line."

He slapped at her retreating buttocks.

"Cheer up," he said to Pilbeam, who was heaving with laughter. "Surgeon comes up to the bed and says, Good morning Mr Smith, first the bad news-we're amputating both your feet. What's the good news? Mr Smith gasps. The surgeon says—Mr Jenkins in bed seven has made a good offer for your slippers."

Pilbeam almost fell off his chair.

"Come on, let's liven things up a bit," said Harry, the three pounds still fanned in his fist, "spoof you for who buys the drinks, eh? Fair dos? What's a few bob to sports like us?"

He grinned at me.

"I'll take a drink off you," said Pilbeam.

I suppose I was drunk but I couldn't see the harm in it. Harry kept firing jokes at us-the Irish expedition that failed only fifty feet below the summit of Everest because they'd run out of scaffolding—and he had actually bought a drink, which showed he wasn't a cadger.

I put three coins in an empty jacket pocket. Harry dropped a match on the table.

The head pointed to Pilbeam, giving him first call. I brought an empty fist out of my pocket, which meant the maximum on display could only be six.

Pilbeam called five, a good shout for openers, giving no indication of what he was holding.

"I'll go three," said Harry.

That told me he was holding no coins. "I'll say none." I said.

We opened our palms. Harry and I were empty. Pilbeam was holding three. As Harry had guessed right he dropped out. Pilbeam and I stuck our closed fists at each other.

Holding one in my hand I called three.

"One," said Pilbeam opening an empty palm.

I broke the agency's brown tenner to buy two large brandies and a large scotch.

Harry said it would 'keep things moving' if we played a round for cash while we were drinking, say a quid a corner?

Pilbeam lost that one and threw a pound at each of us. I bunged mine in my pocket but Harry conspicuously left his on the table.

I kept changing the pattern of my calls but playing against Harry was like standing blindfold in a fast stream trying to catch eels. When he won he left the notes on the table, always insisting it wasn't the money but the sport.

The more he lost the faster Pilbeam wanted to start each new hand, desperate to prove how good he was.

At last my bladder had enough sense to make me leave the table. A person with dyed red hair, heavy eye-shadow, white suit and glitter shoes put money in the juke-box and the crowded room seethed to the lively rhythm of the nation's latest hermaphrodite idol.

In the bog I found myself standing next to Chick Bhalla, a swarthy guitar player when his fingers were working. He was celebrating his fifth heroin cure. Sober we never had anything to say to each other, if you ever can talk to a musician, but being pissed we were great mates. He said he was making big money with a horrible super-group.

"They phoned Baxter up and said they needed a jazz-orientated guitarist," he said, buying large ones. "Know what that idiot thinks they said? He phones me up and says, They're looking for an oriental jazz guitarist—with that dark skin of yours they'll suss you out for a Malayan or somefink—just talk a bit of pidgin English and you're in. That's what he said, man, talk a bit of pidgin!"

It was probably half an hour before I remembered Pilbeam. I took Bhalla with me.

Pilbeam was sitting alone, head floppy.

"I done the lot," he moaned, several times.

We told him the oriental jazz guitarist story.

"I done the fucking lot," was all he could say.

Exquisite came back.

We told him the oriental guitarist story but like a true star's friend he was only interested in Pilbeam's troubles. I said I'd left Pilbeam with Harry, playing spoof.

"How much did he do you for?" Exquisite asked Pilbeam, taking the whole thing far too seriously, as I told him, several times.

"I done the fucking lot," Pilbeam moaned, eyes half-closed, shoulders slumped, arms hanging loose.

"How much was Teepee carrying?" Exquisite demanded, his face angry, as if I was to blame.

"Ninety quid that I know of," I said aggressively, "less what he spent in the Congo. What's ninety to a big star like him?"

"And you let him play wiv that fucker? Harry the Spoofer? That's how he makes his fuckin' livin', you fuckin' Scotch dum-dum."

"Piss off," I said.

"I'm an idiot," Pilbeam moaned. "I wanna drink."

Exquisite put the tattooed hand on Pilbeam's shoulder. Bhalla had evaporated, sensibly.

"You wait here, Tel," Exquisite was saying to Pilbeam. "I know that berk, I'll say somefink to him he won't argue about. You wait here wiv Jock, all right?" He tapped me on the chest. "You make sure he waits here till I gits back, all right?"

"I'm not his wet fucking nurse," I said.

"You just be here wiv him when I gits back, all right?"

I shrugged. Pilbeam just lolled there, too drunk to remember why he was sick. Bhalla came back.

I was cheerfully spending another two quid of agency money when Exquisite reappeared. I suppose he'd been gone about twenty minutes, maybe longer. He became very dramatic, full of winks and nudges and nose-taps, saying we had to get out of there. Bhalla said he was coming with us—I wanted him on my side—but he had sensibly disappeared by the time we got Pilbeam to the pavement.

The next thing I remember is being back in the crab ranch at the Congo, Exquisite with his back against the door. He held up a wad of notes.

"Stan took care owit," he was telling me, "They don't muck about wiv Stan."

"What is it?"

"It's Tel's money, innit? Wot he lost to that spoofin' bastard."

"You got it back?"

"That's wot mates is for, innit? Count it, go on, I don't want nobody callin' me no tealeaf."

"What's the good of counting it, I don't know how much there was. If I was you I'd take ten off the top, you've earned it."

"I won't tell you no lies I already took half a score off the top, Jock, fair dos, I wouldn't have only I'm boracic. You keep the rest for old Teepee in the mornin', he's well pissed now so he'll only probably lose it again."

"Give it to the Black Whoremaster, he'll hold it for Pilbeam."

"Nah, you take it. Less knows wot happened the better."

"What happened? How'd you get it back anyway?"

"I said somefink to him which he agreed to. That's my game, innit, persuadin' an' that."

I remember us shaking Pilbeam awake and deciding we'd go to The Armpit, somebody saying that Decent Don Jago was having an all-night birthday rave. We got Pilbeam to his feet.

Then I remember us being in Bishop Henry Street, starting to walk to Mozart Street. I can't remember where Exquisite went but he wasn't with us.

We may even have gone back to the Congo to find the two black whores.

One thing is sure, we never reached The Armpit in Mozart Street.

Having been to stage six (flakers) Pilbeam made a magnificent recovery back to stage four (walking zombie). I think we kept apologising to each other for getting the needle over nothing, us both being good nuts and proud to be working-class bastards who didn't give a fuck for any of *them* and their smooth bullshit. We covered a lot of pavement but Mozart Street was hiding.

Then Pilbeam decided to have a piss up in the shadows of Holy Man's Cut, a dog-leg alley crying out for Son of Jack The Ripper.

I stood watch at a lamp-post, congratulating myself on having only reached stage three (merriment and memory gaps).

Up sauntered this young constable.

"Why are you waiting here, sir?"

"Waiting on a taxi."

"You'll get one easier in Broad Military Way this time of the morning. Where do you live?"

"Glasgow."

"Working down here, are you, Jock?"

"Just on holiday."

"I'll walk you that way—lots of villains about this late."

I thought I could hear Pilbeam's waterworks from the dark alley, expecting a small flood to come swirling round our feet any minute.

Pilbeam was my friend, a good nut, beneath it all. An arrest for indecent behaviour after midnight in The Rookery wasn't going to encourage the BBC to put him on *Family Favourites*. I set off with the copper.

We went half a mile without seeing a vacant cab.

"There's a rank the other side of Royal Mile," said the young copper. His determination to help was suffocating.

"What part of Scotland are you from? I come from Peterborough, my grandmother was Scotch, I didn't always want to be a policeman but you get a house with the job and what ordinary blokes can buy a house or pay these rents nowadays?"

"Too right," I said, careful to make no false move.

We were passing a brightly-lit entrance when he took hold of me, for the first time, and steered me up the steps of what I quickly realised was Central Nick. He pushed me in front of a desk and said he was charging this man with being drunk in Colman Hedge Lane.

I'd had gins with Sibley, gins in The Maggots, brandies in The Hum Drum with Shand, gins at the pools reception, my share of two magnums in The Congo, brandies in The Abortion Clinic, maybe a few stray ones on the way.

It sounds a lot in a cold-blooded list but I wasn't falling about. Just to prove that my brain was still working—when they took me into the charge-room I gave my name as James Caskie and my address as that Shettleston tenement I'd left ten years before.

Having no driving licence, passport, post office bank book, National Insurance card or credit cards to give me away I knew I was safe to give this fake name, so I emptied my pockets onto the scarred table with a faint smile on my face.

I did have something strange in my possession, though, a creased square of white cardboard with sticky tape curling off each corner.

The big sergeant picked up daintily and read the blue crayon lettering:

"Cheri, new young model, second floor?" He looked at me sadly. "Tore this off some brass's door, did you, Jock?"

"Souvenir for my mother," I said wittily.

"What kind of homes do you heathens come from?" he said, not unpleasantly.

They even lit a cigarette for me before slamming the big door.

And that was how I came to wake up in a cell with seventy quid in my shoes and a head like a box of hungry woodpeckers. Just an average night out on The Rookery scene, nothing to some of the rampages The Beast and I had chalked up.

Then, as big police feet were stamping outside the cell door, I spotted the discrepancy.

Pilbeam's money had been in brown tenners.

Exquisite had retrieved the wrong money—or maybe he robbed Harry the Spoofer of everything he was carrying.

Still, that was all right. Harry the Spoofer wouldn't go screaming for law. He might hire a heavy team to remove Exquisite's toes at the knees but that wasn't my worry, was it?

What was my worry, exactly?

Oh yes, I remember now, I'm twenty-nine and I have to find a way of becoming A Somebody before I'm thirty.

That is a worry, is it? Don't make me laugh.

Blueskin Blake visited Jack and Edgeworth Bess in the New Prison and slipped Jack a file. He cut through their fetters and a heavy window bar and they slid down twenty-five feet by their blankets, Edgeworth Bess in her underclothes to make for easier movement. They then climbed straight up a twenty-two foot high door, using its many bolts and bars as footholds. They dropped down into the street and did not hang about. Jack and Blueskin immediately started planning new burglaries.

7

The hatch slammed open.

"Want some tea?" shouted a giant's face peering in the tiny doll's house window.

I was slow getting off the bunk.

"Think this is the Dorchester—we don't serve it in fucking bed!"

My right hand had time to take delivery of a paper cup before he slammed the hatch, leaving my nose almost touching wood. That's when I saw the crudely gouged lettering again.

The bottom section of the door had been beaten black by decades of desperate toecaps. About halfway up green paint began to reassert itself. The uneven letters were gouged into the paint:

> *Please God*
> *just one*
> *more chance*
>
> B McLaughlin (gbh)

I tried to scratch the paint with a fingernail. As easy to cut a lovers' heart in granite. I looked round the walls, trying to imagine the pathetic crack-up of B. McLaughlin who had committed grievous bodily harm and then couldn't take his own punishment. A brute and a bully, sir. I went back to the bunk and tried not to puke up their stewed tea. In the end I poured it onto their choked lavatory pan.

Not being a brute and a cowardly bully, I lay on the bunk and forced myself to think constructively. I will admit that the small voice of panic called me from around other dimensional corners; half an hour alone in a cell can put you through a psychological spin-drier. Lose control and strange things happen; one minute the walls are coming in to crush you, the next you think your brain is swelling out to fill those hard corners. You think *they* are watching you through concealed peepholes. Every minute is a year of outside time—that year they carelessly buried you alive. You pray for the footsteps that will free you—you cringe in case they are going to kick shit out of you. You go mad staring at your watch. Anything that diverts you for a second is a blessed miracle—an itchy head, a sneeze, a big yawn. Your hands will not stay still. So you scratch your head or pick your nose or bite your nails or pull your wire—and then you see you only filled or killed seven seconds.

I kept control.

I brought out the fivers and tried to read them like a book.

Do you remember those old-fashioned white fivers, the big ones that dated back to the South Sea Bubble? As a boy, when Britain was great, I always thought to own one would be the real mark of growing up. By the time I got among adult money they were out of circulation and in any case I'd learned that the only magic about money is in the amount.

I digress?

In a cell you'll do anything to kill a minute.

I decided to match my brain against that of B. McLaughlin. An ingenious brute—they wouldn't have left a grievous bodily harm merchant with a chisel.

My pockets were empty, save for that crushed packet of Silk Cut kingsize.

"Is it the big morning?" I said.

Now why did I say that? Out loud?

I got up and walked about.

Got it!

Going across to the door I dropped my partial denture plate into my palm and presented the cutting edge of the incisors to wood. I succeeded only in making a faint dent.

The wet dentures slipped from my fingers and bounced silently on the green floor.

Bending down I had an even more imaginative idea. Listening for approaching footsteps I got onto my knees. Distorting my mouth, pulling back my chin, breathing heavily, I tried to gnaw at the rock-hard surface with own canines.

It is, you'll find, impossible to bite the middle of a door.

I lay down and tried to balance cigarettes on end. I even tasted a few shreds of tobacco. In spitting and spluttering I forgot to look at the watch for two whole minutes.

I put my hands under my head and stared up at the high ceiling. Typical of this life, wasn't it, that I was locked up and Pilbeam was kipped up cosily in his own bed? Why the hell did I want to save him from the cop? Ah yes, it's great to be famous, even a little bit famous. Women ask for your autograph. Everybody looks at you. So much money you can stop thinking about bloody money.

And, of course, you can hobnob on equal terms with the Ramsay Shands and Terry Pilbeams of this world. How spiffing.

I heard a male voice singing "The hills are alive with the sound of music."

Where did *big morning* come from?

The hatch banged open.

"Want a wash-up then?" roared the gaoler. I followed him into the corridor. Beside each locked cell door was a small square of blackboard and on each blackboard was chalked an abbreviation of the inmate's charge, rather like cage labels in a zoo. He pointed to a green-crusted tap sticking out of the wall above a slimy little handbasin.

"No thanks," I said.

He jerked his head for me to follow him back along the corridor.

"Don't I get bail?"

"Bail? Oh yeah?"

He looked at me with contempt. "How old are you, eh? Think you'll last long at this rate?"

I moved into the cell and turned. He was neatly shaved. His blue shirt came out in little rucks at the waist, sleeves rolled over elbows of large but flabby white arms.

"My wife'll kill me," I said, ingratiatingly. "You couldn't manage me a light, could you?"

He thought about it. Then he searched truncheon-deep pockets. I took the box. I noted that he was the kind of man who shoves spent matches back in the box. He looked like the kind of man who thought he was holding society together.

"You buggers!" he snorted. "Think we've got nothing better to do than waste time over petty drunks? Know why they arrested you? For your own fucking good. You could've been this geezer who got murdered last night-a knife in the guts, thirteen times! Sneer all you like—half of you wouldn't last two minutes without the bobby."

"I'm not sneering," I said. "What'll happen to me then?"

"The van takes you to court about nine." He frowned. "Don't any of you Jocks have *any* fucking sense?"

I shrugged. He suddenly slammed the door without so much as an au revoir. I still had his matches.

I went back to the bunk and smoked horizontally and told myself things could be worse.

When I'd been bored to madness I couldn't get my eyes to close but now that I had a fag and no fears of a life sentence I quickly fell asleep. The fag dropped on the mattress and burned a black sear on valuable government property. I didn't know about this until I surfaced to a din in the corridor. It was 9.08.

The door was thrown open by a bespectacled sergeant in a flat cap.

"On your bloody way then!" he barked, as if I was trying to establish squatter's rights.

As I was being ushered along the corridor it came to me—my belt! They empty your pockets to stop you committing suicide by swallowing an overdose of decimal currency or slitting your throat with a pound note, but they'd left me with my leather belt. The buckle had a two-inch metal spike.

I didn't ask them if I could go back to the cell to test it.

The big black van was parked tight against the outside wall at the end of the corridor. There was no way to go but up a few steps into a central gangway lined by slim metal doors.

Another copper propelled me into a cubicle and slammed the door shut.

It was about the size of an up-ended coffin. I sat on a small bench, knees jammed against the forward wall. On my left was a frosted window with a clear observation panel. Doors were banged, names shouted. The Black Maria lurched with the weight of each new miscreant. Bolts were rattled. A high-pitched West Indian voice was answered by a rapid gabble in the same lingo. The two blacks sing-songed at each other in great merriment, obviously calling the cops for all the shits in the world. I hoped they'd seen how many stairs there were to be fallen down accidentally.

God is my witness was scribbled in ballpoint on the much-decorated wall, *but he was not in court*. We felons soon learn to laugh at it all, you know. The worst has already happened to us.

I found that I was breathing, always a bad sign, when you notice it. The air stank of ammonia. It was very hot. The van went on sitting there. So tightly were my knees jammed against the wall my legs went numb.

'Wot you in for then?" said the wall, in a cracked cockney voice.

I hope yer coppers balls turn square and fester at the corners, Dave from Dalston 18 mths.

"Hey you, wot you in for Oi'm awskin'?" came the wall's

cracked voice. The West Indian voices shouted and laughed outrageously.

Kicked a rozzer but didn't kick him fucking HARD ENOUGH!!!

"You speaking to me?" I said to the wall.

"Yus, you bin a naw'ee boy then?"

"Drunk."

"That ole? They've caught me onnis church rooft, anney? An' now they're trynna myke summink owit!"

The wall laughed brutally. I said nothing.

May yer coppers pubic hairs turn to drumsticks and beat the living daylights out of yer.

"It's orl a mistyke, innit?" said the wall. "Oi keeps tellin' 'em, doan Oi, wot you keep pickin' on me for then? Oi mean, whoi dunt you fakkin busies git out there awfter them reel hooks steada bovverin' me alla toime?"

The wall guffawed. A slimy throat was cleared. The van started up and bumped out of the yard. Cheek pressed against cold glass, as if that might prevent suffocation, I stared through the slit. The Christmas-shopping people looked well-fed and satisfied. A prosperous woman in a belted fur coat and shiny black boots looked up from the kerb, glancing along the windows of our mobile cage. She was not embarrassed by the attentions of so many disembodied male eyes. I felt randy. I almost threw my neck trying to get another sight of those heavy, booted calves.

The Black Maria made several turns and stops and then came to a silent halt in a sunless, dead-end alley.

The riff-raff of The Rookery night had come to the backdoor of the place of judgment.

Eight citizens sit shoulder to shoulder on a wall bench facing another brick wall painted cream.

A middle-aged white man with numerous blue and red bruisings about his cheekbones and temples, wearing what were once office clothes.

A youth with Christ-length hair, wearing a swastika-adorned American combat jacket and purple trousers fitted into mauve leather boots with built-up wooden heels.

A pimply-faced negro labourer, wearing a black donkey jacket with WIMPEY stencilled across the back in yellow letters to match the yellows of the whites of his eyes.

Two close-cropped youths wearing white shirts without ties, black crombie overcoats, thin olive trousers, blood-coloured industrial boots, the red and white scarves dangling from the waists showing they are Arsenal supporters.

A sharp-featured white man of less than average height, wearing a neat brown suit, stiff-collared white shirt, one normal brown shoe, one brown surgical boot with a five-inch sole.

Ian Mintlaw McGraw (alias John Thompson, alias James Caskie) wearing a blazer-style jacket, light grey trousers, a roll-neck navy blue sweater, shabby suede shoes.

At the end of the line, nearest the metal door of the holding cell, a rain-coated, middle-aged white man whose skin, from neck to forehead, was the colour of lead, as if he had been shaded over by graphite pencil.

Christ: How long do these pigs keep us hanging about? What a rip-off!

Surgical Boot: Allus the fakkin same.

Bruised Man: They have no right to treat m-m-m-m-me like a cri-cri-criminal. Mister Treadworthy the ma-ma-ma-magistrate knows my background. My condition is m-m-m-medical.

Surgical Boot: Yeah—wot's the prescription then, squire, scotch an' gin?

Christ: They busted me in the Piccadilly tube station bog— just one joint. I hate the fuzz, I mean I really hate them. Pigs.

Surgical Boot: Diabolical, innit? Why don't all them rozzers git out there harassin' innocent motorists and leave us fakkin criminals alone?

McGraw: What did you do?

Surgical Boot: Street-tradin' wivout a licence. Ice-cream. Done me twenny-two times this monf already. Nuffink to it, two quid fine.

McGraw: Tax deductible, is it?

Surgical Boot: Tax? Wot's that, squire? Them fines is the only tax old Heaf gits outa me. You know why old Heaf wears a jockstrap then?

McGraw: Tell us.

Surgical Boot: To support the unemployed. You done anyfink spectackellar then?

McGraw: Robbed a bank.

Surgical Boot: Straight up?

McGraw: A blood bank.

Surgical Boot: Funny fakker.

McGraw: I was pissed, that's all.

Stencilled Negro: They said I was pissed and I was only taking sweet stout. Any of you boys manage me a smoke?

Surgical Boot: Wot've you two villuns bin up to then?

First Skinhead: Bit ov knuckle down Stamford Bridge. We wus fakkin unlucky, wunt we, Wayne? Him an' me's all they could collar, there's a whole mob ov us puttin' the boot into this Chelsea berk, wunt there, Wayne?

Bruised Man: You teenagers nowadays, w-w-what's all this football hoo-hoo-hooliganism in aid of, eh? We never be-be-be-behaved like that when I was young. This generation's s-s-s-sick in the head if you ask me.

First Skinhead: Nobody fakkin asked you, stoopid old cu-cu-cunt.

Surgical Boot: How'd Arsenal git on then?

First Skinhead: Won easy, dint we, Wayne? Charlie George scored two. There wouldn't ov been no bower only this Chelsea berk starts provokin' us, don't he, Wayne? I mean, bitta knuckle, you're entitled to expeck that, that's wot you goes for, innit, Wayne? But them Chelsea cunts—they was carryin' meat-hooks! I mean, he's entitled to a kickin', int he, Wayne?

Stencilled Negro: I wouldn't go near no football matches, not me, man.

Wayne: No, you wouldn't would yer, fakkin banana chops?

First Skinhead: Wot's red on the outside an' black on the inside an' gives yer a fakkin big thrill?

Surgical Boot: Yeah?

First Skinhead: Busload ov spades goin' over a cliff.

Surgical Boot: They got laws against jokes like them. How come they got you in this nick if you was down the Bridge?

First Skinhead: We've followed this Chelsea berk onna tube to Picadilly fore we could git him on his tod, dint we, Wayne?

Surgical Boot: It ain't you two wot murdered some ice-cream wiv a knife down Pollett Street last night then? All the rozzers was talkin' about it.

Bruised Man: It's time this whole c-c-c-country got some real discipline.

Surgical Boot: Yeah well, they're makin' a start wiv you, ain't they squire?

Amid all this cameraderie nobody speaks to the man with the leaden face. Some kind of heart condition, I assume.

Going across the big room where offenders are corralled prior to docking I saw Lead Face on a bench. There wasn't enough seating for the assembled miscreants, felons, dope-heads, frighteners and booze-hounds but Lead Face had room to spare, on either side. He was staring at his hands, which were coloured normal. An old granny with thin white fuzz on an eggshell skull tried to tap me for my last cigarette. She was wearing what might have once been a velvet opera cloak. Drink had given her ruddy cheeks. She was southern Irish.

"I've only the one left," I said.

"Ju're a meeserable young fella, are ye?" she asked calmly

"Here—look for yourself."

"I only deals wit gentlemen."

She shuffled away.

The typewritten list was stuck on the wall, a blurred carbon. James Caskie was number five. The list did not specify our crimes but they always put the petty drunks at the top. Scots and Irish names seemed to predominate. A man came close to my elbow, determined to speak, an office-worker perhaps, formal but inelegant, lacklustre grey hair flat with fixative and parted irrevocably in the middle.

"Could I possibly trouble you, old man?" He held up a cigarette in anticipation of a light.

"Sure."

When he saw I didn't have a fag he said, "I say, sorry old man, have one of mine." He went through the old-fashioned routine of tapping one end of his cigarette on a fingernail, as if modern fags were likely to suffer from an excess of tobacco, lighting the other end, taking a first puff with the cautious elan of a connoisseur risking a dubious cigar and then, with no change of tone or facial expression, saying:

"It's the most frightful to-do, actually, I had this pain in my derriere, a touch of constipation I told my better half. I went to the quack for a quick dose of dynamite to get the jolly old pipes moving. Two hours later I was on the operating table! It wasn't gummed-up works, it was a growth in the back passage! They sealed it off and put a tube from the jolly old waste disposal unit—plastic— it comes out here, just below the tummy button, *both* sorts, really the most frightful to-do, old chap, naturally I have no control over my motions, *both* sorts all in this bag strapped to my tum-tum—makes the most revolting pong at times, revolting, absolutely.

People notice, you know.

And then, last Thursday, I popped down into town to do some Christmas shopping—the blasted bag sprung a leak on me! Honestly, I thought I would keel over in the tube. How I got home I don't know. Christchurch! Still, it could be worse, the quacks assure me it was benign, they'll connect up the pipes in a month or so."

"What have they got you here for then?"

"Oh, it's the most frightful nonsense, damned typist says I touched her leg coming up the tube escalator yesterday morning."

"That's a crime, is it?"

"Girl's obviously a neurotic. Imagine—me? Still, I've spoken to a senior police officer, he doesn't think the charge will hold water for a minute."

"Like your bag, eh?"

"It isn't a laughing matter," he snapped, turning away abruptly.

I reached out to touch him—on the arm. He turned, face tightening in apprehension.

"My matches," I said.

He was most frightfully sorry old chap always doing it. Before I could say something pleasant he moved away.

That was when I saw Ramsay Shand. He was on a bench, about ten yards away. He looked like something the bodysnatchers had thrown back in. I edged a yard or so to my left, using a group of three heavies and their solicitor to screen myself from my boyhood hero. It wasn't a conscious decision to dodge him, merely a reflex action to avoid being lumbered. You had only to look at him to know he was a lumber-and I don't mean in the Scottish sense of dating a girl in a dancehall.

The three heavies were listening with mocking deference to their solicitor, an extremely tall young Jew in striped trousers. His clients' eyes were hooded by well-punched flesh. One had a broken nose, one had an arm in a crepe-bandage sling. All three constantly bobbed and dipped their shoulders to rearrange the sloping drapes of their black crombie overcoats. All three wore white shirts with high collars that reached well into the hairline. Their solicitor brayed a little too heartily in a public school accent and they winked to each other. Over their shifting shoulders I caught glimpses of Shand, seeing now how much he had changed since his bigtime days. The big chest was now a belly. The big nose was still the same but the flabbiness of his face brought out the incongruously feminine shape of his mouth, the pinkness of the lips heightened by rusty stubble. In that unshaven drunkard's face it stood out a mile, the poised mouth of an overbred aristocrat or salon fop, not so much weak as pretty.

I shrugged. Meeting him had destroyed a little leftover illusion, that was all.

They started bawling out the names. Lining up with the rest of the cocktail crowd I couldn't avoid him.

"Hullo, Jock," he said, his surprisingly high-pitched voice breaking through phlegm. His teeth were stained dark by wine.

"Have a good time with your reporter friends?" I said cheerily.

"Them reporter bastards? Is that where I met you? Och aye— that club. Those shits, all they wanted was to get me pissed. Hey, you couldnae lend us two quid, could you, I havnae got anything to pay the fine?"

Havnae? This was the man some literateur had once described as Gorki with jokes—Scotland's answer to Eugene O'Neill. Havnae was for my benefit, me being classed in his befuddled but still arrogant brain as a low-class jock of the sort you meet in gutters the world over.

"Yeah, sure," I said.

I dug into my hip-pocket and detached one of the blue fivers from the fold. The note slid from my bunched fingers to his hungry fist yet every drunk in the line saw it—and looked at me hungrily.

I enjoyed that moment. I hadn't done much with my life but he had once been world famous.

"Thanks, Jock," he said as the court officer called his name, "I'll see you outside. This is going to solve all problems."

He had opened his black leather jacket. His dirty fingers patted the sheaf of folded paper he had shown me the day before in The Hum Drum. It was sticking precariously out of his lining-pocket. He winked at me and closed his jacket. The court officer shouted again and Shand went through the door onto the stage of the courtroom.

I found myself standing next to Lead Face. I gave him a smile—but I was careful not to touch.

Magistrate: I'm never too sure if you Scots believe wholeheartedly in Santa Claus. If you do, Mister Caskie, I regret to spread disillusion but despite the proximity to Christmas your festive revelling will cost you two pounds. And I trust that now you've adopted English customs we can look forward not to having the pleasure of your company at New Year. Court titters.

The sergeant opened the brown envelope and slid my stuff across the desk. I gave him back the two pound notes left from my champagne night. He gave me a receipt. I signed another receipt for my bits and pieces.

He didn't notice me hesitating when I wrote the name James Caskie because I didn't hesitate.

Edging past a plainclothes man talking to a uniformed policewoman of girlish appearance I heard him saying, "... made a real mess of him—thirteen times in the abdomen—*and* they'd hurt him something diabolical. . . "

When I reached the pavement Shand was, of course, nowhere to be seen.

Still, five pounds of someone else's money had seemed a bargain for an ego-boost.

For a moment, on the pavement, I felt lonely. Imprisonment has its compensations, you know. It's like being in a play, you perform an ordained part. There are no problems of identity when you've been labelled.

Balls to questions of identity, I snapped at myself. I was hungry, randy, dehydrated, bilious, light-headed, thirsty and randy again, all at the same time. My socks were in a cold sweat and my skin felt dirty and I was still only twenty-nine. My life wasn't going down any anonymous drain. Pathetic bastard, hacking out his snivelling plea for just one more chance. You make your own luck in this game.

Who said that? Wittgenstein?

My first move was obviously to see my tailor.

I headed up a narrow alley into the Christmas shopping crowds milling along the street they used to call The Stony-Hearted Stepmother.

Coming down the steps was the blue-chinned weirdie who dresses as a woman and pushes a rusty pram decorated with white bows, tattered flowers and a curtain. He smiled his way past me in high heels and pink powder on hard stubble.

So what? If he was doing it on a stage, for money, they'd be making him a cult.

In Broad Military Way, as it was called a thousand years ago when I would have preferred to have lived if only because the new names are so boring, the masses who had once cheered the condemned in gallows carts had become flocks of eager consumers.

Where once hucksters and pedlars and patterers had sold St Audrey's tawdry geegaws the modern generation of street capitalists were flogging transparent umbrellas instead of ballad sheets, glass beads instead of anti-plague nosegays, mechanical dolls instead of quack nostrums—nobody had thought up a way of plasticising hot chestnuts.

A short walk along The Stony-Hearted Stepmother. A violent exchange of Saxon curse words between a taxi-driver and a maddened pedestrian. A man who had to walk doubled at the waist. A negro with frizzy hair tinted green at the edges. A craning knot of suckers round a team of three-card tricksters. Newspaper placards, *Bank Robber Shoots Children . . . London MPs Named In Corruption Hearing . . . Famous Music Hall Queen Dies Penniless. . . London's Homeless A Record—Official. . . Third Minister In Call Girl Scandal?. . .*

In the big store I spent five of the blue fivers on new vest and underpants, blue zip-jerkin, maroon cashmere sweater, fawn trousers, Terylene socks (red with black dots). Carrying two large paper bags I went into a cut-price shoe-shop and spent another five on suede Hush puppies, fawn, size ten to go with my big feet. That left seven of the fivers from my shoes. Feckless, that's us bums.

The street seemed noisier than ever. Lines of cars, buses, taxis, Common Market juggernauts moved jerkily round obstructions caused by parked vans, mostly those high-backed garment trade jobs already delivering loads of brand new shoddy for the January clearance sales. But there was another reason for congestion.

Under a low, grey sky the street suddenly became a thunderous tumult of marching men, a roaring, shuffling, chanting, human avalanche stretching as far as Empty Profit Tower. Above the river of heads floated trade union banners of all shapes and colours; heavy placards on twin-poles lurched from side to side like stately howdahs; cheer-leaders barked through battery-operated megaphones, orchestrating the angry voices into cannon-boom shouts; girls leaned out of the windows of offices above the boutiques and dress-shops; the marchers waved and whistled; industrial men in parkas— knee-length moped parkas in khaki with rabbit-fur trimmings; quilted nylon parkas in neon reds and pinks; how about a three-quarter length donkey jacket in light fawn with fake leather facings coloured *beige?* I would have been in a decent industrial union if my mother hadn't wanted me in a collar and tie. You couldn't inhabit The Rookery for long without coming to despise these factory-slaves as mugs, sheep to be fleeced, but that day they had a new virility; somebody was frightened of them—why else was their procession headed by senior police officers, flanked by constables, shepherded by squad cars and tailed by green buses packed with riot-detachment constables?

Burn down the tax office first, comrades!

At the next corner pedestrians were crushed together, some staring, some complaining bitterly. An important middle-aged man in a brown trilby hat forced his way through the column to reach the south side pavement. His face was red with resentment at the mockery which followed him from the proletarian ranks. A side-runner forced a union pamphlet at him. He crumpled it savagely and stamped on it. To all us bystanders he barked:

"Let them try to hold their damned demos in Moscow I say!"

"Keeps the unemployed off the streets, dunnit?" said the corner newsvendor.

"I think they're very unfair to Mister Heath," said a woman to her shopping companion. "It's not his fault everything costs so much, is it?"

I was just getting out of the crowds and into the daytime tranquillity of The Rookery when a blonde girl got in front of me. Cold as it was she was wearing a magenta t-shirt and dirty summer trousers. I tried to side-step but she caught hold of my sleeve. Her face was dirty. She was about twenty.

"We're starving," she said in a hooray voice. "Could you spare us a shilling or two for something to eat? I wouldn't ask but we're desperate."

She looked over to a doorway in which there was a young guy lolling, thin, long hair, white face, bombed.

"He's an addict and they stopped his social security money and we haven't eaten for three days," she said. "Please help us."

"I'm a gin addict myself," I said, pleasantly enough. "I work to pay for mine."

Before I'd taken the next step she had darted to one side and started spieling at two other common buggers who, like myself, would not have been socially acceptable as fiancés when she still owned jodhpurs.

Immediately I regretted this upsurge of viciousness and told myself I must become more relaxed with people. I didn't, however, regret it enough to go back and offer her money.

Major Tomkins, the block manager, was standing on the inside stairs of the Chambers. I picked my way towards him across twenty or thirty red mailbags, all bulging angularly and padlocked.

"Morning Mister Thompson," he said, which was just as well as I was still thinking of myself as James Caskie, "These blinking people are getting out of bounds." He glared at the mailbags.

"Another consignment of porn for the frustrated provinces?" I said.

"The GPO sends a special van for it—favoured customers! It's hardcore, by the blasted ton!"

"What's the country coming to, eh?"

"Never mind the blinking country, they wangled a three-year lease out of me at five pounds a week. For this sort of filth they should be coughing up fifty a week."

"Tip off the cops, have them nicked."

"What—and get the building a bad name? By the way, don't be surprised if your room has been turned over. I've had five break-ins reported this morning. Damn burglars—pity those blinking trade unionists won't work as hard."

Nothing the Major ever said gave any indication that he knew he was commanding The Rookery's biggest fleapit.

He came up the stairs with me. On the first-floor landing a sheet of paper was pinned to the door of Madame Rebecca, Hands Read, Your Fortune in the Cards, Crystal Ball by Special Arrangement. This Madame Rebecca charged thirty bob a consultation to a steady flow of middle-aged women who otherwise looked normal enough; printed on the sheet of paper in shaky capitals was a message: DUE TO UNFORESEEN CIRCUMSTANCES MADAME REBECCA APOLOGISES THAT SHE CANNOT KEEP TODAY'S APPOINTMENTS.

Three nervous Slavs were waiting by the door of the European Gold Investment Co. The thin smell of burning joss came from the entrance to Pataudi's Yogic Healing Surgery, Chronic Ailments Helped Through Divine Power.

The Major went in to try his power on the chronic rent problem. I went on up, whistling 'Look What They've Done To My Song, Ma'. The two words—Big Morning—came back into my silent orations. They seemed reminiscent of something.

On the third floor a man with a brown briefcase was giving a fast spiel to Dunbar St John, a haughty black who, from a room admittedly bigger than ours, ran a conglomerate which included The Third World Flat Finders Service, Glamgals Models, the Angola People's Defence Fund, Songwriters' Co-operative and The Eldorado Loan Consultancy.

It was a rare day when that building didn't echo to the heavy tramp of weary-faced investigators of all kinds, debt collectors, county court bailiffs, inspectors from the rates department, Electricity Board, Social Security, County Council agency licensing department, Post Office—even, according to Neville, the Anti-Slavery League.

". . . the appropriate time of year for helping those less fortunate," the briefcase man was saying hurriedly, "These excellent Christmas decorations—" he opened the briefcase on a raised thigh— "no, sir, only a moment of your time, sir, these are all made by authenticated spastics, sir, a most worthy—"

"I believe you," said St John, closing the door.

It's a hard, interesting world, I said to myself, opening our door and letting myself in. I left the *Cleaner's Store* notice up to fox the man from authenticated spastics.

The room stank of smoke. I plugged in the fire and took off my dirty gear. The briefcase man was knocking on other doors, none of which opened, the tenantry having extrasensory perception for duns and patterers.

The dirty underwear and socks I rolled up and lobbed out of the window in the general direction of the dustbins. I should sit with a book in a laundorama to save pennies? My trousers I folded neatly and laid in my wardrobe, the Oxfam collection on the bottom level of the metal shelving. The blazer-style jacket I hung from a hook behind the door.

I'd keep it for suave business conferences and use the blue zip-jerkin for the cocktail circuit.

Standing on a couple of blank agency contract forms, being totally naked, I pulled on my new red socks with the black dots. Simultaneously, the phone rang and the door knocked. Pulling on my flagrantly blue choice of underpants I lifted the phone.

"What the fuck happened to us last night?" said Pilbeam. "I can't remember a bloody thing after the Congo-"

"Hang on, Teepee, somebody's, hammering at the door."

"Must be the same geezer who's hammering at my head."

New socks sliding and scratching on the carpet, bare shoulders and chest and thighs feeling cold draughts, I pulled the door open six inches and growled:

"No thank you."

But I was not glaring into the eyes of the authenticated spastics man. I was two feet away from a girl with blue eyes, broad cheeks and a pink complexion. The rest of her was only to be guessed at behind a black beret, belted brown coat with grey fur collar, thigh-length suede boots in purple, and black leather gloves.

"Neville Thirsk?" she said in a hooray accent, eyes doubtfully assimilating my seductively bare, ivory-white shoulder.

"No," I said, shaking my head.

She stared at my unshaven chin, my tantalising display of naked arm, and then at the *Cleaner's Store* notice.

"Isn't this the William Toms Agency?" she said. "I was told room sixty-nine."

Hooray is a musician's word, coined from the weird cries emitted by stimulated debutantes at society balls. It means upper-class, public school, the languid drip voice of our over-privileged class. It isn't meant to flatter.

Call a guy a Hooray Henry and you know he is an arrogant imbecile who ought to be hanging from a lamp-post to pay for the sins of his father the capitalist brute who sent our kids down the mine. Like his money, his sins are inherited—no Hooray is capable of earning anything, wealth or damnation, unless in a hooray conspiracy like the Stock Exchange.

Were I not such a relaxed, mature, amiable loafer I'd shoot the fucking lot of them.

"My name's Angela Browne—with an e," she said, becoming impatient. "I have an appointment with a man called Neville Thirsk." "You?" I said, eyes widening. She was the mug, the sucker who was going to be sold a phony partnership in the bent band agency!

I don't suppose Wittgenstein had to make far-reaching decisions of practical moral philosophy while standing in socks and pants at a narrowly-open door facing an unknown beauty with a foul-mouthed disc jockey hanging on the phone and a smalltime shyster selling bogus charity goods coming up the stairs and a healthy stirring in his y-fronts.

I thought I handled it fairly well.

"Can you wait there for a moment? I don't have any clothes on. If that guy tries to sell you decorations tell him to piss off."

I closed the door.

Who was Wittgenstein anyway? We didn't hear a lot about him at Ferguslie Junior Secondary.

Holding the phone with one hand I tried to dress with the other Pilbeam remembered being in the Congo but next thing he could be sure about was being breathalysed by the cops in Hatton Garden while driving home to the Barbican. He also knew he had woken up on his own sofa without any money.

When he finished the dialogue rehearsal I said I had somebody important in the office and would ring him back in fifteen minutes.

"You can't," he said, "I'm off this moment on my north country disco-gigs. Another ten days of bloody piss-ups!"

He rang off.

I pulled up my new fawn trousers, broke the heels of my new hush-puppies and found her leaning against the banister at the top of the stairs.

"I'm decent now," I said.

She stepped inside our room and stated at one of Neville's decorations, a *News of The World* bill: PLEASING OLDER WOMEN, The World's Newest Profession. She frowned. She examined the adjacent *object*, a *People* bill: AMAZING GOAT MILK SEX BOOST.

"Curioser and curioser," she said, examining me. "Why do you have a notice saying this is a cleaner's room?"

"Camouflage," I said, suavely adjusting the neck of my new sweater and sitting down behind the desk. "The bills are alive with the sound of burglars' jemmies."

"What on earth could a burglar find to steal in here?"

She tested both chairs and then decided to rest her buttocks against the window-ledge. I lay back in the swivel chair and put my hands behind my head. She was solidly built. The pinkness of her face owed a lot to cosmetics but to compensate she had a slight Nefertiti squint, the faintest in-turning of an eye that creates an intensity of gaze and is found in many truly beautiful women, usually about the eyes.

"The Beast will be a little late," I said, pleasantly, giving her time to assimilate my relaxed, eccentric charm.

"Who is The Beast?" she asked without passion.

"Neville Thirsk. No Rookery night is complete without the sight of Neville making a beast of himself, lurching into the popular venues, drinking up like there's no tomorrow, falling about and then reeling out again, generally to the chorus of 'Will Ye No Come Back Again *please*'"

"Really?"

My eyes chanced to rest on the desk and there I saw page 167 of *A Bed Of Men*. Blushing but only on the inside, I pushed the typewritten sheets together and dropped then nonchalantly in a drawer.

"Paperwork," I said, dismissively. "By the way I was changing into new clothes when you knocked, I don't normally leap about the office half starkers."

"I didn't notice actually."

"If I'd known you were coming I would have been starkers."

She put on a guarded face.

"Will your partner be long?"

"How long do we need?"

I grinned disarmingly but she didn't. On my desk she put a small black handbag and a folded copy of the mid-morning *Standard*. She lifted her arms and pulled off her beret, shaking out her hair.

She had red hair. Not wish-washy ginger, not a copper tint from a bottle—no, red, as in fire engines.

All my life I'd been nuts about red hair—on women—yet I'd never had it away with a redhead. (I know my attitude to women sounds disgracefully immature but what can I do about it, except grow up? And it's probably too late for that.)

Angela Brown with an e then unbuttoned her coat. She had substantial breasts under a lacy white blouse with a high, buttoned collar. (I know it looks as if I can only see women as sex objects. It must have been all those girls who knew they were sex objects and used the fact mercilessly. Women pay a high price for all that cruelty they inflict on us teenage boys.)

"Do we require somebody to do the introductions?" she said, pinioning my furtive personality with those *slightly* squinting eyes. "You do have a name?"

"You can call me anytime. My name's John Thompson-you can still call me anytime. Do you mind if I shave?" I brought the battery razor out of the bottom drawer. "Handy gadget, eh? It's that well-known brand Fallen Off A Lorry. I bought it in a pub from a man I didn't know and wouldn't recognise again. Of course I had no idea it was stolen." I twisted my manly jaw hither and thither, the battery whirring sexily. "I'm not always this cheerful," I went on, "but I got drunk last night and was locked up by the *polizei*."

She watched me smoothing down my neck. I knew it was nervousness making me prattle but that's why I started drinking in the first place, so that I wouldn't be nervous with women.

"You want to buy into this glamour, do you?" I said.

"Possibly."

"Must be rough where you come from."

"I had a private nursing agency but I have sold it."

"Good racket that, isn't it? Forging their wills and poisoning them and whatnot?"

"It's very hard to convince people you're not running a call-girl service. It became a bore." She looked round the room. "It must be very hard for you to convince people you are not running a junk stall."

"From now on I'll sweep the carpet regular.'

I switched off the razor and dropped it in the drawer. I stared at her. Those eyes! That red hair! Those broad cheeks! Those solidly filled purple boots! One sign that she fancied me and I'd tell her the truth about Neville's swindle and she'd fall into my arms in gratitude and I'd propose marriage and we'd rush off to her luxury flat and she'd cover my face in her red hair and afterwards we'd gaze into each other's wonderstruck eyes and live happily ever after and tell our kids how funny Daddy was that first time Mummy came to his office in that romantically decrepit building in The Rookery.

Knowing I was going to say something dramatic—such as let's go for a quick drink before Neville gets here—I covered my hesitation by reaching for her *Standard*. Why shouldn't it happen like this, I thought, those magazine dum-dums couldn't have invented love at first sight, could they?

I saw the word 'Murder' in a headline.

"There was a murder near here last night," I said, "They've got it here—it was the talk of cell block eleven—"

"Were you really locked up in a police station?" she asked, her voice beginning to acknowledge that I was not one of the faceless.

"If it was a massage kiosk they were keeping the girls well hidden," I said, twisting the paper round to read what was below the fold.

I noticed something else. She had taken off her left glove but not her right. Her bare hand was pink, with no rings.

I started to read it out loud. I got as far as "The body of - " And then my eye was racing ahead and I began to shrivel inside.

He had been beaten and stabbed thirteen times in the stomach. His body had been found by a constable in a pile of uncollected rubbish near the Pollett Street vegetable market. Police had established that he lived in Tottenham and used several names, Harold Francis Whately, Harry Franks, Frank Harrison. He was a metal engraver, 51, with a wife and three grown-up children. His wife had identified the body. Police were checking late-night drinking clubs to trace the dead man's movements. Robbery was thought to be the motive as the dead man had only three old halfpennies in his pockets. Our crime reporter said there were known to be two gangs of vicious muggers working the West End and—

A key turned in the lock and in came Neville, his countryboy's face red with the exertion of running up the stairs, his daily exercise.

"This is Angela Browne," I said, getting up and heading for the lavatory.

William Field, a fence working for Wild, turned in Sheppard and Blueskin Blake and they were sentenced to be hanged for stealing cloth from a Mr William Kneebone, the real crime being not having cut Wild in. In Newgate Prison there was a spiked hatchway between the public visiting room and the condemned hold. During visiting times Jack cut through a spike and two of his lady loves pulled him through the gap while the turnkeys were drinking. They smuggled him out, probably in woman's clothing. A few days later he was arrested in Finchley.

8

I didn't panic.

I thought a lot of nervous thoughts in a very short time but it's only panicking if you lose your bottle.

Did Exquisite murder him?

No—he only leaned on him hard enough to get the money back.

Get the money back? From a hardened old con man? As easy to get shit from a rocking-horse.

Those blue fivers are proof that Exquisite cleaned the guy out.

But Exquisite wasn't carrying a knife.

How the hell do you know? He's an expert at hiding knives, isn't he?

No—he would have been covered in blood. Thirteen stab wounds? He didn't have time to clean himself up.

You being drunk you can be sure of that can you?

Jesus.

It's all down to the money, isn't it? If Exquisite did it and they can trace that seventy quid back to you—

Keep the head, for Christ's sake. You're an ordinary, law-abiding citizen who just happened to be on the scene, that's all.

Oh yeah? I was in the company of a well-known disc jockey (who's just told me he can't remember *anything* great witness he'll make!). But I have the best alibi of all—I was arrested.

Really? You mean you were picked up in the street fifty yards from where they found the body, holding seventy quid from the dead man's pockets? Giving a false name at the nick? Only your real name isn't your real name either, it's the one you use to dodge tax and stamps.

Jesus!

I gave Shand one of those fivers. He paid his fine with it!

Forensics!

Keep cool. The very worst that can happen is they dig you up in their investigations and spread the good word round officialdom that you're only a tax outlaw, not a killer's mate.

That all? So you're locked in a room with hard-faced detectives, the filth. They want to fit up Exquisite for the murder. You are loyal—for a minute and a half. Exquisite is up at the Old Bailey. You get police protection—for a while.

Then Exquisite's loyal friends drop round to give your legs the zig-zag look. Remember that geezer they nailed to a Rookery wall and flogged with barbed wire?

Keep cool. Forensics aren't so brilliant they can prove those fivers were in the possession of The Spoofer. He probably only had them in his pockets for a few hours.

Sweat analyses?

Keep cool.

There was a knock at the door.

"Stop playing with yourself—we're going for a drink," said Neville's voice.

He rattled the door. When I came out, face expressionless, he eyed me curiously.

"You told her anything?"

"No."

"Okay, we'll play it by ear—I'll give you the cues." He rubbed his hands together and gave me a nudge.

"I think she's ripe for plucking, don't you?"

I am facing doom whichever way I turn—and he's merrily dragging me into a conspiracy to defraud, a genuine, premeditated crime?

Which way are the hills? As we came out onto the pavement a trendy girl from the tail end of the workers' demo (straight blonde hair to her waist, small spectacles with metal rims) tried to sell us a left-wing newspaper.

"Read the truth about the Tory property swindlers," she chirped into our faces.

Side-stepping her neatly, Neville said:

"Sorry, luv, I *am* a Tory property swindler."

The girl snorted in contempt. Angela Browne laughed, as so many women did when Neville was being a character.

"Who speaks the honest truth these days?" he said grandly, turning into Colman Hedge Lane. "Tell Joe Bloggs it's stopped raining outside and he thinks you're trying to con him out of his plastic mac. Tell him he's being robbed and he hits you in self-defence. Crazy, isn't it?"

"Especially as you are a swindler," I growled.

"I saw a funny thing the other day," he went on. "I was going down to the ticket agency to get seats for the panto and I stopped to watch this three card team. There's a geezer standing beside me, quite well dressed by Burton's standards obviously up for the day from some fresh-egg dump like Tring. Anyway, I'm in the ticket place, for maybe fifteen minutes and when I come out this punter is running up and down asking people if they've seen a cop. These two rozzers come along. He grabs one of them and shouts that he's been robbed of a hundred quid—his Christmas present money for the wife and kids. He's actually crying on the copper's coat! The cop says, Nothing we can do, mate, they'll have scarpered by now. You shouldn't play these games! See what I mean—you can't tell anybody."

"But you didn't tell him," I said, resentfully.

"Why bother? What kind of mug thinks he'll stroll into the

West End of London and just happen to bump into a bunch of sporting gents having an honest game of chance on top of a cardboard box on the pavement? You can't tell an idiot like that, he learns the hard way."

"I've often seen them playing that game," said Angela. "Don't the police ever catch them?"

"Occasionally they drag a couple of the dog eyes into court, the ones that watch on the corners, just to make it look good."

"You mean they don't really try to catch them?"

"Shocking, isn't it? Oh-oh, let's cross over sharpish."

He caught Angela's elbow and gave her no option but to follow him between a couple of moving taxis. I got through before the next car. Neville was hurrying.

"It's Broken Back Brown," he said to me.

I had a cautious look. They were on the other side, Broken Back Brown, a stocky man with a walking-stick, leader of The Scots Team. Beside him were two other men. I recognised both immediately. One was Paisley Dave, a youngish guy who always wore a white raincoat.

The third was Ramsay Shand.

I couldn't see McMenemy the Enemy or Otto Daffae the German. The last time we'd bumped into them socially they were boasting about how they'd rescued this internationally famous, homosexual, alcoholic painter from the gutter. He was so grateful he started giving them presents of cash, on one occasion a thousand pounds in a supermarket carrier-bag. I remember thinking he would have been safer in the gutter.

To avoid any chance of them catching sight of us we turned quickly into The Three-Legged Mare, a pub we normally avoided.

"I dodge that crowd at all times," Neville said to Angela. "One day I made the mistake of going with them for a quiet drink! We get into this rotten hole—The Septic Tank would you believe—and there isn't much light and Brown, the one with the limp, he puts his hand on a bar stool to steady himself—only the woman's black poodle is sleeping on the stool and his full weight comes down on the dog and it yelps and takes a bite out of his hand. Bit of a shock for anybody. Broken Back Brown don't mess about—he drops the stick, grabs the animal—and breaks its back across his knee. Just like that—snap! Then he hurls it against the wall."

"That's horrible!"

"That's what the dog said! Now then, what's your pleasure?"

The Three-Legged was not a popular pub. It sold the same booze as the others, the decor was equally modern by 1935 standards, and the guv'nor and his wife were friendly enough, being known as Mr and Mrs Vulture more from the shape of his nose than any predatory traits, but in the mysterious chemistry of pub popularity its formula was somehow wrong. You could always get room at the bar, while a hundred yards up the street in The Leafless they were elbowing you in the face to get a drink.

In a peculiar way it seemed fortunate we had come in here rather than the hurly-burly of The Leafless. I was still suffering from shock at my possible involvement in The Spoofer's murder. It seemed incomprehensible, to have his face and his voice still fresh in my mind and yet to think of him lying on a slab. I could feel my flesh curling so vividly could I imagine what a knife going into you thirteen times must feel like? How could he be *dead!*

Turned off, they used to say, just like a lamp.

I felt sick.

Angela and I sat facing each other across a table while Neville was at the bar. It was a small, wooden table, rectangular, the scarred planks slightly warped. Underneath it had a crosspiece of cast-iron. This reminded me of my mother's old sewing-machine with the foot-pedal grille. A Singer. Because of the nearness of the brick walls across the side-street most of the light in the bar came down on us from the highest part of the window, a soft, grey daylight that didn't have the strength to penetrate shadows yet drained colour from whatever it touched; everything seemed timeless and static—the reversed lettering on the outside of the high window, the silently watching men on the bar stools, the crushed cigarette ends in a red china ashtray—static, asleep, waiting for an electric switch.

Harry the Spoofer was still there, laughing and joking and conning us, still there in my head. How could he now be non-existent?

The words Big Morning came back into my head. Why?

"There you go," said Neville breezily, putting down the glasses. She was having a glass of dry white wine and I was having a Bacardi and Coke. Neville, as always, was lining his stomach for the day's intake with a pint of draught Guinness. My fingers felt cold on the curve of the glass. "So where do we start?"

"One thing I've already noticed," she said, holding the wine glass in a gloved hand, "nobody seems to be over-working."

"Nobody's doing much business in Christmas week," said Neville. "And January's a dead month. Next week we'll start getting wheels in motion for February and March dates. Except for Haggis here, he still has his pagan New Year to mark in the customary toxic debauch."

I looked at him with a passive kind of curiosity. My partner? This fair-haired, podgy-cheeked Englishman? Even now it's hard for me to decide what I really think about Neville.

In a conformist, gutless world he was alive, breezy, a guy you'd be glad to meet in a bar anywhere in the world, even if the last time he stole your money and your wife.

Can a rock be a symbol of irresponsibility?

You could certainly rely on Neville—to be scurrilous.

He was indomitable in his search for self-indulgence, stalwart in his rascality, heroic in his drunken foolishness. The only virtue a rock has is that it's always there.

So reliable was Neville's irresponsible misbehaviour he made Gibraltar seem shifty. He intended to cheat this girl and then to swindle me out of my share but he was *there* and three years of my life were there with him.

"I think you could possibly find a more attractive office," said Angela.

"A flash suite—at thirty quid a week plus rates?" he retorted. "You're only paying for bullshit. All we do is screw money out of a telephone. We could do it from a public callbox but for the weather. Let me fill you in. I got the agency from a guy who owed me a few bob—who William Toms was I never did find out-anyway, who's interested in the smalltime operators of yesteryear? What we do is hustle up dates for bands. You ever heard the expression buying and selling?"

"It's quite widely used, actually."

"It means something different in our racket. We buy gigs—band dates—from promoters at one price and we sell them to band agents at another price. The only tangible asset we have is a list of names and phone numbers. Let's say I'm dealing with Sid Greed who's got a few venues in Lancashire. I'll ask him how he's placed for March dates. He maybe has a vacant Friday night. Knowing his venue and what he can pay I offer him a band, Buggins and the Tub thumpers, at a hundred and twenty quid. He says okay so we pencil in the date. Then I phone Buggins's own agent and offer him the date for ninety quid. If the band's free he'll take it. Work's work and nobody is turning down gigs these days."

"You mean he's paying you a hundred and twenty pounds but you're only paying the band ninety pounds?"

"You got it in one. We skin thirty quid off the top. We also take five per cent split-commission of the ninety—four pounds fifty? You'd get muscle-bound ears and starve to death if you tried to exist on the straight commission."

"But don't the bands complain?"

"If they hear about it they sometimes make a moan. But we do separate contracts—one between Sid Greed and our agency, another between us and Buggins's agent. Most of the time the bands don't know what the promoter is actually paying."

"Don't they ask when they get to the hall?"

"A lot of these bands are usually too pissed to know what town they're in let alone get busy sleuthing out the high finance.

"It doesn't sound very ethical," she said, naively.

"Get away," he said, smiling outrageously. He looked at me. "You're the bookworm, me son, come across this word ethical much in your tomes?"

I shrugged.

"And that's all there is to it?" she said.

"Not quite. You do have to be known, get about the scene, keep in touch, make your face fit, know what bands are going out at what prices, keep one jump ahead of dodgy promoters. Most people know we skin a bit off the top but we're not as diabolical as some. You might say they can trust us only to cheat them a little bit."

"And what kind of money do you make?"

"I'll get Walter Just to show you a set of books. Not that they shouldn't be winning fiction awards but they'll show you how much we're paying tax on. It's a caper where you can make exactly how much you want to make—here, me son, remember that day we had the energy virus and bashed away on the phone for six solid hours?"

"Yeah," I said. It all sounded furtive. Was this how my life looked to other people?

"We screwed about four or five hundred quid out of the phone that day. I'll tell you my thinking, Angela, Silent John there and I are a lazy pair of buggers, we like the occasional afternoon off to get round the drinking dens, relaxing, unwinding—just the occasional afternoon, certainly never more than once a day. Sometimes we knock up a ton—a hundred quid—on a feverish Monday and we kind of lose the edge for the rest of the week. But if we had a reliable third partner—"

"To do the slogging while you are off unwinding?"

"Maybe it would give us a new sense of purpose. The lolly is just lying there at the bottom of the well, the bucket can go down as often as you like to turn the handle. I like that, I'll use it in by autobiography when I make my million and retire at thirty-five. You getting the drinks in, partner? Pint of DG for me—Angela? White wine?"

As I was standing up she said:

"Now you've told me the secrets what's to stop me starting the same thing myself? All I need is a room and a phone."

"And six or seven years of falling about pubs and clubs with all the other operators behind you," he said, winking at me. "I'm silly but not stupid, ducks, there are other angles . . . "

No, you're not stupid, Neville, I thought, waiting for Mrs Vulture to take my order. Underneath that clever display of boyish roguery there's a genuine rogue.

Everything he'd told her was true. It worked exactly as he said and we did make four hundred and seventy pounds one day last August. The one thing the sucker cannot legislate for is the intention in the mind of the con-man.

She wouldn't even be able to call cops *afterwards*.

The new partnership would work just as he said, for about three months. Then the rows would start, apparently spontaneous arguments about policy, complaints that she was having to do all the work. The partnership would split up—she might even be conned into buying him out—say another thousand. He would have been careful to keep a good whack of his contacts to himself, promoters she didn't know about. He would rent another cheap room, invent a new agency name and leave her to flounder in a scene she hardly knew. For a small inconvenience of finding a new office he would have screwed two grand out of her. Knowing the bastard well, it was highly likely he'd also have screwed her the other way into the bargain.

And this was the sort of thing I was throwing my life away on, was it? Suppose I died right now? Like The Spoofer—they'd put him down in black and white as a petty con-man, an unlovable thief of The Rookery night. They'd never bother to say he had been a good laugh, even when he was robbing you.

In black and white what would I be down as? A partner in joke businesses, a collaborator in fraud, a drunken Scot?

I brought the drinks back and sat staring moodily. I noticed that she used her bare hand for lifting a glass but her gloved hand for cigarettes, no doubt to obviate unsightly nicotine stains, which wasn't surprising the way she smoked, holding each cigarette in her fingers until it was a dangerous stub.

Neville decided we would go on to The Leafless. Walking behind them to the door I had the haunted feeling that they were in a warm, cosy film and that I was not.

On the pavement Neville did his usual dash, taking her arm and stepping off the kerb. She hesitated. He strode on. I was not surprised to realise I was seeing what he would be like in ten years' time, impatient, arrogant, all superficial boyishness thrown off. I was not surprised because everything seemed to have already happened in my brain one minute before it reached my eyes. I didn't know what was coming but when it did I recognised it. Clearly in my head, especially when I closed my eyes, I saw The Spoofer's dead profile, eyes closed, nose sticking up into the air. Angela stood back nervously.

I stepped into the street, took her hand, led her through the moving gap between a Mercedes and a lorry loaded with bricks.

That hand was not flesh and bone.

As we reached the other pavement and stepped over a spew of rubbish she looked at me expectantly but my face showed nothing as I let go of her artificial hand. Nothing could surprise me any longer.

With Angela between us, her black beret at our shoulders, her small, booted feet doing a skip-step every four or five paces to keep up, we hurried along the pavement. At least Neville was hurrying. Angela was doing her little skips to keep up. If they had run I would have run but I would not have known why. Nothing could surprise me for nothing seemed real. The buildings were already small and old-fashioned, frozen relics in sepia-tinted photographs of the past. The people's clothes looked *dated,* their motives for hurrying and scurrying already made inaccessible by historical remoteness. I might have been a time-traveller.

This sensation of remoteness disturbed me for I could see no valid reason for it. I had always known that psychology is crap mumbo-jumbo for idiots who would save money by going back to God. I had always considered myself a big, healthy layabout who understood everything and was too sensible to care.

When we pushed through the painted glass door of The Leafless Tree we were greeted jeeringly by some of the usual faces; little Roger Parkes the record producer; Thunder-buttocks Watson the struggling comedian (struggling because his natural wit died the moment it was for money); Lennie Drake, a session musician; Tommy something, a music arranger and failed composer (or decomposer, as he said); little Rodney Jackson, a pop magazine writer who yearned for Higher Things.

I asked for a Bacardi and Coke and went to the lavatory, telling myself I would eat as soon as my stomach stopped feeling numb. As I stared at the graffiti ("I am eight inches long and want to be sucked off". . . "How long is your cock?") I frowned, unable to understand why the death of a gutter-rat like The Spoofer should affect me like this. I'd only met him once. He'd stolen our money—how could I feel any sympathy for him?

I just didn't understand it. Me—a hard bastard who didn't even know if his own mother was still alive?

The circle had been joined by John the Baptist and his two sidekicks, No Chance Cheesewright and Fred Matchan. As always in the a.m. Cheesewright's eyeballs were wet and red, the true drunkard's eyes that seemed to have been scraped by the same blade that nicked his raw cheeks. JTB was playing his jolly uncle role, being older than everybody else.

Because it was Christmas and this was neutral ground he and Neville were suppressing their mutual hostility, at least to the extent of ignoring each other completely, although they were only seven or eight feet apart in a semi-circle of mutual friends who talked to them both, often simultaneously.

Could two grown men nurture such venom for each other over a fucked-up deal in pop-star badges? Or was it because J. Talbot Baxter had been known as John The Baptist ever since a famous sneer of Neville's, made at this very same bar—"The way he pontificates you'd think he was just one step ahead of Jesus Christ"?

Did that mean that JTB had a deep resentment at being considered a joke person? Was he, too, thinking of what they'd say about him after his light had been turned off?

I looked at his ridiculous hairstyle and his fat face and thought, It's too late for you, J. Talbot Baxter, your obituary is already written and you can't change a word of it.

I kept looking round as I stood there fiddling with coins in my pocket, listening to the chat, smiling when they smiled, all the time feeling as if I was hovering invisibly a few feet above them. There faces were mobile, integrated, involved; all around were laughing people, in pairs and groups, giving orders, handing over money, passing round glasses; I didn't understand any of them; it was my language they were using but as the words came to my ears I seemed to be frowning with the mental effort of translation.

And all the time I kept seeing and hearing The Spoofer, as though he was here among us. I looked and my eyes saw the gloved, artificial hand of Angela Browne, who had red hair and a slight squint; my eyes moved up and I saw the well-preserved Mrs Wallis, the landlady, being girlishly skittish with two middle-aged executives pretending they were young and lusty again.

". . . yeah, we were in the Jack Ketch having a few and in comes Dennis waving a cheque above his head, smashed out of his skull. He's had a whole half-day on some kids' TV series and this is his first wages in months—a whole twenty-three quid! He skims it over the bar at Lionface the guv'nor and roars, 'Work out how much of this windfall I owe you, landlord, and in the meantime give my friends large measures and a triple fucking gin for me—' and then he flakes out! He's toppled backwards — it was like slow motion. There's these four young people, two blokes and two chicks, all geared up for Talk Of The Town, they're at this table with their revolting amateur drinks—vodka and pineapple, lots of cherries—only next minute they're not sitting round the small table, they're kneeling round eighteen stone of horizontal actor.

The table, glasses, dinky little sequinned handbags, the ashtray—that's all mere splinters under the mighty buttocks of our Dennis. Give Lionface his due, he don't get shirty. He leans on the bar looking down at the struggling Dennis and says—you know that bored look of his—'You owe me another ten quid, Den. I should stay unemployed, these celebrations will harm your credit-rating.'

All the time Den-Den's kicking his big legs in the air and the four young punters are speechless."

A table of laughing girls, secretaries and typists from a film company, were giggling frenetically at their own audacity in having one more round before going back to the office. Shirt-sleeved market men were divvying up their bundles of dirty pound notes and ordering more pints of light and bitter. I saw two old working-class codgers who'd been coming to The Leafless since the days of sawdust on the floor and had held on to *their* pub through all the re-stylings and missing faces. I saw the noisy group of big youths whose sheepskin jackets and hairy heads made them look like fur-trappers but who were a rock band enjoying a fame only little girls knew about, for the moment, until the sound of their money reached us old hands.

I didn't belong to this, did I?

". . .yeah, it's a two-horse race which gives out first, his loot or his liver . . . "

". . . he hates flying so much he gets stoned out of his skull and then the stewardess is announcing in ten minutes they'll be landing at Bombay and he jumps out and tries to get the pilot to take him back to Dusseldorf . . ."

". . . cheer up, the suicide rate goes up ten per cent at Christmas." "I know your trouble, mate, you didn't grow up, you grew in . . ."

". . . no and I don't want none. Kids today? They grow up so bleeding fast you're still reading them Snow White and they're interrupting to say they need an abortion . . . "

". . . he says, take a tip from me, don't grow old!"

I looked at Angela. A white cigarette stuck out of her black glove-knuckles, pearly blue smoke rising in a snaky column until the air from surrounding mouths blasted it into invisibility.

An escaping wisp of red hair was pressed into a flat curl by her beret. Her neck was white. From above and behind, where I was standing, her suede-covered knee was small and narrow.

". . . they ain't all weeny-boppers in these discos, take my word. You know him that manages that new joint in Gunpowder Street, he gets into The Armpit a lot, long hair. Looks like Julie Andrews? That's the one. Julie Andrews? Don't say it to his face! Bloke comes in there last week, well pissed and looking for bother. What does Julie Andrews do? He gets a full bottle of scotch and whacks this geezer on the nut—wham! Julie Andrews? He's in such a rage he then proceeds to put the boot in on this geezer's face while he's flaked out on the floor. He only kicks him so hard he kicks a sliver of the broken bottle up the geezer's nose into his brain, that's all. Julie Andrews?"

Sensing my eyes on the back of her head Angela looked round.

"I think you must be a very moody person," she said.

Without really thinking, but vaguely embarrassed at the attention her remark had drawn from those nearest, I smiled bitterly and said:

"Give me your hand in marriage."

Her eyes narrowed. She turned away quickly. I frowned, wondering why I had been so tastelessly unfunny.

". . . he's so pissed by the time the barman brings back his change he's forgotten he gave the bloke a five-quid note so when the barman keeps trying to hand him the money he suddenly snarls, 'I don't want your fucking charity' and hits the bloke's hand, sending a shower of coins all over the room!"

". . . yeah, I saw it. You see that notice, Rodge, in that doorway just past the Turkish Athletic Club in Bricklay Street? It says No Young Model, in big red letters . . . I will tell you about it if you'll shut up for a minute. It was when one of the Sunday papers exposed this big property company for owning brothels, behind a lot of sub-leases and front companies. So they had to get rid of the whores' gaffs double-quick to save their image. They said they hadn't known what was going on and cancelled all the subsidiary leases. For a public relations gimmick they offered some of the flats at low rents for deserving cases. Kilgallon told me about it if you must know.

So this young couple were flat-hunting and they get offered a two-bedroom deal—in the West End, at ten quid a week? Snapped it up, what do you think. They didn't know the previous tenants were brasses paying sixties and seventies a week. Anyway, their first Monday in residence and the young husband goes off to work and the proud young bride starts her Hoovering—her first day as a housewife in her own little nest-and about twelve the doorbell rings so she opens the front door and this middle-aged geezer pushes past her into the living-room, shoves three quid in her hand, unzips his trousers, lobs out his cock and says, 'I've been a naughty boy, can you wear your riding boots with the spurs?' She starts screaming something diabolical. 'What?' he said, all puzzled, standing there with his chopper in his hand, 'aren't you Miss Du Cane?' So that's why the notice—No Young Model."

John the Baptist bought a round. He said how he'd been sitting in his office when his secretary, Agnes, came in to say there were five Swedish tourists refusing to leave the reception area.

"They'd been strolling down Mozart Street looking for all these sex orgies swinging London is famous for and they're passing our entrance and this tout goes—psst, you gents want to see a filmshow? Their English is none too clever—"

"Hark to Cyril bloody Connolly!"

"You want to hear what happened or not?"

"You've got these Swedes in your office—that was a turnip for the books. Do go on."

"So this fly-boy tells them there's a sex-show on the top floor—and charges them five quid each for admission. Twenty-five quid! So they come wandering up our stairs getting horny at the prospect of all that writhing—and all they get is to clock my Agnes." He smiled at Angela. "She's my secretary. Can you imagine—charging them five quid each to go up to a perfectly ordinary office? Some very sharp operators about here."

"I wouldn't say it's a perfectly ordinary office. There's a lot of people would pay a fiver gladly to see what goes with you and Agnes in a lust-maddened mood—"

"There's nothing like that between me and Agnes!"

A drunk came into the bar, roughly-dressed; he swayed for a few moments then stared at our semi-circle. He lurched forward a step, touched JTB on the back, shoved his bleary face into a gap and shouted:

"Glasgow Celtic's the greatest team in the world, ye English shits!"

I froze inside. My bloody countryman!

Little Roger Parkes, a mild chap on all previous occasions, went behind the circle.

"Is it a fight you're looking for, Jock?" he snapped. "Come on the, don't waste time, I'll punch your bloody head in if that's what you want."

The drink swayed back a degree, blinking in surprise.

"No, I'm just saying Celtic's a good football team," he said meekly.

"You've told us, so piss off."

The drunk lurched quickly for the door. No sooner was he outside than he put his head back through the door and shouted, "If ye hate Alf Ramsey clap your hands." He went off round the corner, singing this ditty to the tune of 'Coming Round The Mountains'.

"How come all them bums turn out to be Scottish, I wonder?"

"Yeah, there was a horrible lush stretched out on the pavement round the corner in Gunpowder Street the other day, he was Scottish. 'Gee us two bob, Jimmy,' he says to Manager Dave and me, 'Ah huvnae eaten for four days.'

Dave looks at him and says, 'Hunger is character-forming, didn't you know?'"

"Tell us, Jock, how come all these wasters are Scottish?"

I shrugged.

"We were all poor and deprived enough in Stepney but we didn't grow up a race of violent drunks, did we?"

"In the army my real mates were all Jocks—great nuts—but two drinks in them and they'd be wanting to smash you in the face with a bottle. Your mates!"

"It's guilt, it's the rantings of John Knox that's to blame, isn't it, John?" I shrugged. Neville winked and went on, "John Knox and all these Bible-thumping mountebanks who laboured so enthusiastically to implant an awareness of Hell in the Scots. I don't know why they bothered—surely every Scot is immediately familiar with Hell from the moment his eyes and ears start to function?"

"Ballocks," I said.

"Yeah—so how come you all want to live down here with us English pigs?"

I shrugged. It was a joke ritual, bait the heathen Scot and see him rage and then buy him a drink and tell him he's a good nut.

But I could no longer see the joke.

It was all true, wasn't it?

Before I could think of anything that would make them stop

and *think* Mrs Wallis came round to our end of the bar to say there was a call for me on the house phone. I ducked under the flap and went through the narrow corridor that led to the stairs. The phone was hanging on the cord.

"John Thompson," I said. "Jock?" I would have known who it was even if he had only cleared his throat.

"Yeah-that you, Stan?"

"Yeah. I wanna see you for a chat, Jock."

"I'm in here right now."

"Nah, not in The Leafless. You gonna be in the offis in the mornin'?"

"Yeah."

"Give us your number and I'll bell yer and fix up a meet. Okay for tomorrow lunchtime?"

"Anything important?"

"Not if we keep our heads."

I found myself swallowing a lot as I went back to the public part of the house. *Not if we keep our heads?*

Jesus.

They looked at me.

"Sibley," I said to Neville. "I told him we'd ring him."

"What, Rentapest? Not if I see him first."

Angela Browne turned on her stool and addressed me too quietly for the others to hear.

"If it's worrying you," she said, "I'll tell you about it. It's made of wood. The thumb has a spring. I can take it off at night. The stump is just smooth skin. It happened on my father's boat when I was twelve, I got it caught in a winch. I've heard every possible pun there is to be made about it and it doesn't bother me any more, except that it's interesting to see how many men have a latent mutilation fetish. Will that satisfy our curiosity?"

I shrugged, unable to think why she imagined I was even remotely interested. What was a wooden hand compared to my problems? Exquisite's menacing phone call had brought me back to practicalities with a jolt.

The sensible thing would be for me to go straight round to Central Nick and ask for the detectives and tell everything I knew. Only that would mean telling them exactly who I was. Not James Caskie, not John Thompson, but Ian Mintlaw McGraw.

At the very least they'd want me as a witness—at the inquest or at any murder trial. The Inland Revenue and the Social Security would be onto me like a shot. How much did I owe those bastards?

I started doing mental arithmetic, never my greatest talent.

Two gypsy-style women with hard, suntanned faces and dyed blonde hair came into the pub carrying baskets of fake white heather on their arms. They wore shawls. They went at each customer aggressively, pinning sprigs of lucky bell heather on lapels before demanding money. Mr Wallis the guv'nor skipped urgently round the corner of the bar and had them on the pavement before they had taken a penny. They shouted something at him and then started to dive at every man coming along the pavement.

That's when it came back to me.

Big Morning.

Feeling frightened and stupid I was looking up at the slice of grey sky just visible above the Rookery rooftops when I became a child again in that one-roomed house in the tenement. I could never sleep well, not really sleep, not the way other people sleep and need an alarm clock, always awake and restless at the first noise or chink of daylight, never drowsy from the moment my eyes opened. Every second in bed after wakening was torture. I felt my bare feet on cold linoleum, aching to be out and doing something. My mother's heavy bed, feeling my way round the kitchen table, teeth chattering if it was cold (I couldn't remember any warm mornings), tugging at her bedclothes, moaning at the mysterious shape under the jumbled blankets until the shape finally stirs; the frightening smell of *her*.

"Mammy, can I get dressed now? Is it the big morning?"

"Eh? Oh my God, what time's it?"

"It's light outside the curtains, mammy, it's the real big morning, honestly!"

If she was in a good mood: "It's not the big morning yet, it's only the wee morning. Come in beside me if you're cold."

If she was in a bad mood:

"Get back to your bed or I'll give you such a leathering!"

"But it's light outside—"

"I'll count to three! You need a real hammering so you do!"

And the boy, me, hurries back round the table and climbs into the cold cotton sheets and tries to make the blanket fit over his feet and lies there, chest heaving with indignation, eyes fixed on the grey slit of light between the curtains over the sink, lips tight with rage and then trembling into sobs, hating her, hating the bed, hating the rasp of cotton sheets on his knees, hating every second to be endured before release.

Standing in the smoking, laughing, swilling bar of The Leafless Tree public house in The Rookery district of London, England, the booze going down into the big lumpy body I now inhabited, cigarettes burning my lips, greasy hair itching, grimy fingers juggling neurotically with slippery coins in the darkness of a pocket, I could smell her.

For several moments I had to fight down the same shout I'd fought down to bursting point in that shaky bed in that other country, a fifth of a century before.

That was where big morning came from.

When I got my breath back I found myself straightening up and tightening my mouth. It was high bloody time I stopped being that whining little boy. I wasn't in trouble because of The Spoofer or Exquisite or income tax or insurance stamps.

I was in trouble because I'd been dreaming my bloody life away.

I watched and waited as my so-called partner sidled round behind the semi-circle towards me.

They took Jack to a room in Newgate called The Castle. He was handcuffed. He was fettered with heavy leg irons. He was chained to a staple in the floor. They knew he couldn't escape this time. At 2 p.m. on October 14, 1724, the turnkey gave him his dinner and locked his cell up for the night. All Jack had was a bent nail. First he squeezed his wrists out of the cuffs. He broke the leg irons by sheer strength. He picked the padlock with the nail. He tied the broken fetters to each leg. There was a chimney in The Castle but it was blocked by a two-inch iron bar embedded in mortar and bricks. With only the nail for a tool he attacked the wall above the fireplace.

9

"I forgot to ask you—how did you get on with Pilbeam last night?" Neville asked.

"I got shoved in the nick," I said. "Teepee was up Holy Man's Cut having a piss and I took a stroll with a beat copper to save him being arrested."

"Yeah? Want a medal? What about the bread?"

"I gave it to Pilbeam. If you hadn't left the Congo so quick you could have squabbled over it in person."

Not recognising my new mood he murmured:

"So what about she of the red hair?"

I glanced down at Angela, who was listening appreciatively to Tommy the decomposer. I looked at Neville. His fresh countryboy complexion was showing signs of wear. At this range I could see the first wrinkles of debauchery spreading delicately round his grey eyes.

"Count me out, she's got a wooden hand, you know."

He looked down over his shoulder.

"So she has. Kinky, eh? What does she do, get her manicures from a carpenter?"

"You want to swindle cripples go ahead. Send me a postcard from the open prison."

"Getting sentimental, are we?"

"Yeah, sentimental over the Hum Drum deal you're trying to cut me out of."

His face did not even flicker.

"I was just going to tell you about that, didn't have a chance till now, it came up all of a sudden."

"You're a fucking liar."

"Just found that out, have you?" He smiled sadly, shaking his head. I'd seen him play this game a thousand times—how can you feel angry at a rogue who is eager to agree with you?

"By the way, I need some money," I said. A light girlish voice laughed hysterically. The Babychams were well into the heads of the rebellious typists. Neville stuck his hand into the hip-pocket of his brushed-cord blue flareds.

"I can give you ten," he said, bringing out a flat fold.

"Thanks," I said, taking two fivers. "I still need some money."

"How much? What the fuck's eating you anyway?"

"Five hundred—just about what the agency owes me."

"Five hundred! A monkey?" Over his right shoulder I saw two girls with long, blonde hair joining the hairy rock group. The girls looked like twin Alices in Wonderland. "We'll have a sort out of the cash situation tomorrow—cheer up for Christ's sake."

"Fuck tomorrow," I said. We were both pretty big—in our prime, I suppose.

He put his hand on my shoulder. It wasn't a gesture of comradeship. He was smiling but not because we were glad to be friends. The hand and the smile were puppeteer's tricks. I came near to hitting him savagely in the guts.

"A few drinks will cure your problem," he said.

"Don't give me that old moody. I'm telling you I want five hundred quid."

"I haven't got five hundred quid."

"Tomorrow will do."

"Piss off. You can't just spring something like five hundred quid on me."

"No? I'm owed that much at least. You going to get it for me or not?" He shook his head. His eyes were smiling. I saw JTB's bunchy face frowning in disbelief at something Fred Matchan was saying. They were all using Angela Browne as an audience.

"You won't get it for me?"

"No can do."

"Right. Now I tell her how she's going to be conned."

"How adolescent can you get? Go on, tell her."

We looked hard at each other and then I turned my head to the right and put my hand on her shoulder.

"Angela—got a moment?" She looked round and up at me and then at Neville. "I think you ought to know something about this deal—"

"Yeah we've decided you're right about us being lazy swine," Neville said quickly. "Ready for another drink?"

"I'm all right thank you," she said. JTB stretched out a pale, boneless hand to remind her he was in the middle of a side-splitting tale.

"You bastard," Neville said to me, "why didn't you say you seriously wanted five hundred? What's it for anyway?"

"Christmas presents."

"I'll go to the bank in the morning. You really would've told her?" "Why not? You fuck me about I'll fuck you about."

He stared at me for a moment then burst into laughter. He put his arm round my shoulder and gave my back a slap and said:

"Don't worry, old son, I'll fuck you about next chance I get. So let's get a few down us. I want to live a little!"

I was disappointed. The old Neville would have let me tell her, just to show how little he cared. But he was serious about conning her. I'd never thought of him as grubby before.

Although I was fully aware I was going to be doing even grubbier things to get my life sorted out. The mental arithmetic always came to around the same figures.

I owed them tax on my sex magazine commission. I owed them on the money I'd drawn from the partnership, say two and a half years at an average of forty-five a week. I owed the Social Security for two and a half years National Insurance stamps.

It all added up to around five thousand that I needed to get myself clear. I needed it quickly, too, for it would only be days before the CID turned me up in their investigations of The Spoofer's murder.

How the hell was I going to make five grand in a hurry? Manager Dave of The Hellhole was holding two hundred for me. I had another three hundred to collect if I could only bash out the rest of *A Bed Of Men*. Neville was going to give me five hundred, although his sacred vows were easily forgotten. Say I got a thousand. Would that be enough to come out of hiding and make the Inland Revenue an offer?

Once I approached them they would know all about me, there would be no going back. They wouldn't bring charges against me as long as I could make them an offer—but the Social Security might. Stamp-dodging was a criminal offence.

How the hell could I get hold of a card without telling them I'd been minus one? It was the first real trouble I'd ever been in. Strangely enough the sensation was quite exhilarating, especially when I knew I was going to do something about it.

Exhilarating is the appropriate word.

I felt so exhilarated I decided to let the rest of that day be my swansong as a layabout.

Let's live a little as Neville said—and when he said it he meant a fullscale rampage.

The rest of that day followed the familiar routine of pubs, clubs and old jokes. Several times I felt like putting my arm around him and telling him to forget the stinking five hundred so that we could be proper friends again. But I didn't.

Late on in the evening, about ten o'clock, we were in The Hellhole, which was packed out with fans of some new tumpty-

tumpty band. Although I had smashed around thirty rums and cokes into my face I was still well under control and proved this to myself by the fastidious distaste with which I watched Neville chatting up an old boiler known as Childish. She had her mate Fall Down Mary in tow and Neville was sounding them out for a fornicating foursome in case he couldn't work the oracle with Angela Browne, whose elbow was next to mine on the bar. Behind us the place was heaving. On either side of us the current generation was struggling to drink London dry.

"Sorry I made a joke about your hand," I said maturely, above the plonking banjo. "I think you're one of the most attractive women I've ever met. I get strange moods occasionally. How about you and me sloping off out of here?"

"I don't think you're a person who knows how to relate to other people. You've obviously—"

"All I wanted was a quick fuck on the office floor, dearie," I snapped; turning and walking out.

Halfway down Colman Hedge Lane I realised I was walking on my own with no certain prospect of meeting anyone I knew. Pride kept me from going back to The Hellhole. This was how it would have to be from now on, a man alone, needing nobody.

Using people, that was what *they* all did.

Passing the all-electric sports garden, which was packed by wasters and riff-raff playing the penny machines, the machine-gun hammering, I saw a couple of black brasses. One was fat and one was thin. They were laughing far too strenuously, in the West Indian manner. They both wore wigs, one blonde with ringlets, the other short and copper-hued. The fat one had thick brown legs. They were in a dangerous night-group of rat-eyed youths, one of whom had his filthy long hair dyed in streaks of green, red and orange. When Neville saw that kind of young degenerate he always said he wanted to kick them for England's sake. Not in the slightest drunk, I stopped on the pavement and let the two blackies see me. The fat one came over, rolling her pelvis. I felt detached but breathless.

"I could make you very happy, daalin'," she said, putting her hand on my chest and pressing into my skin. "Mmmm, you big strong lover. You'll have to give me money, daalin'."

"Bring your friend as well," I said.

Two minutes later we were in a taxi. It drove to King's Cross via the British Museum. I sat between them. The thin one was young and apparently shy. The fat one, once I had given her a glimpse of blue five-pound notes, kept rubbing my stomach and pelvis, always stopping just short of my cock. I paid the driver outside a terraced house with a hotel sign. The fat one went straight in. An unshaven man with a middle-European accent and a rough tartan shirt did some muttering with her and then she turned and told me to give him four pounds. He gave her a key. I followed the thin one up several short flights of stairs.

The room was small and cold. The only light was from a glass bowl hanging from the middle of the ceiling. The fat one, who said her name was Marilyn, asked me quickly for twenty pounds. Pretending to be a merry drunk I skimmed four fivers onto the bed. She picked them up and put them in her handbag on a small bedside table with a glass top. I said there was plenty more where that came from if they gave me a good time.

We undressed individually under the harsh light of the glass bowl. Marilyn had large breasts that distended onto an almost pregnant brown belly. The young one, Roxanne, had long, slender legs, down which she slid her white tights, a slim, smooth arm holding onto the bed for balance. I put my clothes neatly on a basket chair. Marilyn lifted one fat knee and brown thigh onto the brocade bedcover. For a moment she was kneeling on the bed, her breasts hanging. The skin of her buttocks and thighs was rippled in vertical lines of whitish stretchmarks. She kept on her blonde wig. I climbed into the damp sheets beside her big knees. Roxanne came in after me, sliding in sideways. I pushed my face into Marilyn's big warm breasts. Roxanne slid her light arm over my shoulder and wriggled in close. For a moment it was what I wanted, ecstasy, sandwiched between warm bodies, pinned down by shiny brown flesh, smothering in safety, darkness, fat arms, breasts, stroking hands, the sugary smell of negro skin. I must have gone to sleep, probably for only a few minutes. Roxanne was sitting on my pelvis, her thin body rotating round my cock, her slim arms making straight lines down to my chest.

"Ain't you ever goin' to make it, daalin'?" said Marilyn. My blue-veined hands and white arms reached up to stroke Roxanne's delicate thighs and hips and shoulders. She was slim and chocolate. A beautiful, feathery weight.

"Don't stop," I moaned.

"You want to make it all night, daalin'?" said Marilyn. She raised herself on a thick arm and pushed herself across my chest, her free hand pushing her big breasts all over my face. "You'll have to give us more money for all night, daalin', you must give us a nice present."

"Don't stop," I moaned.

"We'll make you happy, daalin'—you like Roxanne? She's only fifteen, does that give you a thrill, daalin'? How much will you give us, daalin'?"

Her other hand slipped under Roxanne's delicate buttocks. Staring down into my face, her huge false eyelashes blinking, she began to twist my testicles until I gasped in pain.

"You want to be our slave, daalin', that what gives you a thrill?"

"Anything, don't stop now!"

"How much you gonna give us for a present, daalin', you bad little slave?"

Money.

I felt myself deflating.

"It's no good, I've had too much to drink," I said.

"We'll help you, daalin', I want you to kiss my beautiful big black bottom, I'm goin' to sit on my white boy slave and — "

107

Money. I was so angry I could have taken it all and thrown it in their rotten faces. Instead I acted the part of a weary, defeated man. I got off the bed and started slowly to dress. Roxanne knelt up on the bed and twisted her slim arms behind her beautifully boned back to fasten her bra, while Marilyn sat cross-legged on the pillow, scratching at something on the cracked, pink skin on her foot. I was careful to make no hurried movements and kept saying how beautiful they both were.

As soon as my feet had crushed past the heels and into the Hush Puppies I was pulling on my new zipper jerkin.

"I think you deserve a little extra," I said, making a performance out of my search for the rest of the money.

"All night would give us a chance to make you really happy, daalin'," said Marilyn, swinging her big legs over the edge of the bed, on the other side.

My hand went under the clothing on the little bedside table. They both had their backs to me, just for a moment. My fingers touched the handbag.

I was switching off the light and halfway through the door before they knew what was happening.

One of them managed to get to the landing before I reached the second flight.

"You'll get killed for this, you bastard!" she screamed. It was Roxanne. It was the first time I'd heard her voice.

My feet skimmed down three and four steps at a time.

Then I was out of the front door and running wildly across the street and losing myself in the shadows.

Three or four minutes later a taxi was taking me home to Everybody's Wife. As we passed the big dark gates of the British Museum, I threw the handbag out of the window.

Kilgallon had taught me that trick. When he was new to the scene he'd gone once to a clip-joint nightclub off Leicester Square and found himself surrounded by five gorillas in monkey suits wanting forty-eight pounds for two lagers and the whisky he'd bought a hostess. He could have paid but instead he suddenly threw over the table and ran head down for the door. He made it too. Being hard wasn't so difficult.

Triumph died within me as the taxi coasted onto Westminster Bridge. The pavements and the road were broad and deserted, silent, the empty planes of nightmare geometry. The street-lamps were floodlighting the masonry so brilliantly and the frosty air was so clear the bridge seemed like an Iron Curtain frontier, guarded by all-seeing sentries out there, in the blackness above the river. I twisted round to make sure I could still see Big Ben. The big, warmly-lit clockface said five past one. I could taste porridge. Big Ben always struck for the nine o'clock news on the radio and that was when *she* made me go to bed, milk on my chin, warm oatmeal in my throat, little husks on my teeth. Big Ben had watched over me all my life.

Then we turned and I couldn't see the warm clockface and the street-lamp shadows flicked smoothly over my lap and I felt cold and menaced. Those girls would be watching out for me from now on.

And Exquisite! That terse, ominous phone call!

The taxi turned into Lindehan Crescent, off Clapham Common.

The driver turned stroppy about changing a five-pound note. I had some single pounds left but I realised he thought I was a common Scots drunk who might be suckered into saying 'Keep the change'. Three pounds!

"We'd better drive back to where you can get fucking change then" I growled.

He decided he could, after all, rake up three pounds.

"Looks derelick," he said, looking up at the tall, terraced house with the flaking stucco front and the ground-floor windows sealed with corrugated iron. "Don't live in that, dooyer?"

"Once they've evicted us it's going to be gutted for luxury flats."

"Yeah, need a bleedin' fortune to live here then, same all over the fuckin' shop," he said, fishing into his church collection bag for silver. "Where's us poor bleeders wot ain't stinkin' rich supposed to live, you tell me that?"

"I didn't vote the bastards in."

"You think Harold fuckin' Wilson's gonna do it any better? They're all the same, Jock."

When the cab had gone I went up the steps and pressed an illuminated plastic button under a handwritten card, *K. Coleman*. The stagily-lit crescent was two-dimensional in its lack of movement or noise.

Her muffled voice barked out of the aluminium speaking grille.

"Who is it? Go away."

"It's me," I said cocking an ear to the grille, teeth chattering.

"Go away."

"It's John!"

"Good night, John."

The old me would have had too much pride to argue with the bitch but I had begun to realise that a lot of this pride crap is pure cowardice.

Hawking a wodge of catarrh out of my throat and spitting it over the railing into the littered basement area I spoke at the grille:

"Let me in or I'll smash this fucking door down."

The first brick was the hardest. After he had made an opening he tore at the wall, covering the cell floor with a cartload of bricks, stone and mortar. This enabled him to dislodge the heavy iron bar blocking the inside of the chimney. He climbed up the chimney until he reckoned he was level with the room upstairs. He tore a hole through the chimney wall and found himself in a disused cell called the Red Room. Crossing it in his bare feet he impaled himself on a rusty nail sticking out of the floorboards.

10

"Oh Christ, come up then."

The door lock buzzed.

It was typical of the old lazy me that I'd never had a key. Already I found myself curious as to what kind of person I'd been *then*. I scuffed through the permanent litter of mail on the lobby floor, window-fronted envelopes with final demands, mail order circulars, blue airmail letterforms, printed cards from junk-dealers and minicab firms, wonderful prize announcements for fortunates hand-picked by the *Reader's Digest* and Automobile Association, all of it useless trash for long-departed victims of London's property racket.

She was waiting for me on the third floor landing, Katie Coleman, no longer a booted glamour item in The Maggots but a stocky girl with bare white legs under a black nylon housecoat.

"There's somebody here," she drawled, pointing to the bedroom door.

"Who? Or didn't you bother asking for a name?"

"You didn't turn up last night. You didn't even ring me."

"I was in the nick. Women are supposed to wait loyally for men in gaol. You? You can't even wait till I get my trousers down."

We were standing in the gloom of the lobby, her bare feet on cold lino. I was so shattered my eyes seemed to be bleeding.

"I thought you'd picked up some slag," she said. "He isn't anybody important, just a boy I used to know in a pop group. Don't be too rough with him."

She went into the kitchen, the little flat's other room, and closed the door. Knowing I was near to collapse I closed my eyes, took a deep breath, hardened my mouth and gave the bedroom door a bang with the palm of my hand.

It swung back, hitting the thin legs of the TV set. The startled face that looked up from the black nylon sheets belonged to a skinny youth whose gingery hair hung in soft ringlets down his white, pimply shoulders.

"On your way, pal," I growled, hands on hips, mimicking the razored Glasgow voice that puts the frighteners in.

"Who the hell are you, man? Where's Katie? What the hell's—"

"You can go under your own steam or I'll sling you down the fucking stairs," I said, unzipping my new jerkin. "I live here, pal."

"I didn't know that, I was asked to come round here, you can't—".

I took a step towards the bed, so weary I could easily have fallen into it and gone to sleep beside him. The skinny youth sat up quickly, a delicately-fuzzed arm snatching at floral pattern underclothes draped on the little folding chair.

"Nothing personal, pal," I said, leaving him alone to dress.

I was leaning against the lobby wall, shivering, when his ringlets bobbed past me and out onto the landing and down the stairs. I went into the kitchen. Katie was perched on the sink, bare thighs splayed wide.

"I'm freezing," I said.

"You look bloody awful."

"It's all this living."

"And that object you're wearing—very adolescent."

"I'm not entering any best-dressed man competitions."

"A jacket like that is a sign of personality mutilation."

"Don't perch there pissing in the sink giving me all that neo-Freudian bullshit."

I used the sink in similar fashion (the lavatory was two flights down) and went into the bedroom. She slowly opened the black housecoat and stretched her heavy-bottomed, fat-breasted, narrow-shouldered, chalk-white body on the low bed.

"I obviously haven't been strict enough with my peasant stallion," she said, in her aristocratic voice. I closed my eyes and shuddered. "Hurry up for God's sake, it's cold," she said, in her normal voice.

I walked out of my shoes. Her heavy stomach creased into folds of smooth skin as she reached down to drag the red Austrian quilt up over her plump, shiny legs.

"Come on," she said slyly, "we won't be able to smell him in a minute."

"That's disgusting," I groaned. "I want some sleep."

"Wait till I get my exquisitely cruel hands on my squirming serf and he won't *sleep*."

"I'm not in the bloody mood for games."

Katie was about twenty-four, almost beautiful, with dark blue eyes and a small, humorous face. She had some useless English Literature degree from Nottingham University and worked in a literary agency. She saw a free National Health psychiatrist every Thursday evening and attended a VD clinic on Tuesday lunchtimes, not for treatment but check-ups, a sensible precaution considering the random way she found men to see her through long night hours when otherwise she would have been moping about rejection by her father, or whatever neurosis was then modish among brain-meddlers.

The Beast introduced me to her, saying he was bored by her promiscuity. When I say introduced I mean I was one of half a dozen blokes to whom he gave her phone number, at her request. In her morbid dread of being alone at night she was willing to cater for most sexual tastes, seemingly having none of her own. She had made one half-hearted attempt to kill herself by scratching her wrists with a razor-blade when a young musician fell out of love with her after discovering her nicknames. This convinced her she would never find a husband.

She talked a lot about Women's Liberation and occasionally stopped shaving her legs.

For some reason the role I had drifted into with her was that of eager masochist. This was certainly *not* a repressed longing of mine; it probably started as a joke; whenever it was actually painful I became the masochist who hit back.

That night I needed mothering not torturing. The more I tried to surround myself with her fat arms and breasts the more perversely determined she was, however, to be the young countess with the slave drooling at her feet.

"Your tongue, dog. Do you want my boot on your neck? The lash on your back? I am—"

"Shut up for fuck's sake. You sound silly."

"I sound silly? It was you who started this countess crap!"

"Was it hell! It's bloody painful, this slave lark."

"You hypocritical bastard! You're a bloody puritan!"

"You're off your head."

We ended up sleeping back to back, cold and isolated in our permissive love-nest, grimly controlling our breathing in case the other might take a sigh as a tentative apology. We might just as well have been married.

Naturally I couldn't sleep. Thoughts ran through my head like a pack of runaway dogs. I'd never realised before that what they call *thinking* is actually the control and suppression of thoughts that exist in their own right. I was too tired to whip them back and they darted out of dark corners, jeering at me, humiliating me, the thought of the shabby drunk in a cell, Pilbeam saying "No, he's with me", a baby boy sobbing because his mother wouldn't let him get out of bed, the great lover who couldn't get it off with two whores but could sneak away with the money, who was scared of Exquisite's big tattooed fist but who posed as a hard man to frighten a teenage guitarist, who thought he had talent but sat in a smelly room trying to write adolescent pornography and couldn't even do that very well, who was Somebody but only in empty rooms, in his own head, who'd posed and clowned and stumbled through a fifth of a century and had now reached a mockery of manhood trapped in another bed, waiting for another woman to say it was the big morning, *waiting*.

I put out my hand but she shuddered violently and pulled herself away. We lay in frozen tension. The phone rang. It was on the floor under the TV set. It rang and rang. I became so angry I sat up, hotly determined to dress and walk out and make my way through the cold, dark streets and to the *Cleaner's Store* room in Nailed Down Chambers and huddle beside the electric fire on the contagious carpet and never see this promiscuous bitch again.

I got as far as the phone.

Picking it up, my bare thighs and legs like white shadows of death, I heard some man's voice.

"Go and fuck yourself," I snarled.

"That might be a friend of mine," she snapped from the bed.

"A friend?" I shouted. "Haven't you got any self-respect at all, you stupid slut?"

I launched myself back across the gloomy room and pulled back the rasping nylon sheets and gave her a punch—on the hip, as it happened. I was berserk.

She tried to scratch my face and I belted her across the cheek with my palm and grabbed her hair and shoved her head back on the pillow. She tried to bring her knee up brutally into my testicles. To protect myself I had to smother her with my whole weight, legs pinning down her legs, forehead jammed against her chin to stop her biting me, hands tight on her wrists.

"I'll kill you!" I was certainly working myself up to doing her physical injury when suddenly she stopped twisting under me and said, calmly:

"Go on then, kill me. I'd rather have that than your feeble attempts to fuck me. Go on, kill me, it might make you feel more masculine."

"What do you bloody mean? I'll fuck you and then I'll kill you!"

Enraged with the delight of raping and humiliating and battering her I rammed myself into her. When I say myself I am not using a euphemism for my cock. Her hole felt like a hard tunnel with ribbed sides and the deeper I penetrated the more it seemed that all of me was being dragged into it by a relentless vacuum force, until my head began to swim with fears of drowning, of being totally absorbed, of vanishing into her body through my own prick.

When I came it was like being turned inside out.

Is all that caused by the mere rubbing of skin on gristle?

"Was that masculine enough for you?" My face was sunk into her left shoulder-joint, my mouth on her armpit hair, the rest of me panting. Drained. Gutted. Skinned alive.

"Very good," she said, giving a grunt as she twisted her shoulder free and wriggled down the bed until she could get her head against my chest and prod my arm to go round her shoulders. "I wish you were always like that. I felt totally helpless."

"So did I."

"No, you were a brute. From now on you'll be my brute."

"Okay—shut up and let me sleep or I'll thump you.

Jack pulled the rusty nail out of his foot and used it to attack the lock. When he got to the Red Room door open he was in a dark passage. Immediately he came up against another heavy door, locked on the other side. It took him half an hour to knock a hole in the wall big enough for his arm to go through. He slipped back the bolt. It was night now and by the time he reached the prison chapel he was working in darkness. Breaking a spike off the chapel door he tried to force the heavy grated door barring his way to the lower leads of the roofs. It seemed impregnable.

11

Even in that rubbish-strewn warren the mornings were good when the sun was up and the big jet-trails were white tramlines in a blue sky and car exhausts hadn't lead-poisoned the street air. I felt ready to attack.

As I crossed the street towards The Hellhole I saw Doorway Doris. She was about fifty, quite matronly in her choice of cast-offs, always with a hat. You wouldn't spot her for a nut at first glance. What she did was haul four shopping bags up and down the street. The bags were crammed with old newspapers, rags and unclassifiable refuse. Carrying two of the bags she went along the pavement and deposited them in a shop doorway. Then she went back and retrieved the other two bags from the last doorway. These she carried four or five doorways farther on, coming back again for the first two, hauling them on a few more doorways, overlapping the bags up and down the whole length of the Stony-Hearted Stepmother. When she was not bending down to deposit or lift two bags she walked close to the wall, staring at the pavement, ignoring people, muttering philosophically.

It was about half-past nine. The Hellhole door was still padlocked. I went back up to the pavement. An office caretaker was sweeping an entrance in his slippers. Two Chinese tots with coal-shiny hair were running up and down the pavement. I went across to have breakfast in The Ancient Grease.

I asked Reet the waitress for two sausages, two fried eggs, beans and a two slice. And a tea. The cafe was quiet and I read the *Mirror* I'd bought at Clapham North tube station, to see if there was anything about The Spoofer's murder.

In the tube the people had been packed so tight their bodies felt like stone, mainly men, dressed for office hypocrisy, unsmiling, surly with suppressed masculinity. My zip jerkin made me feel I was dressed for freedom. I had screwed this good-looking girl in the black fur collar and I wasn't tied to a fucking season ticket. My belly was shoved hard against Katie's hip as I tried to crunch through the news pages. The men in suits and overcoats were all reading the pink *Financial Times* or the black and white *Times* or the grey *Telegraph,* holding them stiffly above their heads.

"What are you looking for so busily?" she asked, mashed pages pushing into her face.

"Just to see where today's demo is," I said, for the benefit of the *Telegraph* reader whose elbow kept touching my head. "I think we got a riot planned for Downing Street this afternoon."

"Communist!"

"Nah, I'm just in it for the lolly."

I don't know if he heard but his elbow steered clear of my bonce for the rest of the journey. I still wonder if he goes round telling people that the Kremlin pays wages to louts. Silly? At least I wasn't reading the *Telegraph,* was I?

When we split up at Warren Street Katie was careful not to push me into guesses as to when I'd be back at the flat that night. Her cheek was cold and fresh.

Reet brought over the rations. You got good big portions in the Grease, even if there was cigarette ash in the sugar bowls. I checked each page of the *Mirror* but The Spoofer's murder was a day old and competition for murder space was fierce; in Hampshire a gent had axed his wife and three kids and then cut his own throat. Mortgage worries, said informed opinion. In Edinburgh a boy aged fifteen had stabbed a crippled man to beat the eternal boredom; in Glasgow three youths had kicked a grammar school boy to death for wearing a snobbish blazer; the bodies of two six-year-old girls, sexually assaulted and strangled, had been found in a gravel pit near Coventry. What chance did a routine Rookery stabbing have? I felt much cheerier. After I'd seen Manager Dave I would have a shave, maybe even go to Polish Joe and have a haircut and shampoo. Four plasterers came in and sat at the next table.

"Them cars was as tight agivver as if they'd been welded agivver, wunney?"

"The rozzers was sayin' it was impossibill a hidentifoy the bodies!"

"I was sick when I got home, straight up."

"They musta bin dooin' a fair lick, wunney?"

I raised my hand to tell Reet I wanted another cup of strong tea.

I was shovelling in the sugar—small, white and deadly as Neville called it since becoming a sucker for the health food racket—when quick movements caught my eye through the steamy window. I gave it a rub with my palm.

She was on the other side of the narrow street, dark hair all over her face, a big hairy jacket, a girl in her early twenties, soiled white trousers and black boots. She was bombed out of her skull.

She took a step off the kerb, took a few steps into the empty street, then reeled round in a circle, out of control. She sat down heavily on the kerb, face to knees, then stood up and walked into the tail of a parked Coca-Cola lorry. She put her hands to her face, screamed something, then staggered off along the gutter, one foot up, one foot down.

The queue at the sandwich and coffee counter turned heads to watch her. One of the plasterers got up and kneeled on a window-side seat. She sat down heavily, threw back her head to laugh, then stood up and shook her hair.

Then she ran for a bit, in that over-balancing way forced on drunks by legs that won't stop. The jerkiness of her movements said pills, not booze. She came to the edge of the kerb opposite the cafe window, stopped, flailed her arms, laughed again and then darted off round the corner.

"One of them fakkin' hippies," said the kneeling plasterer.

"University stoodent more like."

"Wot makes 'em go like that?"

"It's drugs an' that, innit?"

"Yeah but wot makes 'em take them drugs?"

"He's a deep one him."

"Yeah well, makes you think, dunnit? They got all the advantages, doaney?"

"It's all that education, innit, goes to their 'eads, dunnit?"

"That's where it's supposeta go, stoopid berk."

"I don't want no kid of mine gettin' mixed up wiv all that university rubbish. Four more teas, Reet, mate."

"Four Rosie Lees!" shouted Reet along the counter.

I paid and left. Seeing that jerky girl made me feel conscious that valuable minutes were sliding through my fingers.

Manager Dave was at the far end of The Hellhole, changing optics behind the long bar. The night before the band was thumping and the people jumping but now it was just a big, sad-smelling hall. Like all nightclubs in the morning it made you shake your head at the reality behind your good times.

"Watering the whisky then?" I said, rubber soles squeaking on composite flooring. Dave didn't turn. He had a mirror to see who was coming through the door. He bunged a forty-ounce bottle of Teacher's whisky into the optic. For the first time I realised the labels on these bottles were stuck on upside down, so that you could read them when the bottle was turned over into the optic measurer. Clever bastards these booze merchants.

"None of your backchat or I gives you me nut," Dave said, "me flick I calls it, you learn it in the pram up the Holloway Road."

"Yeah, you're beginning to look like Charlie George," I said, refraining from putting my elbows on the bar when I saw that its formica top was still sticky with the rings of the previous night's jollifications.

"I'm only thirty-seven," he growled, back still turned, "I look like forty-seven. I've aged fifteen years in five—owning this place. Not so long ago I wasn't sure I couldn't be turning alcoholic."

"Sure now, are you?"

"I'll tell you one thing, this morning I feel as rough as a zookeeper's boot. Hold on till I get some juniper-juice."

Manager Dave—so called because he owned the place—was the only man in The Rookery I would have trusted to be my banker, and not just because he was in the booze business, the only blue-chip racket left. Almost alone of the men I met every day he did not seem to be wrapped in some private fantasy. Nobody ever saw him pissed, although he never ventured too far from a glass. Nobody ever saw him chasing women although he had been married long enough. Nobody could inveigle him into Surefire Big Money Projects that only required *your* capital to make all of us millionaires.

All this left the sneaking possibility that he was simply a practical man of commonsense who ran a business to support wife and children. Simply? On that scene such a man was about as *simply* as six toes.

He came back from the store-room with two forty-ounce Gordon's gins.

"I don't understand it," he said, "The country's on the rocks, half a million unemployed, strikes, stagnation, inflation, stagflation, house prices rocketing, food going up, beer going up, fares going up, wages pegged but every fucking thing going up—and what happens?"

"Knickers come down?"

"As the nation sinks into poverty the people start drinking like maniacs. Six quarts of gin I sold last night-in mid-week? Beer?

I'm waiting on emergency deliveries to see me through—if the draymen aren't on strike again. I can sell *anything* they like to put in bottles. People are going off their fucking rockers!"

"Must be hell for you. Listen, you know that two hundred you're holding for me—"

"You want it back?"

"No, I might be wanting to give you more."

He stood back and examined his array of bottles. "Look at them-silent sentinels of death! Your partner was chucking the lolly about last night. Stage six!"

"That bad, was he?"

"Stop the pavement I want to get on! I thought you and the ginger piece were getting the old boiling ballocks for each other."

"Angela Browne—with an e? Not my type. She's got a wooden hand."

"A wooden hand! Straight up?"

"Yeah. Dave, I have an idea, I'm wondering if. . ."

"She got the Rentokil guarantee against woodworm? You know who The Beast finally went lurching off into the night with? El Spotto!"

"No? I swallowed it when I saw him chatting up Childish and Fall Down Mary. El Spotto! Here, you know anything about insurance cards?"

"You buy stamps at ridiculous prices and stick them in. Want a heart-starter?"

"No, no booze today."

"Mrs Aitch will make us a cup of tea when she gets in. What about insurance cards?"

"I need to get one—without letting them know I haven't had one for a couple of years."

"Say you lost it. Balls, I'm going to have a Greenshield. You want a pint of lager to wash out your mouth?"

"It's clear-headed day." He poured a small bottle of ale into a glass the professional way, the glass tilted to prevent too big a head. "I can't say I lost it, they keep records, I wasn't issued with one when I went self-employed."

"Half the bums in these bands don't have cards."

"Ah, yeah, musicians—the government doesn't care about *musicians*."

"Somebody was only talking about not having a card for twelve years the other day. I can't remember who it was. There's a wet cloth on the sink, give the bar a wipe, will you, I've got to open the back door for a delivery."

I rubbed at the sticky rings. The new idea had just hit me. If I raised enough loot to make the Inland Revenue an offer I would then have to make enough money to pay off the instalments. Working with Neville I would never get down to serious graft. Dave was the answer!

He came back and watched me wipe the bar. He leaned back and patted the big bottle of upside-down whisky.

"It's all in here," he said cheerily, "laughter, heartbreak, romance, brawls, sore heads, car crashes, gaol sentences. Emotional dynamite—all corked in a bottle!"

We leaned our elbows on either side of the bar. From outside we could hear the rumble of traffic.

"Funny old game," I said, "what's it all about, eh?"

"Keep moving."

"Don't you ever stop to ask *why?*

"Every bugger I meet these days seems to be asking what's it all about. I'll tell you the golden rule for life, will I? Never fuck about with policemen's wives!"

"That's profound."

A brewer's drayman came into the club from the rear entrance.

"Use your blower, myte?"

"Help yourself, it's in the office."

"Cheers."

"You got my lager?"

"Yeah, 'es bringin' it dahn."

He went into the office. I started to tell Dave about my new scheme. The drayman's voice drowned mine.

"Yeah, Wilkins 'ere, I been to six places this mornin' an' I couldn't park at none of 'em and this berk you sent me out wiv won't stir for pickin' his bleedin' nose so I wants you tell Mister Connachie I'm kickin' his fakkin job into touch. All right? Just you give him the message—Wilkins is kickin' it into touch. All right? Cheers."

He came back out of the office.

"Stuff 'em," he said cheerily, "I'll git your kegs dahn, myte, then that's me lot."

"Well done," said Dave.

They had rolled the last metal barrel into the cold room and had their pint and were laughing on the back stairs when the street door opened with a clatter and Fred Matchan came walking up the long floor.

"Wot're you two conspirators mutterin' about then?" he demanded. He put a pound note on the bar. "I'll have a Greenshield. Jock? Dave?"

"I'll have a pint of lager," I said, "just to wash out my mouth."

"That's a shock."

I could see no harm in one pint. It would help to make me less impatient waiting for Fred to leave. I couldn't tell Dave my new scheme until he went, for letting Fred in on a confidence was a quick way of having your secrets talked about by people you'd never met in towns you'd never visited. Fred started off at fourteen selling novelty items off barrows outside football grounds. His family had stalls in various street markets. Fred was over fifty, how far over he never disclosed. Working for JTB as a booker was only a stop-gap until he found himself a 'class artiste' to manage.

Jazz-bands, folk groups, all-girl orchestras, sex-singers — fashions changed, new stars soared across the show biz firmament, twenty-year-old hasbeens were back on the building sites but Fred was always in there managing a piece of something. Duke Ellington was his king.

That morning he was aggrieved at the disappearance of My Boy Billy, a rock singer Fred had promoted into a couple of big hits five years before and who was still worth seventy to eighty a night on the far-flung ballroom circuits.

"I'll kill him when I get my mitts on him," he said, pushing his white shirtfront against the bar. Fred was bow-tie generation. "Never turned up for the band meet yesterday—pissed on brandy with his new sweetheart, don't I know it."

"Who's Billy sweethearting with now then?"

"Tony Tidiman would you believe?"

"He queer?"

"Depraved more like it."

"Tony Tidiman the wholesome all-round family idol?"

"All round the family's correck—he'll charver mum, dad, kids and the bleeding parrot. So wot's the secret celebration."

"We were just celebrating the thrill of it all."

"The thrill of it all, don't I know it. You hear about Harold Wilson, he's the only politician who don't need an interviewer to do *Face to Face* on television."

"The rich are going to squeal when Harold gets back."

"Get back? That bunch of Labour nanas? No chance. I've stopped voting for any of the fakkers anyway. Thieves, every bloody one of them."

"Politicians are no worse than anybody else."

"Yeah but we ain't asking to run the bleeding country, are we? We don't stand up and tell the people a load of lying codswallop, do we?"

"No, only make stars out of Tony Tidiman and your boy Billy."

"That's different. That's rubbish, yeah, but nobody's getting robbed or hurt."

"Only their minds."

"Minds. What fakking minds? The public are cunts."

Dave snapped his fingers.

"Didn't Chick Bhalla have bother over insurance cards?" he said to Fred.

"Insurance cards? That's the least of his problems. I've told JTB we want to get shot of that human pin-cushion."

"Jock wants to know about insurance cards."

"Better ask Bhalla then, if you can find him."

"I was with him only last night—no, the night before. How do you get in touch with him?"

"Find out where they're flogging heroin. Big H, man. That's where he's at."

"He said he was cured—again."

"Hell's like. What a waste that berk's life is. Gordon Bennett! If I had his talent—you know he's one of about two European jazzers the yanks reckon anything to? World class—and what's he do with it—sniffs shit, injects shit, shoves shit up his arse—*and* he's drinking enough whisky, gin and vodka to drown the whole of Alcoholics Unanimous? I don't like the berk but it's a tragedy, with his talent. Give JTB a ring at the office, he'll give you his number."

I put down the money for another lager and two Greenshields and went to use the office phone. I was just in time to disturb a skinny boy trying to loot the desk-drawers. He shot under my arm and hared up the back stairs.

I stuck my head round the corner and called Dave over. He started cursing and checking the cash box while I dialled JTB's office number.

"Yes, John," said the important telephone voice of J. Talbot Baxter, once I'd got past the switchboard girl and then Agnes.

"Hello, JTB, all right?"

"Can't handle it all. You should try working for a class outfit, John."

"I don't dress well enough for your level, JTB."

"Can't afford it on Thirsk's wages I daresay."

"I'd like to get in touch with Chick Bhalla, a personal matter, I borrowed a couple of quid off him the other night and——"

"Forget it, John, he won't remember. Better still, pay me the two quid, he owes me oceans."

"I always like to do the decent thing."

"As it happens I'm seeing him tonight. We've got him an LP contract and there's a top Fleet Street writer coming along to interview him for the sleeve-note. It's for The Leafless around seven. Drop in and we'll dip our noses into something convivial while we're waiting for the bastard to show up."

"Yeah, okay, see you then."

"You can give me the two quid anyway."

I put down the phone. Dave slammed a drawer shut.

"Nothing's missing," he said, "lucky you came in here when you did."

"He could only've been about thirteen."

"It's the school holidays."

"That's okay, as long as he wasn't playing truant."

We went back to the bar. I felt full of beans. If I got some griff on insurance cards from Bhalla I'd at least be on my way.

"This bloke turns to this other bloke and says, Hear the one about the Irish navvy?" said Fred. "The other bloke says, Hold it a minute, you better know I am Irish. That's all right, says the first bloke, I'll tell it slowly."

"Irish jokes are getting boring," I said. "If they're so fucking dim how come the whole British army can't beat 'em?" Then I told a lie, just to get Fred on his way. "JTB was asking if I'd seen you."

Fred didn't want us to think he jumped when JTB cracked the whip. He launched into a story about some musician who'd been playing at a big fireworks carnival night up north.

"The band plays till eleven then the trombone player gets into the bar and pulls one of the local lovelies. Him being a big glamour name from London she agrees to have it away lively and they slip out from the pavilion onto this big stretch of grass and head out into the darkness. He gets her down on the grass and he's giving her a right seeing-to when suddenly it's midnight and they let off rockets and turn on floodlights and they're caught in a spotlight out there on the cricket pitch, his big bare arse sticking up, and as he's staring round at the shock of it all what does he see marching towards them but the massed knees of the Dagenham Girl Pipers!"

We snorted at the whimsicality of it all and Fred left. Dave said he had to shift his tables. I said I'd help him. Instead I jumped up on the bandstand and pulled the canvas off the piano.

"Want to hear my latest number? It's called 'Big Morning Blues'. Listen to this left-hand bit. Reminds me of Jimmy Yancey. *I woke up this morning, but the sky was black as night. . . I woke up this morning but the sky was black as night. . . yeah baby. . . if the big morning don't come soon I'll be dead before it's light. . . big morning blues, you got me in*—well, I'm still working on the lyric. Like it?"

"Don't give up your day job."

"Come on—I know I've only been playing at it but surely there's some . . . not even a hint of promise?"

"With that stuff you've got to start at five. Did you say you wanted your two hundred quid?"

"Oh well, that's it then," I said, closing the keyboard lid and pulling down the canvas cover. "If you can't be brilliant—don't bother. And I thought I was getting quite good, too . . . ah well, fuck it. Listen, I don't want the two hundred back, actually I might want to give you more. Let's have another drink, eh?"

I knew I'd never touch a piano again. That was how it always was with me—if I couldn't be Number One at whatever I tried I suddenly lost all interest. We went back to the bar. I had another pint of lager, stuff I could drink all day without it showing. I told myself the piano was another illusion I was well rid of.

"So?" said Dave.

"Dave—I'm splitting with Neville. He's conning me and I'm getting nowhere. I need to make a lot of money—fast."

"Go on—surprise me."

"The trouble is, I need a company to work through because I don't pay income tax. If I can't be a great blues soloist I'll just have to settle for being a rich business shark. The deal would be—I get the promoters to make out their cheques to your company, you put them through your bank and pay me cash—minus thirty per cent to cover your end of it. Thirty per cent!" I grabbed his arm across the bar. "Like it?"

"Sorry." He shook his head. "No can do. I book all these bands for this place—I can't get involved in a buying and selling racket. Nothing personal."

"What's wrong with buying and selling?"

"Anyway, you wouldn't have to pay the government thirty per cent—not if you got a good accountant."

"I'm into the government for four or five grand. I can't get straight till I've got cash to pay off the arrears."

"Tell them you were moving digs a lot, their demands must've been lost in the post. Tell them you've been sick or you've been working abroad—tell them any fucking thing, if they see some readies they won't put you in clink."

"You really think buying and selling is all that bad?"

"It's okay if you can get away with it but it wouldn't do my reputation any good."

"I see." I wiped my lips on the back of my hand, which I noticed as needing a good scrub. "If you can get away with it—not a great philosophy of life, is it?"

"Never fuck about with policemen's wives! You going to help with my tables?"

"Sorry, I've just pulled a small but integral muscle in my back. See you later."

Dave's attitude was a shock. I had always known this buying and selling of band dates was a mild form of fraud but as long as Neville made it seem like a joke, and everybody else tolerated it, I had never seen the harm. But if the most sensible man I knew regarded me as a furtive chiseller I had to give it up, didn't I?

Only what else could I do? My piano-playing had always been a bit of a joke (although *that* hurt, too) but hustling band dates was my one proven skill. How else could I stay on the gravy train?

Colman Hedge Lane was blocked all the way down by two fire engines, the only visible proof of drama in the vicinity——no smoke, no flames, no women screaming piteously from high windows. I joined the crowd of gaping fishfaces hoping to see flames and women screaming. I say fishes because firemen, with their big black helmets and thigh-length boots, always seem to me to be working in slow motion underwater. Messages boomed from radios. Blue lights flashed with the staccato rhythm of miniature light-houses. Spare firemen grandly ignored us, the audience. The well-known actor Sir J— G— came sauntering past in a grey suit and suedes, a cigarette protruding from his classically severe features. He looked at us bleakly. As far as I could tell I alone in that street crowd of unruly apprentices and rude artisans recognised him. It seemed like an unfair accident of circumstances that he did not know me as someone out with the common run.

"It's one of them gas leaks in the basement, innit?" said a shirt-sleeved packer from a film distribution office.

"They was up here to an electrical fault that killed one of them Chinese last week," said a woman whose hard skin and greasy complexion belied her juvenile taste in platform-soled shoes.

"Good job it ain't a fire," said the shirt-sleeved man authoritatively, "They couldn't get no more fire wagons up this far with all them parked cars. Some day this whole shooting match is going up but they won't be able to get at it, will they? But will they do anyfing about them parked cars? Will they hell as like! They're entitled to, that's what I say."

I turned and walked back towards Nailed Down Chambers. I caught sight of a coarse prole wearing an artisan's off-duty zipper jerkin. It was myself, in a shop window. Looking like that what reason did Sir J— have for giving me a second glance?

On the first flight of stairs in The Chambers wee Mick the cleaner-handyman tapped me for a couple of bob, saying with ferrety sincerity that he'd done all his pay in the betting shop. He said I was a decent big fella, as I'd known he would when I decided to be generous.

Wasn't this what London life should be like for a man of my intelligence, gentlemen of wit and learning ambling through history-rich streets, bowing to famous actors, noting the petty dramas, philosophising on the childish excitements of the lower orders? I yearned achingly for the day when Sir J- would laugh to learn that I had been evaluating the price of his suit while masquerading as a nobody. Dear God, will these wasted days of obscurity *never* end? It is all so unjust—surely I'm at least as clever and potentially talented as a wreck like Shand? It is so lonely Out Here. Right from the start I knew I would only come to life in the magic circle, I have felt it in every cell of my body ever since I—

Shand?

It took less than two flights of stairs for my success story to project itself. Meeting Shand had been the *Sign!* Why the hell had I been so slow in recognising it? All great men say the same thing—it comes once in your lifetime and if you don't grab it you don't Make It. But it wasn't too late. All I had to do was find Shand again—and stick to him. He was a worthless person but he knew the secrets of the magic circle. I would help him out of the gutter. I would guard him from all the parasites. He would show me the tricks of the trade. We would *collaborate!*

Soon I would have learned all he could teach me—but I would always acknowledge the help he'd been in my own development. From my tax-dodger's haven in the Caribbean I might even send him the odd donation, keeping this heart-warming generosity a secret from everybody except my press agent. I'd be so rich I'd never wear the same socks twice.

And to think I only met him by a fluke!

How would it read in the definitive biographies—our meeting

among the common drunks in a London police court? The five-pound note passing hands—almost mystical that would be.

I felt quite breathless. Hardly surprising, it's not every day the cataracts drop from a man's eyes and he sees what destiny had in store for him all the time. To think it had been ordained all along that I should be a great playwright! What else? Do you try to tell me that seeing Sir J— like that, in the street, so shortly after meeting Ramsay Shand, was not *ordained?*

It did just occur to me that perhaps I ought to see a couple of live stage plays, just to get the hang of it, but obviously the important thing was to find Shand again.

Two black men with briefcases edged past me on the third-floor landing. I gave them a reassuring smile.

Success is very relaxing.

I put my Yale key into the lock and stepped into the office, beaming pleasantly on my partner, Neville Thirsk, and his intended victim, Miss Angela Browne with an e.

"Morning all," I said, noting, with a little disappointment, that I had not disturbed them in any lewd act. From their faces, however, it was not hard for a man of perception to see they would have liked rather more notice of my intrusion. Neville had his buttocks against the window ledge while she was sitting in my swivel chair.

"Sir," I said to Neville, "it is commonly supposed that a woman with red hair is—"

"You've been on the booze, you bastard."

This annoyed me a little. He was guessing—and as usual, his instincts were malicious. I smiled patronisingly, preparing to wither him with a Sir, it is—

"No I fucking haven't," said my voice.

"There's some geezer been phoning for you," he said, looking at his wristwatch. "Anyway, we've got to dash, Angela. I'll see you in the Hum Drum around four"

"You had some money you were getting for me?" I said,

ominously.

"Oh yeah—here you are—only fifty here but I'm going to the bank just now, I'll give you the rest when I see you."

The phone rang. I took the money, shoving it in my hip-pocket. She held out the phone.

"It's for you," she said.

"Just a minute," I said to Neville, taking the phone.

"Sorry, we're late as it is."

They were out of the door and away.

"Yeah, who is it?" I snapped, hoping to catch up with the slippery bastard.

"That you, Jock?" said the voice of Exquisite.

"Yeah."

"I've got to see you, Jock, it's Stan, you doin' anyfink about half-one?"

I thought of slamming the phone down and running after them. My instincts told me to have nothing more to do with him. His very voice was dangerous, gruff, anonymous, the kind of voice you occasionally hear on a crossed line and which makes you wonder what terrible things are going on Out There in the big, dangerous city.

"Is it really important?" I said. "I've actually got this—"

"It's about the ower night. You know The Holy Land. I'll be innair about half-one. All right?"

"Okay."

"I wouldn't be phonin' unless it was fakkin important, would I? You be there, Jock. All right?"

"Keep your hair on."

It was half-past twelve. I lifted what I'd written of *A Bed Of Men* out of the desk drawer, telling myself it required only two days' work and then I could collect three hundred pounds.

My stomach turned over at the very sight of the name Wilma. I told myself this queasiness was caused by artistic revulsion, not by fear of what Exquisite was going to tell me.

The grating door had a lock twelve inches wide. Jack picked at it with the nail. It would not yield. He used the spike on the iron lock-plate. It would not come off. He had only one other alternative-to try and tear the metal fillet off the main post into which the door fitted. This metal cover was seven feet high and two inches thick. He attacked it with the spike.

12

Unable to write a pornographic word I left the office, intending to drop in at The Leafless for a drink and a few reassuring pleasantries before meeting Exquisite in The Holy Land, a disreputable queers' pub.

Three or four times I saw men with black leather jackets but none was Shand. I realised I would probably have to comb every pub in The Rookery before I found him—but that would all add to the significance of our relationship, wouldn't it, in the biographies? As I approached The Leafless I saw Neville holding open the painted door for Angela Browne. I had a momentary repugnance at the idea of further involving myself in their petty affairs and walked on past the pub. In any case, I no longer felt the need for drink. I had a future to consider. Besides, it might be clever to have a clear head while I settled this business with Exquisite and freed my life for its most important phase.

I walked on and turned right towards another of my regular cafes, the Alley Baba, a ten-table snackery near the vegetable market. It was fairly quiet. I sat at a window table and ordered my usual meal, mixed grill, tea and two slice of bread and butter. Soon such places would be only nostalgic reminders of my struggling days. I looked round, establishing the scene for future recollection. (I didn't *feel* drunk.)

At a table against the far wall I saw a familiar face, a man wearing a British warm overcoat, a former regular in The Leafless. I had not seen him there for some time.

What was his name again? He always used to be in there ordering up large gins for his cronies from the film companies. So this was where he had been since the British cinema industry collapsed, skulking in cheap cafes while he planned desperate moves that might put him back in the large gin bracket. That briefcase would be full of story treatments and budget breakdowns and plot outlines—none of which would ever see celluloid.

How cruel—not to have a genuine original talent! He must sit in here sipping tea after tea wondering how the hell to keep up the mortgage and pay the fancy schools and give his glossy wife her usual holiday in Portugal.

Sorry for him?

He never bought me any large ones, did he?

I started into the mixed grill. The way prices were soaring most of the cafes were substituting hamburgers for lamb chops but in The Alley Baba they still gave you a piece of liver with the bacon, tomato, sausage, chips and peas, what Neville called a good wodge of stodge. To which I would always reply—we used to win world wars on good British stodge, how many bloody wars have we won since all these health food rackets started up?

I smiled. Even if I said it myself, to myself, I had to admit that I had a neat turn of phrase. Given a few practical tips from Shand why the hell shouldn't I knock out successful plays?

It was a pity about Neville. He had no original talent, of course, and it was inevitable he should turn devious and grubby. Still, when I had plenty of money I could have him as a friend without having to do business with him. I could employ him in some capacity—personal manager, maybe, just to take the sting out of it—and we could travel the world together. Success wouldn't be much fun if you didn't have a drinking mate who knew what kind of life you'd been leading before the big break.

Money. Was that the only reason they invented the bloody stuff, to prevent the rich from being lonely?

A noisy group came through the door. The three women couldn't have been anything else but strippers, with their little square handcases, huge eyelashes and conspicuous professional make-up. There was an old man with them. They took the next table. As far as I could overhear, the old man was the father of the dark-haired one, who seemed uncomfortable at his presence. He sounded like a working-class bloke up from Nottingham or thereabouts to see how his darling daughter was faring in the big city. The other two made a great fuss of him. Mave, the loud one with the lacquered platinum anthill on her head, started waxing indignant, in Birmingham fashion.

"Eet's all thees keenky beet now, yew know?" she said. The other two nodded. Father smiled happily, basking in a situation that had come too late. "I've got to dress oop like a school keed, yew know? Then he's got me playeenk a secreetary, in an offeece, yew know? And I'm to show a beet of thigh and George has to coom on and touch my knee, suggesteeve like, yew know? We don't do anytheenk, yew know. I mean, keenky, that's all eet ees. Eet used to be straight sexee stoof, yew know, playeenk weeth a wheep, yew know? I don't theenk thees keenky stoof ees right, do yew, Reen?"

"Ach it wiz real obscene then," snorted Glasgow Reen.

I paid my seventy-pence bill and gave the waitress a two-bob tip. I could remember when a mixed grill cost two bob.

Crossing Colman Hedge Lane I saw the one-tune, semi-blind flute player, shuffling along the gutter, head cocked to one side, guided by the hand of his partner who walked one pace behind, the other hand holding out the bag. I'd seen them around for years and I still wasn't sure if the one tune was Greensleeves or The Fair Maid of Perth.

Being daytime the queers were absent from the cold, hard interior of The Holy Land, a dull pub used in daylight only by drifting merchant seamen and mistaken tourists.

136

Exquisite was leaning on the bar talking to a lanky young barman with severe acne.

Cold as it was, Exquisite was wearing an open-necked shirt, a thin blue cardigan, big fawn trousers and open-toed sandals over green wool socks. Even without a jacket his sloping shoulders were much wider than mine

He bought me a pint of lager. We carried our glasses over to a table under a leaded window.

"So," he said, "all right, are you?"

"Usual."

"Listen, rememmer the ovver night?"

"Yeah."

We looked at each other. He raised his eyelids so that his brown pupils were completely surrounded by white eyeball. I wasn't sure if this meant he was in a humorous mood.

"You give those readies to Teepee, did you?" he asked.

"No—he was off up North the next morning. I spoke to him on the phone briefly, he doesn't remember anything about anything."

"Lucky old him. You see about that berk bein' done in?"

"Yeah. Funny enough I got nicked that night for being drunk in the street."

"That'll be good for your memoirs. You know the filth's been all round the shop askin' who was seen wiv that spoofin' bastard?"

"He must've been with lots of people."

"I got a china works in that club, he's told me the filth was askin' the barmen and the girls. They ain't been onto you?"

"No."

"They will, soon as they find out about Teepee playin' spoof wiv the cunt. So they're bound to come askin' you. What're you gonna tell 'em?"

"I dunno. The truth, I suppose."

He snorted derisively, eyes astonished and ominous at the same time.

"Can they trace that money?" I asked.

"Money? What money?"

"The money you gave me in—"

"I give you nothin', all right? Lucky you didn't pass it on to Teepee. You spent any owit?"

"You just said you didn't give me any money!"

"Keep your fakkin voice down. Have you spent any, I'm askin'?"

"A bit-in Marks and Sparks."

"They won't rememmer your boatrace. Better give me the est owit."

"I haven't got it on me."

"All right. What you gotta do is git it and shove it down the shit-hole and pull the plug, all right?"

"Why? How can they trace it? He must've been carrying all sorts of money."

"I had a couple off the top of that bundle, didn't I? Lucky I had a good look at them sheets the next day. Snide, innit, slush, queer, Monopoly fakkin money."

"Forged?"

"Look at the fakkin numbers before you pulls the chain. They're all the same, inney? You git collared carryin' more'n one of them duds and they'll fit you up for passin' it. One they let you away wiv—but two's evidence you're pushin' it."

"Jesus."

"That spoofin' shithouse must've been passin' snide stuff— best I've ever seen as it happens. So this is the story, Jock—you just know me from around the scene, all right? You might've seen me that night but you was well-pissed so you can't be sure an' certainly wasn't playin' spoof. I niver give you no money and I niver went out lookin' for that spoofin' bastard. You're respectable, bein' Teepee's manager an' that, they'll believe it from you. Teepee don't rememmer nothin' so that's all right, innit?"

His fingers clamped on my wrist.

"What's all the panic about, ha ha, you look sick you do." He laughed. It was the hand with the blue heart tattoo. "You're the only one who knows anythin' so lissen careful, Jock, you don't know nothin', all right? Cos if you drop me in the shit, Jock, I'll see you git hurt, serious."

We stared at each other. I tried not to swallow conspicuously. His fingers gradually relented.

"Cheer up then, let's have a quick one then you won't be seein' me around for a bit. What's that you're drinkin'—lager? On a cold day like this? Have a drop of scotch, warm you up."

I went to the bar and asked for two large scotches. When I sat down again he said that as I was a bloke who read and that maybe I could tell him the answer to a question that had always bothered him.

"Our family's always bin poor," he said, "old man niver had a brass farthin'—brought up rough we were in Bermondsey. Yet I'm readin' all the time about this Empire of ours. We was lords an' masters over half the fakkin world, wasn't we? What I wants to know, where's all that fakkin Empire money gone to? Eh? I mean, none owit ever got down to us, did it? Must of bin millions an' millions. We niver saw a pound note from one week to the next but somebody was coinin' it in, stands to reason."

"That's capitalism, isn't it?" I said, hardly able to believe we were now supposed to be talking about the Empire.

Realising that I was no great fount of knowledge he said we had to leave the pub separately. He came with me to the door, glass in hand, walking flat-heeled in his sandals.

"If anything happens how do I get in touch with -you?" I asked.

He snorted again.

"You niver heard of me, you berk. Get in touch? Leave me out!"

I nodded and reached for the door. The tattooed hand took hold of my wrist in such a way I couldn't move. Of all so-called moments of truth that is the killer, to be in the grip of a man so much stronger you have no possible chance of fighting him, only the certainty of being hammered. I am Scottish enough not always to be sensible in these matters.

"What did you do to him anyway?" I asked.

"Do to who?"

"Cut out the fucking games," I said, making no effort to free my wrist and thereby hoping to make it look as though I did not notice his grip.

"Leanin' on geezers a little bit, that's all I ever do," he said.

"Worried I'm a man-killer? Nah, it weren't me. But don't you be gettin' me involved—I done enuff bird wivout gettin' sent down for somethin' I niver done. All right?" He took his hand away. "Merry Christmas."

He actually pouted a kiss at me.

Then I was on the street, alone.

This couldn't be happening, not to *me*.

Working in pitch darkness, always listening for footsteps,
Jack ripped at the metal plating with the spike. It took him
an hour to dislodge it from the doorpost. He kicked down
the grating. Immediately he found himself facing another
heavy door—but this one was bolted on his side. Fresh air
struck his face. He came out onto the lower roof of Newgate
Prison. It had taken him six hours to get this far. Between
him and the street was a drop that had killed several
people.

13

I turned into Bishop Henry Street.

Before anything else I had to get rid of the remaining two fivers in my hip pocket.

My hand felt for them, fingers sliding past the thicker wad of fifty singles that Neville had given me in the office. I got the two fivers into my palm, intending to drop them in the gutter.

It's easy to chuck litter about when it's only bus tickets. Not when it's evidence that may damn you.

I was as near to losing my bottle as at any time in my life.

Losing your bottle is rhyming slang, bottle and glass—arse. It makes better sense if you pronounce it the London way—glawss–awss.

Pronounce it any way you like, I was near to becoming a one-man brickworks.

Everybody in that bloody street looked busy—busy in the old sense, as in busybody, nosey.

I crushed them in my palm. My thigh muscles were jelly.

I thought of flicking the crumpled ball into a lamp-post waste-bin. Immediately I could see only derelict men of the type who rake through street litterbins and fill the boredom of their existences by taking mental snapshots of everything and everybody they see.

I thought of flicking them sideways into a doorway but the very next doorway I came to was blocked by three young typists who had *exactly* the sort of cheeky, giggling faces you would see in a *Mirror* picture of the girl Sherlocks whose quick wits helped police apprehend The Rookery Forgery Murder Mystery Suspect.

I came alongside the semi-blind flute-player and thought of dropping the notes into the bag. But they'd remember anybody who dropped in ten quid as long as they lived—and what did semi-blind mean, anyway?

What did I know about sweat-analyses, infra-red fingerprint cameras? These days they had cameras that took pictures of the heat outlines your body left, so that they could photograph you standing in the spot you were actually in yesterday.

I had to get off the streets and tear these notes into a thousand shreds and burn them and crush the cinders and flush the powder down the lavatory.

Of course I was guilty of nothing. That's the worst thing of all to feel guilty about.

By the time I got to the fourth floor of The Chambers my face was frozen as if from novocaine. The building was quiet. From across the rooftops and the blank wall-faces and the windy spaces through which a man could only fall once came the strains of Bob Dylan yelping nasally. *John Wesley Hardin was a friend to the poor*. . some nut played that LP over and over again at lunchtimes, presumably when the other people had gone to eat . . . *he travelled with a gun in every hyand* . . .

I sat in the swivel chair. Exquisite was right about the numbers. I held the notes up to the light of the window. The metal strip was not a metal strip but a dark line printed on the back.

I pulled over the brewery ashtray Neville had pocketed in some bar and got out my matches.

The first one I laid across the ashtray and set fire to the corner. It would not lie down flat but kept humping up in an arch. The flame was bright and reddish-yellow, with white smoke. The arch turned black. When the flame went out there was still a half-inch corner of unburned paper resting on the bed of fag ends and spent matches. I touched the black, crinkled arch. The smoke stopped. The extreme edges had turned a fine grey-white. The charred black arch still had a springy resistance.

I struck another match and held it down on the unburned triangle. It caught alight. In the heart of the flame the curling paper glowed red. The match burned to the very end. Some of the black arch went on fire again but it was still springy to the touch.

Could forensics do anything with that?

I got the red stapler from the drawer and pounded down. A match was flicked into the air, shooting charred crumbs across the desk.

Peering down in the mess I was still able to see, on a black triangle of paper, the queen's eyes and nose.

The last match had set a cigarette end on fire, one of Neville's Gauloises.

I crushed it out with the stapler.

I got a piece of typing paper out of a drawer and tipped the ashtray onto it. Fine dust blew about the desk. Picking up the corners of the sheet I crumpled it into a fine ball, which I dropped back into the empty ashtray. I struck another match and put it to the bottom of the crumpled ball, which was already springing outwards.

The room smelled of autumn bonfires.

I lit one of my Silk Cut kingsizes and sat there, one eye closed against smoke from the fag in my mouth, watching the ball of paper go black but refusing to burn in a way that would totally destroy its contents.

It went on smoking heavily, however.

I got up and opened the window.

A quick blast of air blew black fragments across the desk. I shut the window and then swept the desk clean with the edge of my right hand.

I rubbed dust and tiny particles of black paper off my sweating palm into the ashtray.

I wanted to scream but I kept telling myself that this must be some kind of test ordained to see if I had the moral fibre for success.

The ball went on smoking.

I told myself I was actually being given, on a plate, a brilliant scene for the first smash-hit play I would write as soon as Shand had taught me the basics of drama, like whether to use foolscap or quarto paper.

I still wanted to scream.

I went to the door and looked out into the corridor. There was nobody to be seen, no noise from the other offices, no footsteps on the stairs. I picked up the smoking ashtray and carried it swiftly along the corridor and bolted the lavatory door. I dropped the smoking ball into the pan. I pulled the chain. The pan filled, then emptied in a swirl. The water rose again.

One or two bits of black paper were still stuck to the smooth inner slopes of the pan. I ripped a length of shitpaper off the roll and wiped the pan clean. I pulled the chain again.

The second flush was weaker but the damning evidence had been totally swept down into the vastnesses of the sewage system.

"Follow that, you forensic bastards," I said, standing up.

I had to snort with contempt for this neurotic performance but reassured myself with the thought that men of great talent are often quite silly in the smaller things.

I went back along the corridor, swinging my arms to straighten my back. All great artists are a little bit mad, stands to reason, don't it?

But it was all down to realities now, the finding of Shand, the monastic dedication, the flowering of creativity, the book-lined study where I would pour my distinguished guests a fine old brandy and swop cruel anecdotes about Noel Coward's tax-dodging. Oh yes, it was going to be—

When I discovered that I'd left my keys in my jacket I hit the door with the flat of my right hand.

A working-man in a white industrial apron appeared at the top of the stairs.

"You interested in any foam-backed nylon carpet, guv?" he asked. Hand still flat on the door I looked at him stupidly.

"No."

He hurried past me along the corridor.

I bit my lip. Should I give a loud scream and kick the fucking door down?

The other fiver was still on the desk!

Another man appeared from the stairs, puffing slightly, middle-aged and swarthy, possibly Italian.

"You inrested in helpeeng the blind?" he said, shoving some kind of identification card at me with his left hand and, simultaneously, bringing his right hand out of his raincoat pocket to show me three sticks of male deodorant in triangular packets.

I shook my head.

For a few moments I stood there while the two of them zigzagged along the corridor rattling on doors.

Then I went back to the lavatory. Shutting the door firmly without bolting it I eased up the bottom half of the dusty window and got my right leg over the sill. My hands were black before I got out onto the narrow balcony with the knee-high brick wall.

Between the lavatory balcony and the next was two feet of bare wall stretching down four storeys into the damp, sunless well.

Normally I get trembling knees just looking *up* at heights. But what else could I do?

I stood on the sloping top of the little wall, kept my eyes on the next balcony and took a quick step across the chasm.

It was easy. I passed the window of Chantrey the unfrocked accountant. If he was looking out I must have appeared like a vision, a human being walking in space.

His balcony stopped about three feet from the one outside our window. Between the two balconies was space where only birds and winds could go.

I had to decide whether to step across or jump.

As I was making up my mind I did what they always tell you not to do and looked down. They are fools. A tiled brick on the sloping top of the low wall was cracked in the middle; the outer half was resting slack in its slot. If I had put my weight on it I would have been too heavy for the invisible air currents to catch. Putting my left hand against the coarse surface of the brick wall, which immediately seemed to be actively pushing back, I balanced my full weight on the ball of my right foot and stretched my left leg out across the gap.

I should have let body momentum carry me over but I hesitated and came to a halt, left shoulder pushing hard against brick, legs forming an angle of about forty-five degrees, hands trying to find a suction hold on rough brickwork.

The sky was grey.

My balls started aching. Perhaps they sensed they were dangling sixty feet above the dustbins.

Feeling the bloody building shoving me away, knowing I would fall at any moment, I gave a push with my right foot and jack-knifed my body towards the other balcony, both hands clutching for the low, tiled wall.

I might have been screaming.

I came over the little wall on my stomach. Just for a moment my feet were in mid-air and then I was sliding down onto gritty roofing felt. Never was any woman's flesh so kissable.

I slid up the window and came into the office feet first, shaking but triumphant.

Hands black with grime, new trousers soiled at the knees, testicles churning, I slumped into the swivel chair.

The other fiver was on the typewriter.

I crunched it quickly between my palms and started to roll it into a little ball.

A key turned in the door.

I popped the hard little ball into my mouth and sat back as Angela Browne with an e said:

"Oh! I didn't think you'd be here."

"I didn't know you had a key already," I said, coolly, lower jaw moving slowly in the Gary Cooper manner.

"It's Neville's—I had to borrow it—"

"So you've done the deal?"

"Not exactly, I thought I'd left something—"

She made a show of looking round.

"It isn't here," she said.

The outer edges of the wad were soft now as my eye-teeth took it in turns to grind into the hard centre. I've never tasted the government stuff but forged notes aren't too bad.

Looking at her face I decided she would be beautiful if she cleared all the make-up away. I also had a peculiar notion that if we were lying naked in each other's arms all this stuff about forged money and men like The Spoofer and Exquisite would seem amusing.

She stood beside the desk, her *slightly* squinted eyes appraising me thoughtfully. I've never pretended to be any great shakes at reading women's minds but it did seem, for a moment, as though she was waiting for me to make some utterance of a romantic nature.

"Not coming to the pub?" she said.

"No, I've got some hardcore pornography to write," I said, without smiling.

She thought I was making fun of her. She made a facial shrug and left. I opened the door quietly and tiptoed to the top of the stairs. Her black beret was bobbing down the right-angled spiral of the stair well.

"You can only con people who're trying to con somebody else," I murmured into space.

As I went back into the office I realised I must have swallowed the five-pound note. I should have thought of that in the first place, I decided, getting out the manuscript of *A Bed Of Men* and rolling clean paper and a carbon into the typewriter.

They wouldn't cut you open on suspicion, would they?

Looking back it's easy to see that all this happened while I was half-drunk. At the time I felt totally in control. But in control of *what!* At the back of my mind was the shadowy figure of a man telling me quietly that I was mad.

I typed for ten minutes. Each page was more of an ordeal. What was I doing with such pitiful rubbish? Had I really clawed my way across the face of this building because of a stupid panic over two bits of paper?

The phone rang but I didn't pick it up. I tried to think practically. The only conclusion I reached was that I had turned into a high-class neurotic. Destroying those notes had been totally pointless. If they started tracing the dud fivers they'd find that Shand had used one to pay his fine. He'd tell them I'd given it to him.

Then there was the one I'd forced on that taxi-driver outside Kate's flat. They had plenty of leads to me.

The sky grew darker but I didn't have the energy to switch on the light. People knocked on doors. Urgent sirens cut through the soft swishing noise of the traffic.

I put my head on my arms and tried to sleep. The wooden desk acted as a conductor for voices in the rooms below. They sounded like a speeded-up tape, a fast, squeaky chatter of Disney mice. It became dark. The room grew cold. The phone rang again. I felt totally depressed and alone and futile. The building's front door began to slam, people going home, locking up, buttoning up, saying good night, looking forward to evening meals, television programmes, hot chocolate drinking chocolate, goodnight fumbles, warm beds, pleasant dreams.

And I was left alone in a cold, dark, silent room with no idea *why,* facing the fact that I was a drunken dreamer who had stumbled into the wrong nightmare.

Jack went along the roof to the Northern Tower. This overlooked the flat roofs of houses about twenty feet below, as far as he could judge in the dark, too risky a jump. He needed something to slide down. There was only one thing he could think of —the blanket back in his cell. He had no option but to go all the way back for it.

14

When I woke up it took me several moments to get it into my bleary head that I was not in a tenement in Shettleston, Glasgow, but in an office in The Rookery, London, England, aged twenty-nine.

This was such a relief I found myself singing cheerily. *Bye bye Miss American Pie, drove mah chewy to the levee but the levee was dry!*

I pushed my vest down into my new blue underpants, zipped up, fastened my belt, pulled the new sweater over the belt. I have always thought of clothes as a blind mirror affording tactile reflections of the body. I felt myself to be big and strong. I'd been through an interlude of panicky madness but I was clear-headed again. What was there to fear?

I went down the silent corridor to the lavatory and splashed my face with cold water. I rubbed my grimy hands. It was dark but I could feel the dirt coming off. I was through the fear barrier. Unlike all these other guys I no longer had to live in apprehension of the past. The worst had happened. Already I felt nostalgic for the future. There was nothing I could not do. I would no longer sing a haunted song. This is not the day I'm going to die, this is the night I start singing with exultation.

Yeah. *I'm the biggest fool who ever hit the big time, they're gonna make a big star outa me!* But only I know how foolishly I've thought and acted. Henceforth I am my own conspiracy.

Back in the office I saw the pile of typed sheets on the desk. *A Bed Of Men?*

"Filth, filth, glorious filth," I sang. I banged the pages into shape. Like the forged fivers they were damning evidence and had to be destroyed. When I finally walked in the sunshine with the people Who Counted I would have a secretive smile on my face. The secret smile of success—if only *they* knew that once I was so despicably poor I whored over this kind of crap. That's why the famous have a lurking smile—it's not, as I always used to think, a smile of superiority but a conspirator's smirk. Buried secrets!

I tried to tear the bundle in two but was not as strong as that woman who used to rip up phone books. Joan something. That would have been too easy anyway. A great playwright should bury his secrets with a certain degree of style.

I doubled this load of filth filth filth and shoved it in my jacket pocket, a heavy wad of one hundred and sixty-seven quarto sheets of Croxley 71 g/m Script, and slammed the door.

Mad? I never *felt* better.

A few pages of filth filth filth lobbed into a pile of gutter rubbish. A few pages dropped into an empty cardboard crate against the wall of an Indian restaurant. A few pages posted in the letterbox of a new employment agency for temporary girls. A few more pages into the letterbox of a bank, being unable to get them into the night-safe.

Whenever people approached I whistled 'Bye Bye Miss American Pie' and sauntered past with my hands in my trouser pockets. How were they to know I was the mad postman of the filth filth filth delivery?

The last lot went into the letterbox of the registered offices of a sexploitation film company. I hoped the anonymous fragment would tantalise them out of their minds. My pocket was empty. Nobody could ever connect me with that crap. Now I could find this drunken clown Shand and put my foot on the first rung and start to climb out of the anonymous swamp!

The first pub door I saw was that of The Leafless, where I was supposed to be meeting J. Talbot Baxter. It was not a place Shand was likely to be in but there was no hurry. Besides, I had to clear all decks before my new career got under way and Bhalla was the one who could tell me about insurance cards. Besides, I felt exhilarated. I wanted to stand in the company of those who thought they knew me and to practise the faint smirk of one who alone can hear the countdown to lift-off.

I went through that painted glass door like a fist with a smile on its face.

"Ah, there you are, John," said J. Talbot Baxter, beckoning from the wondrously reliable semi-circle at the end of the bar of The Leafless Tree. "What's your pleasure?"

Gathered round J. Talbot Baxter alias John the Baptist were Roger Parkes, Junior Waddell the ace scribe from North of The Border, and Tony Stringfellow, ominous grease of a music trade paper. I gave *him* the kind of grin that says seconds out. He was tall and dressed like a woman in male drag. I mean, the gear he wore was individually identifiable as normal male attire but on him it looked like the ensemble the butch showgirl rushed out to buy the day after her sex-change operation.

In print he was everyone's oldest, bestest, dearest mate but in speech he was all sneer. He had once referred to me in the Hum Drum, when I wasn't there to give him a friendly slap of the kind that bruises kidneys, as that 'fish-eyed sidekick of The Beast's'.

"So where's the mainline, sorry, mainstream jazz genius?" I asked.

"Late. Is he ever anything else?"

"As I say, I've got this fella to meet in The Jack Ketch," said Stringfellow. Quick as a flash I said:

"Another rocker whose favourite colour you need to know?" He withered me with a glance. I counter-glanced with a scorching flame-thrower.

"I'll have to hang on here till Chick comes," said JTB.

"There *are* no ugly women at midnight," I said, for no other reason than to amuse and edify.

"What's that apropos?" said my countryman, Junior Waddell.

"Bacardi and Coke, ta."

"Junior's going to write the sleeve-note for Chick's new album," JTB said to me.

"Make it a large Bacardi and Coke then," I said.

Junior Waddell I could do without. Five minutes off the Glasgow train at Euston and he knew the lot. They have no humility, these Scots. This one was nobody's fool because nobody would have him.

I gathered that he'd only decided to give newspapers a boost by racing quickly up the Fleet Street career ladder before launching into a music-industry and/or television success story, injury having ruled out his certain prospect of playing outside-right for Celtic and Scotland. He was tuned-in lingo-wise—'k' for thousand instead of grand, 'hassle' for trouble instead of aggro or bother, 'rip off, 'heads', 'uptight' and 'hang-up'.

He was growing a droopy moustache and his trousers were flared and like all the pop stars he referred to the scrubber he was living with as 'the old lady'.

Mainly I disliked him because he was me before I understood that we were all tiny dancing figures on the edge of the Seventh Seal's big black hill.

"Don't sweat," said little Roger Parkes, when JTB again checked the time on his watch with the time on the pub clock. "He always does show, eventually. Remember that time I had him down for a studio session and he arrived at three in the afternoon—with twenty session men sitting round reading their *Angling Times* and *Popular Mechanics* since ten in the a.m.?"

"Don't I?" said JTB. "At eight quid an hour for every man jack of them? Plus the studio rent? I could've murdered him."

"It wasn't you who had to pay the taxi. He comes rolling in, half-pissed, popped to the eyebrows and says, Settle the cab bill, Rodge, there's a mate. He's only taken it from St Albans via

Putney to pick up his instrument. Or as he calls it, the axe."

Parkes I did like. He was short and cheery, an all-round musical utility man who could sight-read, get a tune out of any form of musical instrument, think up sounds for pop groups, tell them what notes to stumble through, balance the tracks, edit sixty-seven takes into one chartbound version and then head for a pub where sane men told stories about Louis Armstrong and Duke Ellington.

"I'll have to go across to The Jack Ketch," said Stringfellow.

"Another profound rock singer with a message of universal love to give the people?" I said. "Better hurry before he starts smashing chairs."

Mainly the reason I disliked him was that he could give me five or six inches. Taller men always make me feel like a specimen.

"I could go off you," Stringfellow said.

"I didn't know you wanted to get on me, duckie," I said, putting a wrist on my hip and fluttering my eyelids.

He left, disappointingly.

"I don't suppose you'll get this into the sleeve-note but you ever hear about the time Chick and Dick Bernstein gave themselves the Chinese cure?" said Parkes. "They booked a room in a Bayswater hotel and took their stuff—heroin mixed with water in two bottles, one each-they knew that if they didn't have separate bottles they'd end up by cutting each other's throats. They were in that room for seven days— occasionally they got a sandwich sent up but they never went out. The idea is that every time they fill their hypodermics from the bottles they replace it with water from the tap. In a week they're onto straight water. Chick told me he felt marvellous. He took his wife to Brighton to celebrate—he said he could feel the rain and wind on his cheeks for the first timein years. So they go to the pictures—I'll never forget him saying it was *The Vikings* with Kirk Douglas. So he's sitting there all cured and feeling great, his wife's ready to forget the hell he's put her through—great! So he has to celebrate, doesn't he? Know how? He creeps off to the cinema lavatory and gives himself another shot."

"All is forgivable in people with talent," I said, mockingly, "learn to strum a guitar and they'll lap it up when you behave like a monkey in the fucking zoo. I think I must become famous."

"Strum a guitar? Chick Bhalla's a fucking genius, mate, and don't let me hear otherwise."

"A genius of the plectrum! A good enough reason indeed for turning himself into a chemical freak. In us faceless men it would be mere self-indulgence but—"

"How about the time he got that job in Paris? He was registered by then so he picks up his scripts in advance—one thousand, six hundred and sixty pills of heroin, one hundred and thirty grains of cocaine. He has to walk about Paris at night to find dark doorways for the fix—he says, 'Them frog bogs are too open for my purposes, man.' He uses the fortnight's scripts in five days so he takes a day trip back here to pick up more."

"Where the bloody hell is he? The aggro I've had with that geezer!"

"You know all he's eating by that stage? Couple of times a week he bought a Mary Baker chocolate cake and covered it with half a pound of strawberry jam and wolfed it down. His sole nourishment, man!"

"Great player though. Every yank says it, he's the one guy in Europe they reckon in their own class. Look at the polls he's won."

"You know what his average was at his peak—two hundred heroin pills and thirty-two grains of cocaine *a day*—"

"Plus he's drinking enough to be in the alcoholic class."

"He told me the other night he was cured," I said, knowing this would raise jeers and grimaces. I was sick of hearing about Bhalla. "They're never cured, mate. They get dragged down so low they're dizzy in the gutter."

"Here, is that clock fast? I make it half-past seven."

"You get it all the time with these blokes, one minute they'd lick your arse for a plug in the paper, one minor hit later they're too big to spit on you—"

"Don't compare Chick with pop musicians in my hearing," snapped JTB.

"This is real talent. One of the finest musicians this country ever produced."

"The public don't—"

"What the fuck do the public know? They like what they're sold, that's all."

"That Beaulieu time, Chick's supposed to be getting a lift back to London next morning but he gets so stoned he decides to walk! All he remembers is sitting in a gutter somewhere in Hampshire, laughing his bleeding head off. He thinks he got onto the train at Southampton, he couldn't swear to it. Next thing it's Waterloo station and the ticket collector is calling an inspector because Chick's only got a platform ticket and the inspector screams for the railway police. There is our Charles drugged to the eyeballs, half drunk into the bargain, no ticket and enough junk in his pocket to turn on half the population! What happens? They pat him on the back and tell him to take care of himself!"

"And I have a few drinks and they arrest me on sight?" I said, ironically.

"Maybe they didn't spot your hidden talents," said Junior Waddell. The sneer was only partly hidden by his stupid moustache.

"Maybe I've got some to hide," I sneered back, immediately regretting that I'd allowed him to rattle me. Recovering my faint smile I said, "One should never confuse creative talent with superficial eccentricity."

"Nah, thank God you're one of my kind of people," said JTB, putting his arm on my shoulder.

He glared at Junior Waddell. "John is a good nut. There's not many blokes I'd rather go into the jungle with." He gave my shoulders a squeeze. Junior Wadell took the sneer off his face. It was a very seductive moment. Not just to be liked as one of the crowd but to be *well* liked.

"Well, it's the long long road a-winding to Theydon Bois for me," said Roger Parkes.

He left. It was after eight and JTB could think of no more places he could phone for Chick. Junior Waddell let us know he had several exciting spots where vital people were eagerly waiting to have drinks with him but at nine o'clock he was still there with JTB and myself. JTB had been knocking back the vodkas at a fast rate. He said he could drink neat Vodka all day and night without it affecting him but he began to sound a bit woolly to me.

He was at stage three—arms permanently round my shoulders and protestations of undying mateship—by the time Junior Waddell decided to let us in on A Big Secret, A Surefire Scheme! I smiled on him tolerantly. He was only trying to re-ingratiate himself with JTB and me, the two good guys who knew what it was All About.

At first he didn't want me to be privy to this brainwave but JTB would have none of that.

"Anything you want to tell me tell me now because John is my friend—I'd trust John before I'd trust my own mother."

"Her that kites dud cheques?" was Junior Waddell's quick sneer.

"My mother? Dud cheques? You think this fellow-Scot of yours is pissed, John?"

"Nah, he's from Edinburgh."

It was very funny at the time.

"All right, know what I'm going to do?" said Junior Waddell emphatically. "The Chick Bhalla Story! It's a knockdown cert. All those junkie anecdotes? It's a book, a real book for once about a jazzer. I've got it all worked out in my head."

JTB and I shrugged faces at each other.

"Told properly it's a great story," said Junior Waddell. "I've been into jazz since I was this high. I know the scene. I'll tell it how it is!"

"And how is it?" said JTB.

A book, I thought, frowning. Who ever heard of a book about a British jazzer? Chick Bhalla? I knew him—how could he be bigtime enough for a book? What did this Junior Nobody know about Bhalla anyway?

"I'd tape it," he said, nodding wisely at his own dynamic.

"I'd get him for a whole day at a time, follow him about, get it all down on tape, jazz, junk, women, the lot! I'll get a publisher—Confessions of a Jazz Junkie! By Chick Bhalla and Junior Waddell!"

"Sounds a possibility," said JTB, turning serious and taking his arm off my shoulder. "Any idea what kind of money publishers would pay?"

"I'll do a straight split down the middle with Chick. So the hardback advance isn't much—but the real loot comes with serialisation. The Sunday populars will go crazy for it. We can auction it between them! Then the paperback rights!"

"What sort of money do Sunday papers pay for that kind of thing?"

"We'd want ten k—rockbottom."

"Ten grand?"

"Ten thousand pounds! Tell you what—I'll get down to it with Chick and produce a synopsis, then we'll take that to a hardback publisher and see how much bread he'll put up front for us to work on it. I'm telling you—it's a knockdown cert!"

"Yeah, sounds interesting," said JTB. "What d'you think, John?"

I shrugged indifferently. Inside I felt resentful. It was me who was JTB's friend.

"I've spent too long with The Beast to get the horn over Surefire Projects born late at night in boozers," I said, disparagingly. "Chick isn't the biggest name in the world and the papers never go much on jazz, no—"

"I'll make him big," snapped Junior Waddell. "I know about newspapers, that's my bag."

"That's your hard luck," I said. "Anyway, I've got to go, I'm meeting Ramsay Shand the playwright—we're possibly going to collaborate on a play."

Just for a moment it was the most important moment of my life, to see which of us JTB could do without.

"We'll have a quick one in The Jack Ketch, John," he said. To Junior Waddell he said, "I'll think about this scheme of yours, mate."

"It's a winner," said Junior Waddell.

And you're the loser, I thought. I really felt good. Why did I ever think JTB was an idiot?

He asked Alex the charge-hand to send Bhalla round to The Jack Ketch if he showed after we'd gone.

"It isn't company policy to divert trade to other premises," said Alex, another bloody Scot but the morose, silent type.

"You'll want rid of this one, matey."

We left Junior Waddell on the corner looking in all directions for a taxi. Serious men don't have Surefire Schemes for easy money, I told myself, they have longterm *plans*. They are liked for themselves. Least of all do they need fame to make them feel they belong. As JTB and I crossed The Avenue we heard the hysterical shouts of a woman. We spotted the source among the over-dressed theatre crowds, a young brown girl with very long, thin legs under a shortie raincoat. I say brown, I mean a spade. Pushing through the fur coats and the American haircuts she kept jerking her head and screaming abuse, apparently at nobody in particular.

"Poor tortured soul," said JTB.

"She think she's the only one?"

"No sentimentality in the Scots at all, is there?"

"Until we're boozed and start wailing about the heather mountains and Bonnie Scotland we'll support ye ever more? It's real sentiment we're short on, JTB, for boozy sentimentality we're the greatest." I clapped my hands in the staccato football rhythm. "Scot-land! Scot-land!"

He stopped and took a grip of my bicep.

"I like having you around me, John, you're a good nut."

"You're pissed!"

"Is that all you can say to me, John? Course I'm pissed. That's when you speak the truth, isn't it?"

"Yeah."

"You've never lied to me, John."

"I wonder why not. Maybe because we haven't done any business together."

"I know we haven't. But we should have. Come and work for me, John."

"All right. But you'll have to loan me some money. I'm way behind with my taxes—and I don't have an insurance card. You can fiddle me a card, can you? I'd need a lot of money, JTB, I'm in real trouble."

"I'm glad you came to me with your problem, John. Let's have a drink on it. Where will we go?"

"We're going to The Jack Ketch now, as it happens."

"Right then, that's where we'll go. I hate the place but if that's where you want to go, John, that's where we'll go."

"No, it's where you wanted to go."

"I hate the place. We'll go there anyway, it's the nearest."

At lunchtimes The Jack Ketch served as local for a certain part of the music trade but once the agents and managers and publicity men had downed their quick ones and headed off for the commuter stations it became an impersonal barn of a place for the faceless passing trade. It was also one of those pubs which the brewers had decided to turn into a snack-bar. With so many trays of pickle and salad and sides of cold roast beef and piles of sandwiches and hot sausage machines and plates of scotch eggs it was a struggle to find a stretch of the bar for mere drinking.

The barman and the straggle of customers were staring in our direction as we came towards the bar. I didn't think JTB was all that drunk. But it wasn't us they were clocking. The old freak with the red roses behind his ears had slipped into the saloon bar behind us. You often saw him about The Rookery, generally well-pissed on cheap red wine from dark bottles without labels. He sold roses to tourists who also gave him tips to take his photograph. Most of the time he cursed them for a load of fucking foreign bastards but they thought it was colourful local patois. In a sane society he would have been getting treatment.

As we reached the bar he took a dark wine bottle from his pocket and balanced it on top of his skull. He started to do a soft-shoe shuffle.

"I told you to gerrout of it!" snarled a young Irish barman.

He waltzed towards a couple of Americans.

The barman got his knee on the ledge under the bar, leaned across and with a savage sweep of his right arm knocked the dark wine bottle off his head. It bounced on composite flooring, spurting red wine.

"Out—before I sling you!"

The old freak scuttled to the door.

"A large whisky and a large Bacardi and Coke," JTB said, with some dignity. He looked at me with slightly glazed eyes. "The young are very cruel," he said heavily.

"Did you mean that about me working for you?" I said.

"You want to work for me? Wonderful." He pressed my arm again. The barman put down our glasses. "Have one yourself," said JTB, handing him a pound.

"Thanks. That'll be another ten pee."

"What did you say? I gave you a pound."

"You're having large ones. And a coke. And my bottle of steeout."

"Here," I said, sliding a tenpenny piece at him. "Cheers, JTB."

"There's no problem I can't solve, John."

"I need five grand to pay off my back taxes. And the card."

"Insurance card? Simple. What we did with Bhalla was

drop a word in the right ear. That's what my talent is, John, oiling the way. You don't have a card? I'll get you a card. Simple."

"Great. But five thousand—I can't make a move unless I have that much to pay my back taxes."

"Ah. Now. Five grand. It isn't lying about in the petty cashbox. Is it? But—you give me ideas I can work on and I won't quibble at five thousand. Ideas, that's what's in short supply."

"I'll give you one as a present."

The door opened.

The old freak with the roses poked his nose into the big room. He was crying wet tears all down his grubby cheeks.

"You shouldn't 've done that, you know," he whined, "I am some mother's son you know."

We heard him running away.

"Next time I'll see to him sure enough," said the young barman. "Dirtee ould bastart'"

"I'll give you one proposition for starters," I said to JTB. I'd thought about the moral and practical consequences for all of one minute and each time the conclusion was—*why not?*

"Kilgallon is having to sell the Hum Drum because of his blood pressure. He's supposed to be selling it to Neville Thirsk for nine grand. Nobody else is supposed to know. Neville is scratching round to raise the loot. You could get in quick and cut him out. Kilgallon will sell to the first geezer who bungs readies in his face."

Slowly JTB shook his head while gazing into my eyes.

"John, what did I tell you? Ideas! We've only been talking seriously for thirty seconds and you've come up with this. What did you say you needed? Five thousand pounds?" He took my hand in both of his. "There's nothing we can't do together. Let's go somewhere for a proper drink."

We decided to make for The Amorous Congo.

Going along Bishop Henry Street we came to the door of The

Rats' Castle.

"This'll do us," said JTB, grabbing my arm. Knowing who was likely to be in there I slipped his grip and stood back on the pavement. The door slammed behind him. I waited for him to reappear so that I could explain about The Scots Team. After a minute or two I realised he'd probably forgotten all about me. I pushed through the door and found him trying to attract the wee barman's attention. As I was taking his arm I saw, at the other end of the bar, Broken Back Brown's gingery skull. I was not surprised to see that he and Paisley Dave were talking to Ramsay Shand. After their lucrative interlude with the famous painter those guys obviously associated culture with easy pickings. I hated to think what they'd do when they discovered Shand was not a rich eccentric but a genuine penniless bum. They'd kick him to death just to save face.

And I'd been thinking about becoming the great playwright with the help of a slob like that? I must have been drunker than I knew. The creative artist fantasy. Look at him—filthy clothes, pissed out of his skull, nothing to show for one life but a little bit of fame that everybody else has forgotten. Look at JTB beside me—a middle-aged square, yeah, but a man who could hold his own in the jungle, who could get pissed without coming apart at the joins, who knew that a real man gets a few bob in the bank and doesn't expect any other bastard to buy his drinks.

There was no choice to make.

Funny, isn't it, the crazy ideas you get out of bottles?

I got JTB to leave before that riff-raff saw us. We made it to The Congo. No sooner were we at a table than JTB got up and disappeared. I ordered a large vodka for him and a Bacardi and Coke for myself. After the shabby rabble of The Rats' Castle the Congo's air of sleek villainy appeared sensible and grown-up. This was where I wanted to be, with the men. JTB came back. I wondered if I'd done enough already to clinch this deal about working for him because the place was filling up and I could see a couple of big black mamas between whose mighty bristols a slim white body might enjoy a few precious moments of relaxation from the constant challenges of the grown-up rat-race. I knew JTB wouldn't be game to make up a jolly foursome.

On the other hand I didn't want to leave him until I'd heard a bit more about this five thousand quid.

"John, could you do me a deep favour?" he asked, thickly.

"As we're now in business together—anything."

"You've met my wife Betty, haven't you?"

"I haven't had that pleasure, JTB."

"Ah. Well—listen, I won't hear a word said against her! But— she gets funny ideas. She thinks—where do women get these funny ideas—she thinks there's something going on between me and Agnes—you've met Agnes my secretary, haven't you?"

"Briefly."

"Wonderful woman. But my Betty—I swear blind it isn't true—she thinks I'm seeing Agnes outside the office. Know what I mean? Outside the office! You doing anything much tonight?"

"Well, actually—"

"I tell her it's purely business—you know it's purely business—thing is, if I brought you home she'd know I was only having a few drinks with the lads, wouldn't she? Look, why don't we hop in this fucking minicab I just phoned and nip up to my gaff in Dollis Hill and have a few drinks in the comfort of my house and put on a few good records and have a long, sensible talk? Eh? Why don't we?

I'd known this was coming. He was a right bore when he was drunk but he was my friend, wasn't he? How many men do you meet in a lifetime who'll tell you straight out they think you're good enough to go into the jungle with? You tolerate the little weaknesses of your friends, don't you? It meant I couldn't wallow in those big black mamas but it wouldn't kill me to be his alibi for one night.

Besides, there's no easy way of making five grand, is there?

Maybe I was a bit gone, too, but I do remember talking in my head to Ramsay Shand and saying, with a sneer, 'When was the last time anybody willingly invited *you* into his home, you pathetic creative wanker?'

Passing the trail of destruction he had made on his way to the roof Jack went back through the chapel, along the passage to the Red Room and down the chimney to The Castle. Among the rubble of what had been the chimney wall he found the blanket and his shoes and hose. He then went back up the chimney, through the Red Room, along the dark passage, through the chapel, onto the lower leads and along the outer wall to the Northern Tower. This afterthought had taken him a full hour. He used the spike to fix the blanket into the lead coping. He slid down and dropped onto a flat roof. It had a garret door. He was free of Newgate Prison.

15

As soon as we were in the minicab, which was driven by a jolly Nigerian who tried to bore us with his optimistic views on Enoch Powell, JTB said:

"I'm the loneliest man on earth."

He said it at least six times before we reached Marble Arch.

"I'm just a fat little ugly man," he said, "I know what I look like. Don't you think I'd give my arms for a tenth of Bhalla's talent?"

"What the hell's Bhalla got to do with it?"

He put his hand on my knee and stared at me intently—as far as I could tell in the constantly shifting light from the Edgware Road lamp-posts.

"Why do you think I let Chick Bhalla shit on me regularly? I wouldn't take it from anyone else—"

"He's a genius, I know—"

"He is a mess!"

"Whatever you say."

I looked at my watch. It was only half-past eleven. What the hell was I doing in a minicab heading for Dollis Hill this early?

"JTB, I've just remembered, I was to meet Neville—"

His hand pressed on my knee.

"You shouldn't be mixed up with a slag like Thirsk. Why don't you come in with me?"

"I thought we'd agreed on that."

"Great! We'll have a few drinks and put on a few records and discuss it seriously."

"Yeah." It was the longest session I'd ever had with Baxter and I was beginning to find him a drag. Still, for five grand did I expect laughs as well? Does a drowning man care if the reaching hand has dirty nails?

"You want to know why I let Bhalla treat me like dirt? Maybe you can tell me. I have been a father to that man. Why does he do it?"

"He says you called him an oriental jazz guitarist."

"Lies again. Why does he make up these lies about me? I know I'm just a fat little ugly man but I've been like a father to him. And I *respect* him, you needn't laugh—why does he want to be a human drain for every poison known to man? I should be on drugs and drink, I'm just a fat boring businessman, I can't express myself in music. Why does Chick do it?"

"Because he's a self-indulgent idiot."

"He has more talent than all of us put together! You know he's forced himself to take five cures? You know what hell a junkie goes through on a cure?"

"All right, he's a fucking hero."

"Exactly. Why else do I respect him? He has more than talent, he has *guts!* I know that man. Will I tell you something?"

"Go on. I could've been a contender, you know?"

"What?"

"Go on—Rod."

"What? He knows he has to dry himself out before he starts a cure, right? So for his fourth try he decided to walk. Just that— walk. He showed me on a streetmap. He started from his gaff in Notting Hill. He walked to Kings Cross station, He walked from there to Fleet Street and had a cup of tea in an all-nighter. Bhalla-drinking tea? Then he walked to Baker Street. Then he walked to

Gloucester Road? You think I'm making this up? Go on, say it, you're drunk, JTB, you can say it, John, I'm squiffed I know. Listen, he showed me on the streetmap! You don't think that journey isn't stamped on my brain? It is. He took the first morning tube from Gloucester Road to Willesden Green, just for a rest. He then walked all round Cricklewood. Cricklewood? Chick Bhalla walking round Cricklewood at dawn? Too much! He then walked back to the West End. Another cup of tea. He walked for thirty-six hours non-stop! Could you do that? I couldn't. Chick did. His arms look like dartboards, you know that? You wonder why I want to be a father to him?"

"No, Leopold."

"Leopold? I don't get it. You called me Rod a minute ago. I'm sorry, John, I don't have a sense of humour. Don't you think I wish I had? I'm just a fat boring businessman. Talent, John, that's the thing we must respect, we haven't got it. I'm a fool, John. But you're a good nut, John. Why don't you leave Thirsk and come in with me?"

"I'll think about it."

"Great!"

Then we were at the front of his semi-detached villa in Dollis Hill and I followed him through the stained-glass door.

Immediately a woman's voice barked at us from the top of the carpeted stairs.

"Veronica's sickening for something," were the words. You ever heard anybody whining at the top of their lungs?

"Again?" he muttered thickly.

He took my elbow with unwelcome intimacy and steered me into a cold living-room. "Help yourself to a drink," he said, eyes glazed, arm waving at a white leather and brass-studded bar with a mock awning in red regency stripes. It more or less filled one end of the room. It was not a large room but it had all the trimmings—colour television, hi-fi speakers, tropical fish tank, white Swedish-style bookcases, glass-topped coffee table, prints of Chinese horses, a fireplace of real Purbeck stone, and a three-piece leather suite that would have been large by St James's club standards.

There wasn't a lot of room for walking about. I came to severaldead ends but finally reached the bar. The sheer absence of noise made my ears buzz. When I bent down to look under the bar for a glass my head went on a merry-go-round. The labels on the bottles kept changing places. I held onto the one bottle I recognised and poured about half a pint of Gordon's gin into the tumbler. A search for ice and tonic seemed impossible. I started to chew on cashew nuts from a leaf-shaped tray. The solid little fragments made my throat jump, just because they were solid. I spat them into my palm and wiped it on a hard-textured napkin, which I re-folded to hide the mess.

Baxter came into the living-room and closed the door carefully.

"Let's have a drink, never mind what she says," he whispered, defiantly. He went behind the bar. Immediately he looked like a dreary little barman—in his own home? I had to blink a lot to keep him in focus. He glared at me.

"Don't think I'm under the cosh," he said. "My Betty is going through a difficult stage, that's all."

His waving hand managed to get quite a lot of whisky into the glass. He asked me for a cigarette. I found I had none left. He said there was a machine about half a mile away. Then he remembered he had some cigars. We lit up a couple of very large Jamaicans. In getting mine out of the box he managed to crack the outer leaf. It wouldn't draw, so I broke it in half and lit the jagged end. An outer leaf curled almost to my lips. I asked him what kind of records he had and he said would I mind if we didn't put on the player as his Betty was a difficult sleeper. We sat opposite each other in mock leather armchairs. Immediately my buttocks began to sweat. Yet it was extremely cold. He kept flicking his large cigar end at an ashtray on the glass coffee table and missing. Embedded in the glass was a dark-tinted split-globe map of the world with Latin lettering.

I couldn't make out where Britain was. He said, several times, "This is better, eh?"

My ears were buzzing something chronic. He said there was this Jewish shopkeeper who found one of his girls stealing stock and said he would have to call the police only she begged him not to saying she would do *anything* and he'd fancied her for ages so he said get in the store-room and get your clothes off and after he'd locked up he went in and started to screw her only he was too old and after a couple of hours trying he pulled up his trousers and said he would have to call the cops. He waited for me to laugh. I did try.

He then said he was a misunderstood man because people didn't know the struggle he'd had because he was born in the very poorest part of Bingley, Yorkshire, only his name was Thomas Baxter, only he changed Thomas to Talbot when he went into dance-bands before the war because he thought it would sound better when he got his own orchestra like Geraldo or Ambrose only the war came and when he came out the big bands were dying so he got into the agency racket and he put the J. in front of his name because Talbot Baxter sounded kosher and while he had nothing against Jews and liked most of them for being knock-out blokes to do business with you always had that funny thing about them, didn't you? He was telling me all this because I was a good nut and could keep a secret between friends, only you had to tell somebody, didn't you? I kept blinking to focus my eyes on his face. His head seemed to be swelling up to fill the whole room and then shrinking away to a little point. I forgot about the gin and then swallowed most of it in a gulp and felt a bit better. He asked me why I didn't want to work with him and I said I was short of money and he got out his wallet and made me take six pounds. I took it and said what I really needed was five thousand pounds and he said that was a lot of money but that I was a good nut and he would see me all right. I thought about calling a minicab to get me back into the West End but he said there was a bed made up for me and that

169

his Betty liked having people to stay so we went to bed. I wanted to stay up drinking but it was very cold and my eyes started closing.

The spare bedroom was upstairs, bang next door to their bedroom. He took a long time about leaving me in the little bedroom, which was very cold, starting to tell me once again that Bhalla was an ungrateful shit. When at last he left me I put out the light and closed the door and got in between the cold sheets in my vest, underpants and socks. The door had swung open of its own accord and light from the landing cut the little room in half. I was in the dark half but I couldn't get my eyes to stay closed.

"Is Veronica asleep yet?" I heard her saying, as clearly as if we were in the same room. "If she starts coughing again I'm going to call the doctor, I don't care how late it is."

Mumbles from JTB. I drew my legs up into the foetal position and hugged my shoulders for warmth. I heard him leaving their room. I wondered if she had big breasts. He came into my room and put on the light.

"Comfortable?" he said thickly, looking a lot less dapper in his heavy, striped pyjamas. His stiff tonsure was sticking out sideways and his mouth was fallen and puckered, without the support of his dentures.

"Fine thanks," I grunted.

"Only if you need more blankets . . ."

"No, I'm fine thanks."

He closed the door but forgot to put out the light. I got up and turned down the switch. As I got back into the sheets the door swung open again.

"For God's sake don't waken her up!" called Mrs JTB, in a voice capable of reaching Wembley Stadium.

The child's bedroom was on the other side of mine. I was right in the middle.

"All right, ducks?" I heard him saying.

"My cough's better but I've wet the bed," said a child's

melancholy voice. I heard him bumping about her room. Then he said good night, several times, and went downstairs. Silence. I tried to force myself to get up again and close the door. It was very cold in that little spare room. He came back up the stairs.

"What did you do with the wet sheets?"

"They're drying."

"They don't want *drying!* The smell will get *everywhere.* They'll have to be *washed.*"

He went down the stairs again. I thought I heard a cat mew. He came back up the stairs again.

"I've put them in the washing-machine," he said. "You'd better do it in the morning."

"I'll have to, won't I?"

Silence

The light went out!

I turned over and hugged my shoulders for warmth.

The child started coughing.

"Where were you tonight anyway?"

"A top Fleet Street writer wants to do Chick's life story for a book."

"Take all this time to discuss a book about that man, did it?"

"You know what Chick's like. He got drunk. John and I had to take him home."

"Who is John? Is he the—"

"Sshhhh, darling."

Silence.

I straightened up. My tongue had found a piece of something stuck between my back teeth. I probed at it until it was sore from constant twisting but I couldn't stop it. What the hell was I doing here?

"It'll be another big deal like your stupid German marching songs," she said.

"You saw the price they paid for Hitler's autograph."

"You're mad. Nostalgia for the SS? You're mad."

"You'll see."

"If they're going to make so much money why aren't you actually doing something about it?"

"Give me credit, please. I produce an album without establishing the copyright position and some ex-German song publisher turns up on the next plane from Tel Aviv and flashes contracts from before the war and wants the thick end of the royalties? Give me credit for knowing my own business."

Silence.

Apart from the child's dry, strict tempo coughing.

Then they were shouting at each other. He came into my room and put on the light.

"Will you come in and tell her I'm not carrying on with Agnes?" he demanded. I lay still, the blankets fortunately covering my head.

"What more do you want?" he shouted at her, hitting my bed with his knees. "You wanted to live in Dollis Hill, didn't you? Because the school was convenient for Veronica, because the people seemed so nice—why the hell don't we ever see the nice people, eh?" He sat down on the bed and put his hand on my shoulder. I didn't move. He shouted again. "It's up to you to make an effort to get to know them—invent excuses for going to their doors—I don't know what wives do—hold Tupperware parties for God's sake! I even gave up smoking cigars because they affected your throat! What more do you want? Please, John, come in and tell her I'm not carrying on with Agnes."

I was running out of oxygen under the blankets but suffocation was better than the alternative. He shook my shoulder.

Then he crashed out of the room.

I heard them mumbling and then my ears were buzzing with silence. Again. For a solid hour I lay there desperate to go to the lavatory but not even risking a yawn, knees jiggling to keep my bladder's mind off its determination to waken the whole house again.

Besides, I didn't know where the lavatory was.

Then I remembered seeing a small wash-basin in the corner of the room. I got up, testing each step ahead of me with delicate feet in case of cracking twigs, arms crossed ahead of me as the blind cross their arms to stop an open door hitting their faces.

The relief! Of all the places that wrinkled old retainer had been none had ever been so *beautiful* as the cold porcelain on which it flopped while my warm, uneasy load tinkled off into the pipes of Dollis Hill.

Of course I could never go to work for that man sleeping through the wall. John the Baptist, indeed! What a mockery all these colourful nicknames were. We weren't soldiers together or Runyonesque criminals. The man's real name wasn't even picturesque. J. Talbot Baxter? Thomas Baxter, from Bingley! Telling me when he was drunk—which showed he thought about it all the time. Aged fifty-two? At least I was only twenty-nine.

By Christ! It wasn't a Sign, it was a terrible warning.

"Ian Mintlaw McGraw," I said—immediately biting my lip and listening for answering sounds from the bedroom. At last my bladder had no more to give and I felt my way back to bed.

That was when it hit me. The solution to it all! Of course! Staring me in the face all the time. The night hadn't been wasted. God bless you, Junior Waddell!

I could hardly bear to go on lying there waiting for the morning. All my troubles were over!

On my slink out of the house before the J. Talbot Baxters stirred in their nuptial couch I met the child coming out of the bathroom. Giving her a cheery, avuncular wink I said:

"Tell your Daddy I had to leave early. Which way is it to the tube station?"

She pointed. Her eyes were both melancholy and hostile. She looked exactly like her mother.

But I never saw her mother?

Some faces you don't need to see.

There were quite a few of us on the dawn Bakerloo line tube south. Having neither a paper nor cigarettes I read the adverts for highly-paid secretaries and audio-typists rather than be ill-mannered enough to stare at the legs of a large West Indian cleaning woman. She had beautiful calves, extremely large with hard lines. When she caught me looking at them she gave me a critical stare, obviously thinking I was only an unshaven white sex maniac.

I closed my eyes and pretended to be sleeping. This helped me concentrate. Shand had been A Sign, all right, only I had mis-read it. The hell with getting involved with an idiot like Baxter—Shand was worth five thousand to me, just for the effort of picking him up out of the gutter!

Opening the roof door, Jack crossed an attic room and reached the stairs. His leg irons clinked. A woman's voice said, "Oh lud, what was that?" A man's voice said, "Perhaps the dog or cat." Jack went down the stairs. As he reached the ground floor the front door opened, from the outside. Jack scuttled back up the stairs and hid in the garret. He went to sleep. When he woke two hours later the house had settled down for the night. It was midnight when he reached the street. He walked west to the fields at Tottenham Court Road and hid in a cowshed.

16

Merely as a postscript to Dollis Hill: around half-past ten Baxter phoned me at the office. He remembered little of what had happened in his house. He made no mention of the six pounds he had loaned me. He was phoning to find out if he had made a fool of himself in any of The Rookery spots. I said I, too, had been too drunk to remember much, giving myself an alibi in case he later remembered the six pounds.

I thought he owed me that much, for having endured his hospitality.

"I did a terrible thing, John," he said, after a little pause, to let me know this was important. "You were sleeping but last night my little girl wet her bed and I changed the sheets and I put them into the washing-machine so that my wife could wash them this morning. She just slammed the washing-machine door shut and pressed the buttons. She's just phoned me in a fine old state. The cat had climbed into the machine during the night, John. When she pulled out the sheets it was in there with them."

"Dead?"

"What else after a hot wash and two spin drys? A fifteen guinea pedigree Siamese, cat that was, John. I told her a mangy tabby was good enough but she insisted on a Siamese. She's in a state of shock—well, can you blame her? I mean, pulling it out with the sheets!"

"Jesus Christ," I said, not knowing if outright laughter would be acceptable.

"John—" meaningful pause. "We must have a chat—soon, John. Is Thirsk there?"

"At ten thirty in the a.m.?"

"John—I'd like to put this idea in your head—how would you like to come and work for me, John?"

"Funny you should mention that, I thought—"

"Think about it, John, seriously. Then we'll have a chat over a glass of something convivial. In fact—I don't normally do this but I feel rough this morning—how about joining me for a heart-starter in The Leafless?"

"I can't," I said. "I may see you in there later."

"Okay then. And John—think about it seriously, won't you?"

I put down the phone. It rang again, as if it had been waiting impatiently.

"Nev," said Neville.

"Morning."

"Oh Christ. Let's expunge yesterday from the human records. Where the fuck were you all day?"

"I was here all afternoon. Working. You know—w-o-r-k."

"Okay, I'm a lazy good-for-nothing as my mother puts it. I'll see you in The Leafless in half an hour—a man's entitled to relax now and then, isn't he?"

"You will go to the bank and get me the rest of the money, won't you? Four hundred and fifty pounds."

"Jesus Christ, mate! Yeah, okay."

After I'd put the phone down I rubbed my hands together and decided I was enjoying this new me. I'd been to the public baths in Pesthouse Close. I'd been shaved, sheared and shampooed by Polish Joe. I had typed three copies of a single-sheet contract that was going to make Ramsay Shand *mine*.

Wasn't I the lucky bastard? It might have looked like aimless drifting but all the time the Guiding Hand had been on my shoulder. But for Sibley I would never have gone to The

Maggots that lunchtime and would never have met Shand. Even being arrested had been part of the Grand Design. That forged fiver I'd given Shand to pay his fine was going to be the best five pounds I'd ever spent.

Never mind, pussycat, it was a clean death.

Exactly seven days later, while his escape was still the sensation of all London, Jack drove round Newgate Prison in a hackney carriage, for a lark. He had his usual quota of two women with him. They peeped merrily at the prison walls from behind the carriage curtains. That night Jack went on a tour of the gin houses, making no attempt to disguise himself. He was too drunk to use his pistols when Newgate turnkeys grabbed him and took him back to the condemned cell.

17

The answer to all my money problems had come to me with over-powering suddenness while I was waiting for dawn to activate the Bakerloo Line and free me from J. Talbot Baxter's happy home.

Conversations from the past few days were still going on in my head. Thinking of that obnoxious whizzkid Junior Waddell describing how he would make big money writing Chick Bhalla's story I had come over hot with resentment because I felt I knew Bhalla better than that Scottish upstart. And because I had not come up with the idea myself, although I *knew* I was a cut above the likes of Junior Waddell.

Then it had hit me.

Ramsay Shand!

If Bhalla's story was worth ten grand to a Sunday newspaper what would Shand's story be worth? Bhalla was only an obscure musician, a jazz genius maybe but who knows anything about British jazz geniuses?

Shand had been a front-page celebrity. The newspapers had not forgotten him, either, or those two young smoothies would not have been assigned to feed him with booze.

Of course I'd never written for a newspaper but I'd met enough idiots who did to know it couldn't be all that difficult.

How I boozed away quarter of a million—by the Wild Man Playwright from the Dundee building sites? What kind of headline would they give it? Booze, Brawls and Beds! *Today I am a shambling wreck of a man. Doctors have told me the next bottle will kill me—but once I strode through the smartest hotels in the world, a glint in my eye, a curse on my lips and a bottle in my fist!*

Anybody could write that crap—even a failed hardcore pornographer. Most of it could be taped. He would remember me as the generous big chap who loaned him five quid to pay his fine. He might still have an agent of his own but I'd dangle drinking money in front of his face—and once he'd signed these contracts he would be *mine*.

Of course I wouldn't cheat him. We'd split every penny down the middle. He was very lucky that it was me who'd hit on the idea and not some smooth English shark.

And the snags?

I could see one.

Maybe The Scots Team thought he was *their* goldmine.

So I headed for The Rats' Castle feeling not exactly scared but sensibly aware I wasn't dropping in on a Boys' Brigade cocoa night.

Scared?

The first time Neville and I found ourselves exchanging brittle cocktail chat with The Scots Team was a lunchtime when we decided to try some of the pubs we normally avoided, The Jack Ketch, The Three-Legged Mare—and The Rats' Castle.

As we came through the door this stocky man with the cropped ginger hair and hard blue eyes took one look at us and then grabbed hold of Neville's arm.

"I don't remember you in the Legion, chief," he barked, flicking out Neville's tie.

A man who acts as confidently as that with total strangers—who themselves don't reckon to look like fairies—is not to be slapped away with a quick sneer. Guardedly, with just enough hostility commensurate with dignity, Neville said it was a Lancashire County Cricket tie he sometimes wore for fun.

"Zattafack?" said Brown. "Good job ye wasnae pretendin' to huv been in the Legion because me and my mate Otto were sergeants in the French Foreign Legion—aye and we've got papers to prove it."

When Brown and Otto Daffae and Paisley Dave and McMenemy the Enemy learned we were show biz agents they took to us warmly. My being from Glasgow helped. Their smalltalk was, one might say, boisterous. None of them had a job. Brown had worked for half a day on a building site at Vauxhall, got drunk at lunch time, fell off the scaffolding and now walked on a stick to prove that he needed state sickness benefit.

I did ask Paisley Dave outright what he did for a living in London; he was about twenty-five, fresh-faced, always in a white raincoat, always very clean. Out of the side of his mouth he replied:

"Don't ask too many questions, pal."

McMenemy was the biggest and youngest of the team, a six-footer with shiny black curls. He reminded me of Elvis Presley, which would no doubt have pleased him immensely. Otto Daffae, the German, was a big blonde who laughed all the time. He and Brown had served five years in the Legion and liked to tell anecdotes about how they shot Algerians in the stomach because basically they were too kind to let them fall into the hands of the Deuxieme Bureau.

The four of them we gathered, lived on what they could pick up from tourists and queers. Pick up is literally true for they generally knocked these parties down first.

The Rats' Castle—which they called Bar Linnie—was the one pub in The Rookery which had not barred them.

Barlinnie is Glasgow's Bastille. They were not without a certain wolfish humour, these genial Scots monsters.

180

Scared?

What reason did I have to fear these men, in broad daylight,in the heart of a heavily-policed city, in an ordinary pub? I had a couple of whiskies before I started out, I can tell you that.

I had them with Neville in The Leafless. As it happened he could, inevitably, give me only a hundred pounds cash but promised to give me the rest the next day.

"So what's all this loot for?" he demanded, watching me stuff the notes into my hip-pocket.

"My mother's sick," I said, smiling eccentrically. "The surgeon's asking if she wants the vital operation under anaesthetic or on the National Health."

"Keep the corny jokes for someone else," he said, genuinely annoyed.

"I'll tell you about it tomorrow," I said, "don't forget the three hundred and fifty, will you?"

"Is it a woman?"

"A gentleman never tells."

I went to the lavatory, locked myself in the stall and put a hundred in fivers and singles into my shoes. When I came out again I saw Angela Browne with an e talking to Neville and Thunderbuttocks Watson.

But for her arrival I might have weakened and slipped back into that warm, boozy semi-circle of amiable loafers. Maybe it was her red hair, maybe the wooden hand, whatever the reason she made me feel edgy.

Outside there was a wind getting up. The sky was grey and it was cold enough to make me blow into my hands. On the corners loose papers were flying about in invisible whirlpools. Air currents lifted bits of paper above the heads of the people. The piles of rubbish were spreading across the pavements, making people walk in single file.

I wasn't scared.

Lonely, maybe.

Not because I was alone but because I didn't really understand why I was so determined to carry out this scheme. I told myself the reasons were obvious and practical. I had to get myself straight with the tax and the insurance card.

Practical reasons. But there was more to it than that.

One night in The Hum Drum, before thieves jemmied the steel door and had it away with Kilgallon's colour set, we happened to find ourselves watching a TV documentary about Glasgow violence. One man still had the scars of razor slashes that required fifty-three stitches on the lower part of his face.

He said he'd been in a pub when three neds came in and told him they wanted whiskies and beers. *On the demand* it's called. This man wasn't terrified enough to pay for their drinks. They said they would get him outside. When he walked out of the pub they were waiting on the pavement. After a kicking they held him down and slashed his chin, mouth and cheeks.

"But why didn't you run- away—or leave by another door?" asked the 'puzzled TV interviewer. (Naturally he had a posh English accent—you need educational qualifications to do anthropology.)

"Run away?" said the man with the scars, incredulously. "Let mahself be known as the man that ran away? Ye think I'd ever huv been able to walk about the street again?"

Neville and the others said they didn't understand it. They had the true London philosophy—where's the sense in crime or bother unless it's for cash?

I told them it was a cultural difference. For a few moments it made me feel quite virile, speaking in the same accent as that man. (Of course I would have run away by a side exit *and* sneaked to the cops for help. I was not stupid. I lived in London by choice!)

What does this explain? Merely that I was not being over-fanciful in seeing that short journey between The Leafless Tree and The Rats' Castle as more than a change of brewery labels.

There's even a different face for being Scottish, you know that? The lips tighten and the lower jaw steps forward.

The outside of The Rats' Castle was no dirtier than most of the buildings in Bishop Henry Street. The woodwork was brown, under a greasy film of street dust. The windows were tall and painted with tawdry gold and chipped enamel lettering. The bottom sections of the windows were opaque to ensure a certain amount of old-fashioned privacy.

The moment you tested the strength of your arm against the stiff street door you became conscious that more separated the interior of The Rats' Castle from the busy pavements than sheets of painted glass.

Out There was now, slimming crazes, oil crises, rising fares, man-made fibres, Royal journeys and all the other imagined reasons for keeping the people busy.

In Here was for ever.

Scared?

It should be obvious that this so-called Scots Team were not ferocious monsters but merely feckless inadequates, semi-articulate victims of a society based on educational competition, social flotsam, potential case histories for the soft sociological porn that so stimulates the liberal responses of quality newspaper readers and paperback intellectuals.

Let me tell you. Sociological jargon is no defence when the case histories are living, breathing wolves eyeing you suspiciously as you come through the door that opens into a seemingly timeless world where policemen and penal reformists don't count for a lot.

No, I wasn't scared.

Two whiskies were helping.

The interior of The Rats' Castle was slightly colder and bleaker than the street outside. It was a long, rectangular bar the size of a small hall, split down the middle by a ceiling-high bottle gantry. On the counters were no displays of civilising sausages.

The wall was lined by wooden tables separated by low partitions, remnants of old-style booths. Generations of boots seemed to have put all furnishings and woodwork to the test, giving the big, cold room the battered badge of indestructability.

There was only one barman serving on the saloon bar side of the gantry. He was about five feet two inches tall and wore thick-lensed spectacles which made his eyes disproportionately large for so small a man. He had coarse grey hair cropped army-style. The sleeves of his white shirt were rolled up past the elbows; his skinny arms were knobbly and decorated by hard old cut-scabs.

Leaning against the bar was a girl of about sixteen or seventeen.

She wore an ankle-length woollen cardigan over blue micro-pants, shiny brown tights and open-toed shoes. Her heavy black eye-shadow was streaked as though she had been crying, although when I came in she was laughing insanely. Her unsupported breasts hung heavily in a white, roll-neck sweater. Leaning on the bar beside her were two scruffy youths with long hair.

Standing a few feet behind the girl and the two youths were Broken Back Brown and Paisley Dave. Brown, stiff-backed, gingery-hair cropped flat on a wide skull, was not so much leaning on the walking-stick as using it to emphasise his gestures, like a stage prop. He was wearing a dark green tweed suit, with a check shirt and tartan tie.

Paisley Dave, fair-haired with an outdoor complexion, wore an unbuttoned white raincoat over a black polo-neck sweater, sports jacket and crisply pressed chino trousers.

As I passed them, Brown, who was tapping one of the long-haired youths on the shoulder with his stick, looked at me without recognition.

The big German known as Otto Daffae came out of the men's lavatory at the rear end of the room. He was wearing an American-style college pullover, white with red and blue hoops round the biceps, sky-blue slacks tucked casually into calf-length paratroop boots. He walked on the balls of his feet, humming and rubbing his hands together.

The little barman said something sharp to the girl, whose head was lolling from side to side. He came up the bar towards me.

"Pint of lager," I said quietly, in as neutral an accent as possible.

"Pineta laagerrr, right ye urr Jock," he barked, reaching under the bar for a glass.

"Hey, do I no' know you?" came the staccato voice of Broken Back Brown.

Both hands resting on the bar I turned my head and gave him a non-committal nod. Paisley Dave examined me.

"Aye, I met you in here a while ago with my partner," I said, careful not to indulge in anything so prematurely extravagant as even a smirk.

"Got you! From Glasgow?" He limped round behind Paisley Dave. I wiped my nostrils with the ball of my thumb, fingers raised, just to let them know I wasn't soft. The little barman shoved a no-handle pint glass across wet formica.

"Have this one on me," said Brown. He gave me a nudge with the hand that held the stick. "We're in funds the day, Jock." He winked, one of those winks that require the lower jaw to shift sideways and the cheek to move up an inch. He threw a note onto the wet bar. "Aye, I remember now, you're in the music business, right?"

"Sort of, just a small agency."

"No' another o' they big yins, for Goad's sake!" said the barman. "Give us one of they singles I gied ye for change the last time."

"You speaking to me?" Brown said very quietly. The barman immediately backed down and gave Brown a sheaf of notes and silver.

"What's your name again? I'm Jackie Brown—this is Paisley Dave—and that's Otto. Him and me were in the French Foreign Legion together."

"Aye, so I believe," I said, lifting the big wet glass, "I was too yellow for the British fucking Legion. Here's to us, wha's like us?"

"No many," said Brown, "just as well."

"My name's John Thompson," I said.

"That's right, I remember—like the Celtic goalie. You a left-footer, are you?"

I was a slick London operator there purely to do a deal and promote a scheme and all this Scotch stuff was as relevant to me as Big Chief Sitting Bull's ballocks but just for a moment I had never left Shettleston. I took an inch off the top of the lager, licked my lips and gave him the unblinking stare.

"I left Scotland because of all that religious rubbish," I said, firmly but without any suggestion of a challenge.

"Quite right, too," said Brown, looking quickly at Paisley Dave. This could have been a signal for up boots and in so I got there first.

"Done any dog-fancying lately?"

"That fucken poodle? Were you there that day? Jesus Christ, the noise of that fucken pooch!"

"My partner was with you."

"Aye, so he was. Hey, Dave, he's asking if I've been doing any dog-fancying lately."

Paisley Dave eyed me without expression. Dressed so neatly he might have been a coming young doctor. I felt sorry for him, strangely enough, to be so young and nifty-looking and yet be living this pointless gutter existence. I was just in for a quick snatch job, I would get hold of Shand and make myself five grand and then I would have a future to plan. What did he have? Timeless days in this dump?

Sorry for Paisley Dave?

These Christ-like notions are apt to get you nailed up, I thought.

He didn't know enough about me to trust me and stiffened noticeably when Brown started to tell me how he and

McMenemy had made a good killing a month or two before by allowing an American queer to pick them up in a bar.

They went back to the American's hotel, where he set them up a bottle of Glen Grant and all the champagne they could slurp for chasers. When he fell down drunk they took his wallet and left without incident, although McMenemy, according to Brown, wanted to punish the American for Vietnam by kicking his face in. In the wallet was a new book of American Express cheques. They could have sold the book for fifty quid to a pickpockets' fence but instead McMenemy stole a small van and they drove up one side of Broad Military Way and down the other, going into every likely shop to buy clothing and accessories with American Express cheques, both of them putting on American accents, always a source of pleasure to your true Glaswegian

When the van was full they drove it to a fence in Walthamstow, selling him van and contents for four hundred and fifty quid.

"There was about two thousand quid's worth of gear in that fucken van—plus the value of the van itself," said Brown. "These fences never give you a square deal, thieving bastards."

"Why don't you complain to your MP while you're telling the whole world?" said Paisley Dave.

"He's a suspicious individual," said Brown.

"Suspicious of me?" I said aggressively, the only reaction that would satisfy him. The girl fell off her stool backwards. The two youths caught her before she hit the deck. Both of them handled her enthusiastically as they brought her and the stool back to the perpendicular.

"You lie down for me, darleeng?" shouted Otto, grinning cheerily.

The girl screamed abuse at him.

"Hey, Bobbie, there no' a law against selling drink to minors?" Brown shouted.

"Aye, coal-miners," Bobbie growled in a hoarse Glasgow

voice. He put his hands on the bar and jerked his head for us to draw near. In a confidential voice no louder than a bus hitting a wall he said, "Pills, that's what she's oan."

I was bored by all this. There is no glamour in bestiality, not for the mature man, certainly not for a mature man impatiently waiting for five thousand sheets to come lurching through that door. By Christ, when I got into the real money I'd never be found in a place like this, with people like them. My blood-brothers? Ignorant monsters. Noel Coward was right, get the hell out of it to the sunshine, the hell with this brawling, drunken country and its brutal tax system.

"Fuck you bastards," the girl shouted.

One of the youths looked over his shoulder and in a Liverpool accent said to Brown:

"Leave 'er alone, woolya?"

"You speaking to me?" Brown said, quickly and quietly. In the films it was the moment when the bartender starts lifting bottles down below the bar and the poker-players sidle for cover.

"I only says—"

The brass ferrule of the walking stick smashed down on formica an inch from the boy's back. He tried to jump away, with his head still turned to watch Brown. The girl raised an arm to shield her face. Brown swung the stick down again—bang—on the bar. Then he pointed it at the boy's face, like a one-arm soldier holding a rifle.

"You—out!"

He aimed the stick at the door.

"What 'arm did we do you?" the second youth said, plaintively.

Brown took one step forward, the stick still pointing at their faces.

"You fucken deaf?" he said.

The three of them left hurriedly, with a certain amount of muttered bravado—when they were safely at the door. Brown gave them a farewell wiggle of the stick. The door slammed shut.

Brown turned, smiling. When he saw the barman's face he snapped:

"What're you looking so moody about?"

"Och—youth must huv its fling," said little Bobbie. "Not in here when I'm drinking," said Brown.

"That stick clatterin' doon on the bar—gave us a fright so it did."

"Only a poor cripple's crutch, that's all," said Brown, raising the stick to rub its dark yellow shine against his cheek. "You be glad I'm improving the moral tone of this midden. Teenage trash. How about a drink then?"

I was careful to let my face show no reaction. Big Otto thought it was the biggest laugh since the war.

Five minutes later the street door opened. Brown made his usual careful examination of the newcomer, a cocky little chap aged about fourteen by the size of him but considerably older in his aggressive movements. He had a thin face that needed square meals and a pair of eyes as edgy as those of a fox interrupted while gnawing its hind leg free of a gin-trap. He came straight up to the bar and spoke to Bobbie.

"Any blokes frum Glasga in here?" he demanded.

"Get a load of Oor Wullie," said Brown, who now had the stick hanging from his forearm, as old-fashioned gentlemen did prior to taking snuff.

"Mah pal tellt us there wiz a loata Glasga fellas goat in this boozer," the boy said.

"What's your pal's name exactly?" said Brown.

"Dennis Scalley—frum Coatbrig. We wiz in Boarstal thegither."

"That's no' the Scalley that was doing five in Peterhead is it?"

"Naw, his brurrer. It's Bennie's in Peterheid. You know him, do ye?"

"I ken a lot of folk, Sonny Jim. Needing a drink, are you?"

"No, Ah'm no a sponger. You tell us where Ah kin make a few quid, quick like? Ah havnae any bread."

"Thieving?"

"Aye, anythin'."

"Go on, have a drink."

"No, I doan't waant wan." "Good on you, kid. Tell you what you could try. There's a pub round the corner, big place with green doors. They're always looking for barmen, just—"

"I doan't waant tae fucken *work!*"

"Who mentioned *work?* See the big gaffer round there? Mr Wallis? He's a big nancy. He'll give you a couple of quid for a quick sucking off up the stairs. That your kinda line, is it?" Brown winked at the rest of us. "He's an ugly big bugger."

"That's his hard donald, intit?"

We watched him leave.

"Besta British Donald Duck, kid," Brown shouted.

Paisley Dave looked at me. "I remember you now," he said quietly. "Big Joe thought you could be law."

"What—me?" I snorted, a genuine reaction for the first time in that den. "I never saw him carrying his white stick."

Paisley Dave gave me a clean-cut grin. It occurred to me he might know he looked a lot like Jeffrey Hunter the film star.

"You want to watch the wisecracks with Big Joe," he said. "He's a people-hater."

"Aye, lot of them about," I said, with a manly nod of self-confidence.

We talked about the footballers of our respective youths back home. Brown had a brother who'd known Charlie Tully well and we all told our favourite Tully stories (said the yank in St Peter's Square: "Who's that guy in the white up there on the balcony beside Charlie Tully?"). We told our favourite Rangers-Celtic stories (the bottles started to fly down from the upper terracings and Wee Erchie says he's off home to safety and Big Aleck says did he no' remember what they said in the war, you wouldn't get hit by a bullet unless it had your name on it? And Wee Erchie says, I remember it bloody well, my name's MacEwan! This being the name of Scotland's biggest brewer).

Wee Bobbie the barman had actually played for Partick Thistle before the war. A lot of them have that fantasy but Brown told us it was true, he remembered his father talking about Bobbie Deakin. Otto the German must have grown tired of our reminiscences and developed an obsession with the silent juke-box. Bobbie found him a plastic-handled screwdriver to repair it. Stray drinkers came and went.

We told each other our various reasons for being unable to live in Scotland, mainly because of the hopeless drinking restrictions. Brown told us a few yarns from his Foreign Legion service, all of them gothic horrors.

The few lonely ones at the tables got up to buy themselves drinks and then sat down again. I learned that Brown had been ready to go to Glasgow University but had joined the army instead. I must have showed some scepticism—when Brown next limped theatrically to the lavatory Paisley Dave told me the university stuff was true.

"He comes from a well-off family," he said, "you know, frootina hoose and naeboady seek?"

"Come again?"

"Glasgow definition of rich—fruit in the house and nobody sick. You never heard that?"

"Ach, I left Scotland when I was just a boy really."

"We both went to visit Jackie's folk a couple of Ne'erdays ago—we got as far as the front door in Bellshill and his father wouldn't even speak to him. Wouldn't even let us in the house. Jackie was a captain in the HLI, know that? His father threw him out of the house when he was eighteen. I've seen him in bloody tears about it—but don't tell him I said so or he'll be curing your dandruff with the stick."

This seemed to show I'd been classed as reliable. When Brown came back I said, casually:

"I got nicked the other night for being pissed in the street and you know who I saw in the court? Any of you blokes remember a writer fella called Ramsay Shand, from Dundee?"

"You're joking!" exclaimed Brown. "Know him? We've been nursing him! He's been coming in here all week. First time Big Joe wanted to put the slipper into him for being sarcastic. He's a big hopeless lush but he kept calling us illiterate Scotch morons so Big Joe gets the needle and says we'll take him round the alley and see what he's got in his pockets and then kick fuck out of him. I says, He's a famous Scotsman, you big cunt! We'll take care of him, poor bloody lush that he is. Dave gave me a hand with him, we carted him up that alley round the corner and put him to bed under a load of papers."

"He put the bite on me for a coupla quid to pay his fine," I said, shaking my head ruefully.

"You can say ta-ta for ever to your two quid," said Brown. "He doesn't have a sou—just a bum. He was in here last night on the tap."

"Aye—and Ah'm no' lettin' him here again," said Wee Bobbie.

"How not?"

"The boss catches me lettin' in alkies Ah'm for it."

"The boss?" said Brown. "When did you get scared of him? If he tries to throw out any Scots you refer to me, right?" He gave me a nudge. "The gaffer here's a lush himself. That's the only reason this wee nyaff has the job. Nobody else would employ him—would they, you wee rascal?"

Bobbie grinned, almost proudly.

"He gets a good jobs and then vamooses with the takings. They caught him once in Blackpool—five quid left out of nine hundred. Spent it all in three days on rum and teenage hoors—didn't you, ye wee Glesca eejit?"

Bobbie winked at me.

"Right enough but," he said, "Ah'm basically an irresponsible person, a doctor wance tellt me Ah'm immature so he did."

"Time you were closing this hole," said Brown, lightly tapping the bar with the stick and looking round the silent people at the side tables. "Throw all these unemployed vampires the hell out of here and we'll have a wee sing-song."

I should have gone away when the doors closed. Shand would not show again till the evening. I had established the important point—that they weren't looking to make cash out of Shand. I didn't go because I liked it there. I like Jackie Brown. I've always liked grown men who attack life like eighteen-year-olds. And when Paisley Dave finally trusted me enough to say what he did for a living I felt I'd passed a vital test.

"All right, I'll tell you," he said, "I'm a burglar!" He emphasised the word burglar, conveying a certain surprise, as if I should have realised. Or maybe saying, Isn't everybody?

"He shits on their carpets," said Brown.

"No, I don't, I sniff their panties."

So the four of us Scots and Otto Daffae stayed in the saloon bar of The Rats' Castle all afternoon, one thickness of painted glass hiding us from the street, the little triangle of blue sky turning purple and then grey and then black. We could not put on electric light because that would have alerted the passing constable to our illegal enjoyment. We sang together, self-consciously at first, and we told well-worn jokes and we described our memories of home, of Wilson's tenement zoo in Glasgow where the one decrepit lion had to be hit with the cleaner's broom before it would move over a weary inch to let him sweep the cage, the door of which lay open all the time he was in there, and Ibrox Park when the bottles flew like crows darkening the sky, and sweetshops that sold dry cinnamon stick and liquorice root and Barr's Irn Bru, and women schoolteachers who were heavy with the belt, and big family reunions at New Year, and the first time we dared enter the big men's world of the pub.

We crooned songs like 'The Star o' Rabbie Burns' and 'The Girl That I met On The Road to Dundee' and 'Nancy Whisky'. At one point I was glad of the darkness to hide a tear. Wasn't it tragic that we should all ache for the place we said we hated so much?

I hadn't forgotten why I'd come there but it no longer seemed important. This was what counted, being with men who could laugh and fight and fuck the system. Five thousand like us and we'd set Scotland free.

Then it was half-past five and Bobbie was opening the streetdoor. In the lavatory I splashed my face with cold water and told myself staunchly that at last I had fallen among *men,* of my own blood.

The bar had been open about ten minutes when the boy came back. He insisted on buying us all a drink.

"How did ye get on then, chief?" asked Jackie Brown, a true Legion sergeant on whom half a day's whisky could not make a dent.

"No' bad," said the boy. "The big fat gaffer says start the night so he takes us up the sterrs and shows us the barman's room and then says, Ah'll gie ye three quid if Ah kin suck yese aff. Awright, Ah says. Anyway, Ah get three quid aff him and Ah'm gaun doon the coarridoar an' his big bride pokes her heid ooota door and says, Come in, so Ah goes in and she gets me tae screw her—an' she gives us five quid!"

"Eight quid—not bad, chief," said Jackie.

"Eight quid nuthin'! Ah cleaned oot the till when Ah come doon the sterrs! Ah've goat thirty easy."

"You'd better on your way then fore the polis turn up," said Jackie, paternally.

"Aye, ach Ah only come doon tae London tae seefa could make a few quid. Ah'm aff hame on the train the night."

Off he went.

"Youth will have its fling," said Jackie, as we moved up to the back end of the bar to avoid the evening crowd.

We stood quietly, the jokes and the memories all used up. What else in common did we have? The country that gave us the accent had given us nothing much else except our imagined reasons for escaping to another country, where we did not live so much as find ways of compensating for the lost country. Would we ever be happy anywhere? I kept watching the door for Shand so that I would have an excuse to leave.

Instead, through the street door came the most dangerous man in The Rookery. He had no name and I had never seen him before. He could have been any one of ten thousand identical men. This one wore a mass-produced fake leather jacket with greasy nylon-wool collar. He was not a criminal or a professional hard man but he was to be avoided at all times.

You know that man?

He is still young enough to feel the pain but old enough to know there will be no more magic round the next corner. His hair is going and his face has hardened and nobody is attracted to him any longer. He has come to The Rookery for escape. He goes into pornography shops but that only makes him feel despicable. He goes to striptease shows and feels branded as a sucker. He goes from pub to pub but there aren't going to be any more romantic miracles. He goes into sex-shops and sees only ointments and aids for the lucky ones. He knows it's stupid but he goes into clip-joints and this time the hostess appears to be honest and he gives her five pounds to buy her temporary freedom from the relentless boss, and as he waits in vain for her to come to the hamburger joint on the corner he sickens with shame at his own gullibility.

Soon he knows he will be confirming his own hopelessness by climbing the narrow stairs to pay three pounds to a woman who openly despises the endless crowd of failures who trample desperately through her life.

It is his night of escape and its minutes are ruthless.

By the time he reaches The Rats' Castle he is a desperate man. The next face that sneers at him is going to be smashed to a pulp. How else can he keep a man's self-respect?

The tension coming off this one was almost radioactive. He shot terrible glances at people who brushed against him at the crowded bar. He picked up his glass and decided to sit at the end table, nearest where we were standing. He gave us a glare, thinking we were sneering at him for being alone.

I was just telling myself how safe a dangerous world could appear when you had mates like Jackie Brown and Paisley Dave when the door opened and in came Big Joe— McMenemy the Enemy. I took a deep breath.

McMenemy came straight towards us, black shiny curls, white T-shirt under a seaman's jacket, mouth hard set, head turning for narcissistic glances at the mirror behind the barmen. He looked hard at me. "Who are you?" he demanded.

"Fine, hoo's yerself?" I said.

"Fucken wise guy, eh?" he said.

"He's a friend of mine, John's his name," said Jackie Brown, with more detachment than I would have liked. McMenemy was well over six feet, a strapping great lump of hair-trigger temper.

"I'm just buying," I said. "What do you have?"

McMenemy looked at me.

"Ah remember you," he said. "Clever cunt."

"You thought I was police," I said easily.

"Don't tell me what Ah fucken thought," he snapped.

Jesus!

I had taken one step towards the bar when Wee Bobbie put both hands on the formica and started shouting at the man in the fur collar.

"What're you lookin' at me like that for?" Wee Bobbie yelled above the din. The man stared back. Then he snorted contemptuously and pretended to spit. Wee Bobbie vaulted straight over the counter and ran at him. He grabbed his fur collar in both hands, shouting:

"Don't you fuckin' look at me like that, ye horrible bastard!"

The man's shoulder movements were hampered by the fur-collared jacket but he managed to get a right-handed punch up at Bobbie's face.

Big drops of dark red blood immediately ran down his upper lip, as though they had been waiting for the signal.

Big McMenemy gave me a push with his left arm. Instinctively I closed my eyes prior to butting at his nose with my forehead but his hulking big body forced past me.

He grabbed at the seated man's fur collar, bawling:

"You hit my pal, Ah'm going to waste ye, cunt."

The man in the fur collar threw his beer up into McMenemy's face, simultaneously pushing himself to his feet in the narrow space between the bench and the table. He smacked at McMenemy's face with his pint glass. It was the dimpled kind, with a handle. It didn't break. He ran for the door. McMenemy ran after him.

People hugged close to each other against the wall and against the bar, leaving a clear path for McMenemy's long-striding dash.

"Youth must have its fling," said Paisley Dave, turning his back to lean both elbows on the bar.

I followed Brown to the door.

Looking over his shoulder into the frost-bright street I saw McMenemy gripping the man by his hair, the man trying to duck away while kicking out at McMenemy's legs.

McMenemy's right hand came out from under his seaman's pea jacket holding a big knife. For a moment, as they twisted under the street-light, I saw it clearly, a wooden handle, one straight edge, one curved, sharpened edge.

"Leave off, Joe," shouted Brown.

"Ah'll cut your fucken heart out," McMenemy screamed at the man in the fur collar, whose arched body twisted from side to side as if the hand on his head was screwing him into the ground.

For a slow-motion moment the dull steel blade moved towards the struggling silhouette of the man in the fur collar. I could feel my skin wincing.

Then Brown took a step forward. He swung the stick down smartly on McMenemy's wrist.

The knife fell to the pavement, metal scraping on stone. McMenemy yelped. The hand that had been gripping the man's hair massaged his injured wrist. His big young face stared at Brown, a shiny black curl falling over his forehead.

The man in the fur collar ran across the street and disappeared.

Brown took a step forward and kicked the knife into the gutter.

"What the fuck d'ye do that for?" McMenemy demanded, biting his lower lip as he rubbed his wrist.

"Didn't I tell you to drop that chiv in the river?" Brown snapped. He walked across the pavement and looked down into the gutter. I saw him kicking the knife with his right foot, pushing it along the gutter, guiding it with the stick.

I edged clear of the doorway and walked off without turning my head.

My countrymen!

My own blood?

No!

Was I glad to get to the door of The Leafless? I could have hugged all of them! Even Stringfellow.

Matchan said he was in the chair, what was I having, why was I looking like that?

I said I had just seen a knife-fight outside The Rats' Castle. Stringfellow said it could not have been so sickening to watch as what he had seen in the gents bog at Waterloo Station when six tearaways were kicking shit out of an old bum, with twenty or thirty commuters too scared or too pressed for time to do anything.

From now on I belonged here, I told myself. The hell with Ramsay Shand, I wanted nothing to do with anything remotely Scottish. I would change my voice until it no longer reminded me of razors and prisons and bottles flying over the heads at Ibrox Park. I would make it up with Neville. Or go in with JTB. Or anything. I would pull on the cosy, old slipper warmth of *Englishness*.

Brandy in my shaking hand—the least Scottish drink I could think of—I stood quietly and listened.

". . . this Chinese geezer sat beside her so I was just thinking hallo hallo hallo, don't often see a chink trying to pull a white woman, do you, when she passes him a roll of fivers you could've used for the fence at Becher's Brook. He was the collector for the heroin racket, wasn't he?"

"Stands to reason, Chinese heroin!" ". . .listen, you great pillock, I said, my pockets are all to let, I can't lend you a sausage. Some people have no bleeding shame, do they?"

". . .yeah, Coyne gave us a card and said show it to the head waiter and he'll let you drink till all hours being as you've friends of mine, so Chick and I got into the place—real clip-joint—prices? Diabolical! We show the bloke Coyne's card and he says he'll let us have a bottle of scotch at the table for eight quid—about half price by their standards if you're a punter buying it by the glass. So Chick says, How about those chicks, man, you recommend? And Coyne's pal the head waiter says, Nah, they're all thieves, lads, don't bother. Cost you too—I have to charge you five quid the moment her kneecaps touch the table-cloth!"

"Like it! Five quid the moment her knees touch the table-cloth!"

"I still can't believe it—Chick? You know, I really did honestly believe that bloke was indestructible."

"What about Chick?" I murmured.

That was why he had not turned up for his meet with Baxter and Junior Waddell. While we'd been recounting our Chick Bhalla stories and Baxter had been phoning all round to trace him, Chick had been dying. He'd been drunk all day and then taken too many sleeping pills.

Sleeping pills!

Not heroin or cocaine or alcohol. He had lived with them for twenty years.

Sleeping pills?

I felt sick.

"But when you saw this helpless old bum being duffed up I'm genuinely interested—why do you think it was you didn't go to help him? No—seriously—look, I wouldn't have helped him but I keep asking myself why not."

"I'm not ashamed to admit it, I was too yellow."

"No, commonsense. You start playing Sir Galahad to every bastard you see getting kicked and thumped around here you'd be spending your whole life at it."

"I think we'll need to set up vigilantes—"

"Don't be stoopid! If any government would declare war on bad housing and terrible schools—"

"Don't give us all that socialist crap, half of these apes don't come from slums—"

"You don't understand. Poverty is relative, what—"

"Yeah, I've got a lot of poor relatives—"

"Poverty is what other people have got, and what you haven't got, even if you've got enough to live on—it's comparative—"

Was it the brandy, on top of all those pints of lager?

They babbled on and I couldn't escape the fact that I was bored. They didn't seem *manly*. Rabbits, rabbiting.

Was it the brandy? Three small measures?

I bought my round, said I might be back, and lurched off back to The Rats' Castle. No brainless psychopath with an Elvis Presley fantasy was going to interfere with my plans.

Shoving through the crowd inside the pub I went straight up to the four of them, poked my index finger into McMenemy's hard chest and said, in my best Shettleston voice:

"See you, you big balloon?"

On November 16, 1724, Jack was brought out of Newgate Prison to the gallows cart. He was smiling. Hidden in his clothing was a knife. He intended to cut the rope round his wrists and jump off the cart where the crowds would be thickest, in Holborn. He knew the people would help him by hindering his pursuers. He was London's hero. Two hundred thousand people were lining the route to Tyburn, to cheer him. Just as they prepared to leave Newgate a busy warder called Watson decided, on impulse, to search Jack. He found the knife.

18

To this day that moment makes me sweat with shame and anger. The humiliation! McMenemy's face broke into a grin. He was jeering at me! I had been ready to fight to the last drop—feet, knees, head butts, even bite his ear off. But he just grinned!

That was when I realised that Ramsay Shand was standing behind Jackie Brown.

"See me?" said McMenemy. "I only fight with proper men!" He pointed at Shand. "I've got a sister that's got more guts in her wee finger than that object." He then pointed at me. "Away and join the Girl Guides." He laughed.

Jackie Brown silenced whatever I might have found to say by pushing the brass ferrule of the walking-stick into my chest.

"On your way, pal, while you're still able."

Humiliation? To this day I clench my teeth and curse myself for not having a gun! In that one moment McMenemy destroyed me.

"Aye and take this garbage with you," said McMenemy, stretching out one big arm and giving Shand a push in the chest. Shand sat down heavily.

I think Brown moved in front of McMenemy to shield us while I helped Shand to his feet. His eyes were dead.

"Make a great pair, don't they?" laughed McMenemy as I steered hand towards the door. As soon as we were on the pavement Shand started to struggle. He wanted to go back inside. He didn't know who I was or why I was taking him away from his friends. I got hold of him by the lapels of the black leather jacket and shook him savagely.

"Those guys are killers, you stupid bastard! Don't you have any brains at all? I'm the only friend you've got in this whole bloody world! Come on, I'll buy you a drink—just try and keep a grip of yourself for Christ's sake!"

The Three-Legged Mare was crowded but the manager spotted us coming through the door and when we reached the bar he said, without any hypocritical politeness:

"Not serving you in that condition," looking mainly at Shand. "I want you to leave right away. *Out.*"

I looked round. Shame upon shame!

"What about all this lot?" I snarled. "They all look bloody pissed to me."

"Nobody's drunk in my house and if they are they spent their money here. Out!"

So we went, possibly arm in arm.

"Don't you live any bloody where?" I growled when Shand refused to give me an address where I could take him. We were stumbling along Bishop Henry Street, possibly towards The Leafless.

"I was flung out. Friends? They aren't friends, I don't have any real friends at all." He lost his balance. I caught him by the shoulders of the leather jacket and hauled him upright. All the time I kept closing my eyes and clenching my teeth and cursing the name McMenemy.

Then I saw a taxi with its light on and waved it down. The driver had a good look at us before deciding to pull in.

"Lindehan Crescent off Clapham Common," I said, revolting myself at the easy way I turned on a false, smiling charm. "It's all right, my father's just been celebrating my mother's funeral."

The bespectacled driver grunted something about making us pay if anybody was sick in his precious bloody cab and off we went to Kate's gaff. I started to tell Shand how he was a human disgrace but that I could make him some money. He passed out before Trafalgar Square. His big head lolled against my shoulder. I stared grimly out of the window, seeing nothing but my own weakness and cowardice and humiliation. I wanted to hire people to smash McMenemy into the ground, to kick in his face, break his arms, shatter his kneecaps. I wanted to see him roasting over a fire, screaming for mercy. I wanted to make so much money I could pay to have him blown apart with a shotgun.

Shand fell down a couple of times between the taxi and the door. I pressed Kate's buzzer. There was no sound from the speaking grille. It was only half-past nine. Why the hell didn't I have my own key?

Shand sat down heavily and dropped his chin on his chest and then toppled sideways. I pulled him farther into the shadows in case of a passing cop and sat on the doorstep beside him.

It was the coldest hour of my life. He was snoring but I was coming apart at the seams. Hugging my shoulders, breathing between clenched teeth, I sat there and vowed over and over again that my drinking days were over.

My blackest hour?

Compared to some of the hours to come it was sixty minutes of sunshine and laughter.

Katie was not overjoyed to see what I had brought home but I was in no mood to be subtly persuasive.

"Help me get him up the stairs or I'll bloody strangle you," I snarled. We got him to his feet.

"What do you intend to do with him?" she asked in an icy voice.

"Get him a basket and a box with cat-litter—what the hell do you think?" We started him up the stairs, me with my arm round his waist, Katie coming behind ready to prop us up if his weight overbalanced me.

"He's worth a lot of money to me—you'll get a share of it. I'll find him a place to stay tomorrow. I've got to get a tape-recorder. This man's famous, you know, in Scotland, you never heard of Ramsay Shand the playwright?"

"That's Ramsay Shand the playwright? Really?"

"Why, you think all big writers wear velvet jackets and sip Napoleon brandy? He's an alcoholic. You know he boozed his way through a quarter a million pounds sterling—before inflation?"

"I know quite a lot about him. I've even read his plays."

"That's good, you can give me the *Reader's Digest* plot summary so that I can hold rewarding conversations about his art. Let's put him down for a rest."

We sat him on a stair, shoulder against the wall. His lips were caked with brown stuff. He opened his eyes, stared at us blankly and then passed out again.

"It was the only way I could make sure of not losing him again," I said by way of an apology. "Just for tonight—he can kip on the floor and tomorrow I'll find him a bed-sitter round here somewhere."

"I don't mind," she said, looking down at him.

"Look at the poor tortured artist," I said, sneeringly, barely resisting an urge to kick his inert bulk. "What's wrong with these guys, they think typing out a few crummy words entitles them to double rations of debauchery?"

"His plays weren't crummy," she said.

"Gorki with jokes? I don't care about his plays, it's his life of sin and degradation I'm going to turn into money. The bard of booze and broads! The millionaire in the gutter! Who do you think I should approach first, the *People* or *The News of the World?*"

"Just your level," she said. "Come on, let's get him upstairs."

"Oh, becoming quite maternal, are we? They do say that fame's the greatest aphrodisiac there is. You mean that holds good even if you're ex-famous?"

"Jealous?"

"Of this human disaster? You're joking. Steady your end."

"Everybody is jealous of an artist," she said.

His eyes opened again when we started to take off the leather jacket and slide him onto one of the two single mattresses that made up her double-bed.

"Where the fuck's this?" he mumbled. "Don't you steal my bloody play or I'll, I'll. . . "

He closed down then for the night. We covered him with one blanket, his jacket, her dressing-gown and her raincoat. I found that I didn't like touching him but she got down on her knees to take of his disintegrating shoes.

Leaving the electric fire on we got into bed, her on the single mattress, me on the lower level of the bed itself. This made it difficult to cuddle against her for warmth so I started to climb on top of her but she pushed me back.

"Not with him in the room," she hissed.

"That dead body? We could have the massed pipes and drums of the City of Glasgow Police Force in here and he wouldn't know. Come on, I'm freezing."

"No."

"All I want's to get warm."

She compromised by sliding over on top of me. We held each other tightly under two inadequate blankets and fell asleep, lulled by the soothing rhythm of the bard's catarrhal snortings and snorings.

In the morning, coming back from the kitchen sink, I slipped my hands into his assortment of bedding cover and probed around until my fingers touched the wad of paper in the inside pocket of his leather jacket.

With both windows closed and the electric fire having been on all night the room was at oven temperature. Lack of oxygen seemed to be making our bodies sweat whenever we touched so I took the lower level and switched on the bed-lamp to read the masterpiece he had waved in my face on the first two occasions we met.

There wasn't a lot of it, twelve foolscap pages, typed so badly and with so many ballpoint insertions and corrections that it was a struggle for the eyes to move along each line. It was supposed to be a play about two tinkers being arrested by the police in the heart of Dundee, for cadging in the street.

The message wasn't very subtle—the tinkers were supposed to be free spirits living the old life before the money-blight, the coppers representing the dead hand of property. The dialogue wasn't very funny or brilliant, as far as I could judge, but when I came to the end of what he'd typed I found myself disappointed at not having the rest of it to read.

I'd only been to Dundee once, when I was fifteen and Rangers were playing in a Scottish Cup game at Dens Park, and the impression it left on me was of a cold and violent city where the police boxes were made of iron to prove it. I could well imagine the warmth and hospitality the Dundee constabulary would show to a couple of tinkers. Poor tinkers, living in low tents on grass verges and going to Scottish farmhouses to sell clothes pegs or cadge a cup of tea and a scone, like Red Indians on the edges of those big American cities, people who were living by the wrong calendar.

Reading Shand's stuff made me shiver in that overheated, airless room, thinking about Scotland and the cold wind whipping off the North Sea up the grim Dundee streets and the big cops in their three-ton police boxes that only an anti-tank gun could penetrate. You'll hear a lot of talk about Glasgow being a rough place but it's a warm bath compared to Dundee where they don't even have smiles on their faces as they kick each other to death.

Shand had got the feel of the place, right enough, but even I could see the weaknesses. Besides, when did they last put a play about tinkers and Dundee bobbies on in Shaftesbury Avenue? Poor bastard, I thought, looking over at the untidy bulges of his sleeping body, this isn't going to get you back to the Hilton rooftop with champers in the bucket and a nymphomaniac on each arm.

Still, that wasn't my worry, was it?

Shand woke up as Katie was leaving for her office. He stared at her without saying anything. I was still in the bed. I could see that he was looking up her legs, dirty old drunk that he was. She must have known he was looking up her legs but she just stood there above him "John can make you something to eat," she said to him. "I'll be back about half-past six, you can stay if you want."

He grunted.

"Tatty byes," she said cheerily, leaving the room with only a quick glance at me.

"Where the fuck's this?" Shand said in that incongruously squeaky voice of his.

"Remember me?" I said.

"I met you somewhere, didn't I? How the hell did I get here, wherever this is?"

"I brought you home last night. My name's John Thompson. I met you in The Maggots that day and took you to that club and then we bumped into each other in the court-remember I gave you a fiver to pay your fine?"

"Two for the fine and three for the publican. I'm dying."

"This fell out your pocket," I said, showing him the typed sheets. "I was reading it—don't mind, do you?"

"Course I mind," he snapped, rising on one elbow and then having a partial collapse as the headache blinded him. I threw the wad of foolscap onto the carpet beside him.

"I think it's very good," I said.

"Good?" he gasped. "It's fucking brilliant. I was just an entertainer before, a public clown—"

"Look, I do a bit of writing myself, nothing as good as you—"

how do you fancy me helping you to make five grand?"

"Five thousand pounds? If only."

"Seriously."

"I've heard the tale every way known to man. Success? When you've got a hundred thou you draw them like flies. I'm a walking testimonial to the old adage that you've got to be trained to handle money. Oh Christ—you know what would do me a power of good right now?"

"What?"

"Any whisky about?"

"No, sorry, there's only a bit of gin—"

"That'll do, where is it?"

"On that bookshelf just above your head."

It almost made me vomit to see him scrambling to his knees, coats and blanket falling off him like a statue at unveiling, grabbing the half-bottle of Gordon's and not so much drinking gin as letting gravity carry it down his throat. He drank a quarter of a bottle, without stopping once.

Then he lay down again, sighing.

"Quite good, neat gin," he said, as calmly as if commenting on the weather. "You're a writer yourself you say?"

"No, not me. I have done a bit, just enough to let me know I'm not a writer. Not a proper writer. But listen, I do bits and pieces—we have a music agency, you see, and I ghost columns for one of my clients, Terry Pilbeam—the disc jockey, you know?"

"No, I don't know any fucking disc jockeys, brainless buffoons the lot of them. That's not a world I care to bother with. Pop culture, leave all that to those Sunday newspaper intellectuals, so-called."

"So how do you fancy me ghosting your life story for one of the newspapers?"

"Oh, that's your ploy, is it? Not on, friend. You don't think I haven't been asked? A thousand times. I always told them the same thing—let me write it the way I want and print it without changing a word and then I might consider it."

"Okay then—we'll tell it exactly the way you want. Listen, quite apart from the money, I was a fan of yours when I was a fifteen-year-old boy in Shettleston in Glasgow, you know that? You were my hero—an ordinary building site labourer who wrote international stage hits? I thought you were better than Glasgow Rangers."

"Of course I was. Scotland's whole trouble is Glasgow bloody Rangers. I've never been to a football match in my life—and I'm proud of it."

"That must be a record—or else you're a big homo, as they say in Glasgow."

"Aye, I've been that as well. Love between men—what's wrong with it? And listen, while we're being personal—I was only working on that building site for one summer—they said I had a spot on my lung and I needed fresh air. I was all set to go to St Andrew's University. We weren't working-class at all, my father was a haberdasher, it was all publicity, the press agent for my first West End production seized on that building labourer crap and said it would go down big with the moronic newspapers. My father died, luckily. He would have been livid.

Christ, I was the dux boy of my year at the academy. Everybody I meet tells me how wonderful I am to be so literate for a navvy! Listen, my father was a very well-read man, we had all of Sir Walter Scott and Balzac and Tolstoy and Theodore Dreiser in our house.

There was one bitch critic woman in Edinburgh, she got hold of me at a party one night and started telling me I was only an accidental incidental—some magic spark had passed to me when I was a semi-literate labourer and wasn't it amazing how Scottish culture was kept alive by the unlikeliest vehicles? Listen, woman, I said, I'll give you a pound for every novel you've read that I haven't read starting with James Hogg's *Confessions of a Justified Sinner,* taking in all the French classics, the Russians—then I'll give you ten pounds for any line you can give me from any

Greek drama. Stupid bitch—it turned out she'd never even read a line of MacDiarmid's. Never even read *A Drunk Man Looks At A Thistle*! Comedians and football players, that's all they know in Scotland. I think personally MacDiarmid is an elitist and an intellectual fascist but when he says he's not interested in the Glasgow mob and their unexamined lives I know exactly what he means. It's not just a case of bad housing and unemployment, it's poverty of the mind.

Scotland, the Sahara of the north!

I see myself suffering exactly what Robert Burns suffered, this ploughman label, the guy was a bloody intellectual! The only reason he had to plough fields was because the Scottish bourgeoisie were too moronic to buy enough of his books. Now Burns wrote a lot of pawky, *Sunday Post*-mentality shit but he was a major poet, even if it's only the Russians that realise it. I chose the stage to write for because it seemed to be the most immediate way of getting to the people's minds, albeit that pretentious, snobbish, braying minority that goes to a theatre in this land of Philistines but I'm in direct lineal descent from Burns and Dunbar and Hogg, artistically speaking. You say I could make five thousand from a newspaper?"

Jesus!

"Yeah, easy. I tape it, I write it—just to save you the bother—we split the dough."

"I don't know anything about you."

"Oh, I'm just an accidental incidental. Listen, I don't like to be rude or anything but when exactly was the last time anybody offered you a newspaper deal?"

"Don't think I'm forgotten! Those two feature-writers the other day—that shows you I'm still very much in their minds—"

"Did they write anything, in the end?"

"I don't know, I haven't seen a paper for I don't know how long. I mean, why should I let you do it when I could go to a newspaper myself and let them write it and collect all the money?"

"You could do. They wouldn't write it the way you want, though. The bard with the birds and the booze. The labourer who pissed away quarter of a million. What I was thinking was, I might pay you some money now, money of my own, just to keep you going until—"

"How much?"

"I could let you have fifty quid—if you're agreeing to the deal."

"Fifty? Better than nothing I suppose. What time's it?"

"Just after nine."

"That all? Fucking hell. If I don't get a big wet pint into me soon my face will burst. Okay, I'll agree to your deal."

"Great. I've got a little letter of agreement we can sign—just something to show the newspapers to prove I'm actually doing it with you."

"I'll have a look at it. They open about ten round here, do they?"

"No idea. I've never used these local boozers. I was actually thinking we could get started right away, work out a synopsis I could show to the newspapers."

"Aye, sure, but we can talk in a pub as well as anywhere else. We'll have a quick one in the nearest and then head up to the West End, that's where most of my friends hang out."

"I'd rather not go near The Rookery for a while if you don't mind. Keep this to yourself but there's just a chance I'm involved in a murder case—the worst of it is I don't know what to do, you think if—"

"Wake'me up when it's ten o'clock. I'll spend some of that fifty on a couple of bottles of good malt whisky if we're going to be staying here. I detest this working-class dependency on pub opening-times. It isn't fucking civilised."

Jesus!

The only thing about my ex-boyhood idol that wasn't a fake, it seemed, was his thirst.

"Didn't some doctor say you would die if you didn't stop

drinking," I said, tentatively.

"Yes but she didn't tell me how to stop," he proclaimed, from under the blanket.

Even that early I think I had a glimpse of the far-off gates of Hell.

Jack Ketch the public hangman turned off the life of Jack Sheppard on the Tyburn Gallows but Jack's friends grabbed the body and rushed it to a pub called The Barley Mow, where they tried to revive him. This time, however, there was no escape. So demented was the London mob over the death of its hero a regiment with fixed bayonets was required to put down that night's rioting. Jack Sheppard was twenty-three.

19

Some boys were playing football on the Common. Shand had a cigarette in his mouth and the collar of his leather jacket turned up, a squat bundle of a man not nearly tall enough for his big square skull. He had not shaved for two or three days and already his black stubble had the inevitable red Scottish tinge; by covering his cheeks and chin and throat this rough beard made him look much younger and even virile. The hard ground was so cold I could feel it through my shoes and socks and this, coupled with the shouts of the boys and the wispy condensation steaming from their mouths, reminded me so strongly of the countless frosty mornings I'd spent playing football as a boy that I found myself wanting to put my arm round his shoulders and saying. . . I don't know what, something to the order of 'Aren't we silly to let these adult neuroses sidetrack us into self-imposed gloom?'

When their plastic ball came bouncing in our direction I suddenly ran at it, jacket flying behind me. Flicking it up with my right instep I smashed a volley shot at the boy between the jacket goalposts.

My left foot slipped and I fell heavily on my hip. That pain, too, was so evocative I could not believe that it was thirteen or fourteen years since I had last kicked a ball. *Thirteen years?*

"Oh yeah, the old skill never leaves you," I said to him, biting my lower lip as I massaged my hip-bone.

"That your hidden talent is it?" he sneered, walking on with an abruptness that was downright autocratic, even though his dark trousers were lop-sided and recognisable as trousers merely because they were covering his legs. I had to trot to catch up with him, resenting these continual sneers that were supposed to remind me that he was The Artist and that he had been Up There among the secrets of success and that I was merely an untalented operator.

The pub was one of those that tries to resemble a cosy lounge, with Christmas decorations and witty signs about the banks not selling beer so don't ask us to cash cheques. Shand wanted a whisky and a pint of best bitter. The landlord—moustache, cardigan, a joke for every regular customer—radiated an unmistakable hostility but he served us and I let him know with a couple of ingratiating pleasantries that we were not two Scottish trouble-makers. I asked for a tomato juice, to which Shand reacted with another sneer.

"I want to keep a clear head today," I said as we sat down at a table near the door. "If you want to go ahead with this scheme of mine I'll have to start buzzing around like a blue-arsed fly."

"It's not the sort of thing I should be doing at all," he said, lifting the whisky glass and throwing it down in one gulp. He shuddered and groaned. For a moment I thought he was going to be sick. Then he took an inch off the beer, noisily. Brown foam lay wetly on the stubble round his lips. "Fifty quid, you said."

"I've got that much I can give you just for living on while we're getting the thing started," I said. "It'll take two or three days to get an outline of it on paper. Then I can find out if the Sunday papers are interested. Suppose we say we'll do it for anything over six thousand? We'll ask for ten but we'll make six the rock-bottom, you think?"

"I wouldn't be interested in anything less than ten

thousand—that kind of cheap sensationalism won't do my professional reputation any good. I was cursed by rubbish publicity in the first place. I need another whisky."

Yes, autocratic was the word. He was a wreck and he hadn't produced a play for ten years or more and most people thought he was dead, if they thought of him at all, but he had been where I hadn't, in the magic elite.

I got up and fetched him another whisky. He was turning out a lot harder than I'd anticipated and it didn't come naturally to me to play the ruthless negotiating game. How the hell would Neville handle this? I watched him throw over the second whisky. He lit a cigarette without offering me one.

I brought the folded sheets of my typed contract out of my inner jacket pocket and flattened them on the table. I brought out the wad of notes Neville had given me and counted off ten fivers, keeping them in my hand.

"This is the fifty I'll give you out of my own money if you'll sign the agreement," I said. "If nothing comes of the project you keep the fifty. If you don't want to do it let's say so now and forget the whole thing, no hard feelings. I'd like to do it and make us both some money but it's up to you."

I sat back.

He read the typed contract. He looked quite tough.

"You've got us splitting it fifty-fifty! That's not right. It's my name that'll sell it—I can find plenty of short paragraph journalists to knock it out!"

The cold tomato juice was reminding my stomach that it was starving. I felt cold and isolated, far from the warmth of familiar faces. It was ten to eleven and up in The Rookery, where I was *known,* Neville was waiting for me with three hundred and fifty pounds. This alleged boyhood hero was an all-round shit. All I had to do was shove the fifty quid back in my hip-pocket and walk out.

Why didn't I?

Because he had a beard to hide the disintegration and looked like the kind of tough but clever man I'd wanted as a friend all my life? Because he made me feel I was getting near at last to the secrets of success, of fame? Because I had obstinately decided to prove I could force this scheme to work?

Or because I was frightened by what might happen to me if I let myself drift back into The Rookery, taxes still unpaid, pursued by police and black whores and brutal friends of Exquisite?

"What kind of split do you think's fair then?" I growled.

"Oh, I dunno, I always left that kind of crap to my agents," he said disparagingly, neatly making me feel like the one who was low enough to bicker over percentages. "Get us another pint and a whisky."

I realise now, looking back, that he was not playing a clever psychological game—I had the money and he had the alcoholic's simple logic—if he didn't get another drink he would *die*. Fortunately I was unable to prevent my resentment from boiling over, accidentally making the right negotiating move.

"It's your bloody round," I snapped.

"I haven't got any money," he retorted, accusingly, as if I were both stupid and mean.

"That's your own fucking fault, isn't it?" I said, shoving out the hand holding the fivers.

"But you want fifty per cent! Look, just lend me a fiver till we discuss it properly, eh?"

"I lent you a fiver the other day to pay your fine! You think I'm Andrew bloody Carnegie?"

Other people were coming into the bogus snuggery and from their faces I realised we both looked exactly like the kind of shabby Scotch bums who always mean trouble.

I snorted contemptuously to cover my embarrassment and shoved the sheaf of notes into my jacket pocket.

"All right, give me a pen and I'll sign your wee bits of paper."

"Aye—but you're not going to take the fifty and then disappear into the night."

"If I sign my name that's my word and I've never broken my

word to a living soul," he said, speaking quickly, almost desperately, hand stretched out for a pen. By Christ, he had a knack of making me feel ashamed of myself. As soon as I realized he had caved in I became uneasy with guilt, seeing myself as a big, hard bully, no better than McMenemy the Enemy.

We each signed our copies. I gave him the first carbon and kept the top copy and the bottom carbon. He folded his unevenly and rammed it carelessly into his hip pocket and grabbed the fivers.

I felt as if I was robbing him.

"You don't want another horrible tomato juice, do you?" he sneered over his shoulder.

Just to restore the illusion of friendship I said I would have a pint of lager. I heard him making a joke with the landlord. This man, who had been suspicious of me, immediately started treating Shand like an old pal. I had to get up and go across to the bar, where Shand made me feel I was intruding on their jolly intimacy. Before I had finished my lager he managed to tell the landlord he was Ramsay Shand the well-known playwright, and although the landlord had obviously never heard of him he was definitely impressed. One thing about Shand, once he had fifty pounds in his bin he didn't squabble over whose turn it was to set them up. I supposed you could call it generosity. He was The King and money was just stuff to throw down at us petty nobodies.

I ached more bitterly then for some fame of my own than at any other time in my life.

I had one more pint of lager and said I would have to see my partner to make some arrangements, wondering whether I could get Shand in and out of The Rookery without being dragged through the very pubs I had to steer clear of.

But Shand would hardly listen; a wider circle of customers was now laughing at his merry tales. He didn't want to leave and said, dismissively, that I could do my bits of business while he stayed there and enjoyed himself. I managed to get the landlord to one side and tell him that Shand was, indeed, the famous playwright and that he had been seriously ill and that I would be much obliged if he could keep an eye on him until I got back.

The landlord seemed to think I was unjustly smearing the reputation of his new friend.

I got a taxi to Nailed Down Chambers. Two pints of cold lager in my guts made me feel that the whole city was one big shiver. I told the driver to stop on the corner and approached the Chambers cautiously, looking for any sign of danger. I passed the entrance once and then slipped inside and went quietly up the stairs, passing three workmen repairing the jemmied lock and splintered door of Dunbar St John's office.

My Hush Puppies made no sound as I arrived at our door. I listened for a moment but heard no voices. Instead of using my key I knocked, ready to say to any police inside that I was looking for a different office.

Neville opened the door.

"You look terrible," were his first words. He sounded hostile. He went back to sit at my desk.

"You look utterly desirable, of course," I snapped back, closing the door.

He didn't smile.

"I've been doing some sums and it doesn't look as though the agency owes you anything like five hundred quid," he said, "I'd say a hundred and fifty top whack."

I wished we could smile and put everything back the way it had been but even as I was thinking of telling him about Shand—perhaps cutting him in to do the newspaper negotiations and turning the project into a jolly Surefire Earner—I found myself looking at him with Shand's eyes. The world was full of chisellers with fake smiles on their greedy faces.

"Got it on you?"

"Here you are." He licked his thumb and counted fifteen brown tenners. I decided I would take them over to The

Hellhole and get Manager Dave to change them into fives and singles. A ten-pound note was too conspicuous to produce in the kind of dumps I'd be forced to use until I'd finished with Shand. Only the other day I'd heard a barman making a fuss about changing a tenner—where the hell was that? I'd been in so many pubs over the last few days they were all jumbled together in my mind.

Everything had been simple, before, when Neville and I were mates.

"Got a bit of news for you," he said. "I've left my wife."

"Get away," I said, walking over to the window and looking down into the shabby canyon.

"Met Miss Right, didn't I?" he said, behind my back.

"El Spotto?" I said, with a sneer.

"Do me a favour! No, actually, Angela Browne and I have decided we were meant for each other. I've moved into her gaff, as it happens. She thinks it's love."

"Angela? You're joking!"

"Why, you think she's too good for me?"

"No, but—"

"Fancied her yourself, did you? Thought you probably did. Surprised you didn't try your luck. It was there for the asking. She says she rather fancied you, originally, I can't imagine why. Oh, by the way, you got any idea why the cops were ringing to ask where Pilbeam is?"

Jesus!

"What did they say?"

"Just wanted to know where he was and how they could get in touch with him. I told them he's in Blackburn today."

"Probably about his breathalyser."

"Oh yeah, that night you went with him to the pools thing. What happened that night with you two anyway?"

"I was too drunk to remember much. I spoke to Pilbeam the morning after, he didn't have a clue where we'd been either. I know we met Chick Bhalla, I still can't believe he's dead."

"I never thought he was anything else. Is there life before death, eh?"

A grey pigeon landed on the little balcony, cocked its head, saw my face, blinked and flew off again.

"What the hell's going on with you anyway?" Neville asked. "You suddenly get the needle about something?"

I shrugged.

"Maybe I got neurotic sitting here for three days trying to write that pornography crap while you were doing big deals."

"You bloody Scots! Why the hell can't you just get on with life and stop torturing yourselves with all that old moody? Listen, I was only fantasising about owning that bloody cesspit. I heard a whisper that Kilgallon was having to sell because his polluted blood can't move through his clogged-up pipes. A few drinks in me and it seemed like a good idea. You imagine the state of me owning my own bar? Jesus wept. Tell me, you think this paranoia of yours is temporary?"

On the ledge of a dummy window half way down the building opposite, five motionless pigeons were huddled together on a platform of their own white-caked shit, their necks sunk into their shoulders. Comfort is only comparative, I thought, pointlessly.

"Angela is the best thing that ever happened to me," Neville said, coming to the window and standing at my shoulder. "I'd never have found the energy to leave that other cow—she was making me doubt my own existence. Never marry for money, old son, the wages are very poor. But now—let's face it, you and I have both been doing a good imitation of drunken wasters— these joke schemes! The pen-pal bureau! Angela's right—why waste time on jokes when the same energy can get you in the real money? Look at all these brainless cunts who manage to screw fantastic money out of this show biz crap—don't you think we could do better than them?"

"Like Baxter, maybe?"

"We know the truth but just think—out there millions of

suckers would consider that Baxter is a success. By average reckoning he *is* a success."

"I stayed the night with him. I'd rather be a roadsweeper."

"Me, too, if I didn't think I could leave Baxter far behind. What do you say—give it a try, eh, new leaf and all that?"

"Remember we were going to write a musical about the Duke of Wellington?"

"Happy days."

"Why shouldn't we have? It would have been worth at least a try."

"You think we ever showed the slightest sign of talent? Did we hell. Come on, let's get down The Leafless and start planning moves—what are you doing over Christmas, eh? Why don't you and Kate and Angela and me get together—Angela's got a knockout pad in Marylebone High Street, Chinese restaurant downstairs, good little pub on the corner—we can get in a few bottles and smoke some hash and leap about!"

"No, I don't fancy it."

"Why the hell not?"

"How can you say we didn't have any sign of talent? We never bloody tried."

"We didn't have to. Us? We're not the type. A couple of uncomplicated ravers, that's us, old son, goodtime Charlies."

"You don't really *want* to be a businessman, do you?"

"Why not, if that's the way it's got to be?"

"So you make a pile. So what? You end up like Baxter, eating his heart out because he's jealous of Chick Bhalla?"

Neville turned away from the window and sat on the swivel chair, banging open a drawer.

"The creative artist kick now, is it? Oh well, give us a shout when you've won the Nobel Prize for *A Bed Of Men.*"

The old Neville would have been joking. When I looked there was no humour in his eyes.

"I threw that crap away," I said. "If you want to fix up deals for pornography you try writing it yourself."

"Beyond your capabilities, was it?"

"At least I wasn't scared to try."

"What—me? Scared to write that crap? Who the hell would want to?"

"Oh—but it was all right to shove it onto me, was it?"

"I thought it would give you a thrill. At least get this creative rubbish out of your system."

"Why the hell do you take it for granted I don't have any creative talent? I mean, what the fuck gives you the bloody right to dismiss any chance I might have of—"

"Because I know you, that's why."

"You don't know the first bloody thing about me!"

"Hidden talents? Okay—how's about me fixing you up with something more appropriate to your artistic soul than porn—I know—jokes for Christmas crackers!"

I shrugged and walked to the door. Our eyes did not meet again and I left the office without mentioning the rest of the money.

It wasn't until I was buying a tube ticket for Clapham Common, carrying a small Japanese tape-recorder and six forty-five minute tapes in a parcel, that I remembered intending to change Neville's ten pounds. I could have gone back to The Hellhole but I didn't want to leave Shand on his own in the Clapham pub any longer than I could help. I would hide this money in one of Kate's books and tell Shand nothing about it.

It was while hurrying down the big escalator that I remembered where I'd seen a man changing a brown tenner for a round of drinks, in The Rats' Castle, that first lunchtime I'd gone looking for Shand. Jackie Brown put down a tenner and wee Bobbie the barman said, "Not another o' they big yins for Goad's sake."

Not *another*?

The knife!

Why else would Jackie Brown have taken the trouble to knock the knife out of McMenemy's hand and kick it along the gutter and then poke at it with his walking-stick until it slid between the bars of the drain?

The tube rattled from station to station and I gradually realised I knew the whole story of The Spoofer's murder.

My first instinct was to find a phone and ring the Yard and put an anonymous finger on McMenemy but the more I thought about it the more I saw that the only safe thing for me to do was disappear. There were a lot of black faces on the Northern Line and they only reminded me of the two whores I'd robbed and by the time the train reached Clapham Common I had a terrible urge to run.

Wild was arrested exactly three months after Jack
Sheppard was hanged. He was taken to Newgate. The
indictment was lengthy; he was a confederate of thieves;
he divided London into areas and appointed gangs to
run each area; he used illegally returned deportees,
who could not give evidence against him, and many of
whom he had hanged to maintain his reputation as
Thief-Catcher General; he had been a fence and joined
in robberies; he had warehouses for storing stolen goods
and a ship for exporting them to Belgium; he employed
artists in precious metals to alter stolen jewellery; he
only returned stolen property if the owner gave him
half its value; and he sold human blood, by giving false
evidence against people who might give evidence against
him, or whom he simply didn't like, or for the
government reward.

20

Shand had not only out-stayed his welcome but rubbed their
noses in it. He was still trying to make them laugh but they
couldn't understand his slurred monologues. Beer and dribble
trickled from the corners of his mouth. To make them listen he
was grabbing at their arms and lapels and as I came through the
door the landlord was preventing a couple of young blokes in
sharp suits from dragging him outside as retribution for spilling
beer down a pair of Cecil Gee strides.

I put a pound on the counter to buy them a drink and told the
landlord. I would take Shand home. Shand tried to push me
away. Luckily there was no strength in his heavy but slack body.

The parcel with the tape-recorder under my left arm, I got my
fingers round his bicep and coaxed him to the door, followed by
mutterings and threatening looks from the gang he had been so
recently entertaining. "I don't want to see him in here again
thank you very much," the landlord shouted as I forced the door
open with my shoulder.

We were lucky not to meet any police on our way across the Common. Shand was raving, trying to hit me, desperate to get back to the pub, enraged to tears at having lost his audience. I got him back to Katie's flat only by giving him a yarn about the whisky we had up there. Even then he tried to hit me as I closed the front door. With only one hand free I had no alternative but to shoulder him heavily in the chest, sending him back against the wall and then to a sitting position. He started to cry, rubbing his eyes with his fists like a little boy.

That revolted me so much it required some self-restraint not to kick him. Instead I forced him up the stairs, sometimes telling him we were going to have a party, several times threatening him with a punch on the face. Inside Katie's room I pushed him down on the single mattress on the floor and put the tape-recorder on the highest book shelf, resting on her collection of Tolkiens.

What the hell was I going to do now?

If I left him to fetch a bottle of whisky he would only try to slip out again. If I didn't go for whisky I was going to have to hold him down physically, at least till Katie came back from the office. He didn't look ready to pass out.

It took at least ten minutes to get it into my head that I was dealing with a *thing*, and that I needn't feel embarrassed about tough handling him.

"I'm going to get a bottle of whisky," I told him, three times, speaking as if to a deaf foreigner, "you wait here, right? Give me your shoes and your trousers, I'll get them cleaned for you. Okay?"

Embarrassed? Even writing this today makes me sweat. To get his trousers off I had to crouch over him, one knee pinning down his chest, hands working in disgusting intimacy with his dirty clothing. His legs were white and thin and completely hairless.

I left his shoes under the bath in the lavatory on the first-floor landing and went to find another pub, Shand's trousers bundled under my arm, running most of the way. When I got back to Lindehan Crescent he had done nothing worse than piss in his revolting underpants. I would have abandoned my scheme and him there and then but for Katie.

I gave him whisky in a cup. He drank it in one gulp. I gave him another. He started to drink it and then stopped to make some retching noises, fortunately producing nothing. Then he took a deep breath and, to my amazement, asked me quite lucidly if I could put some water in the cup.

Then he sat in the armchair and blinked a lot and sipped the whisky and gradually sighed his way back to comparative normality. I could only-stare at him in disbelief and horror. He asked me for a cigarette.

"Aye," he said, allowing me to light it with a match and then blowing smoke straight in my face, "I occasionally get these wee giddy turns."

I phoned Katie at the office and asked if she wouldn't mind buying some gents' underwear and some shaving gear. With Shand now watching me calmly I could hardly tell her what had happened but I said I would start finding a place where Shand could stay.

"Stay there for all the difference it makes to me," she said, "I'm going home tonight anyway for Christmas."

"You didn't tell me you were going away," I said, complainingly, having been counting on her to cheer things up a bit.

"Should I have asked your permission?"

"So I'll have Christmas on my own? Charming."

"Not on your own, you have your man of letters to keep you company, I'm sure you'll have a spiffing time together."

"Jesus Christ."

She came and brought him two pairs of underpants and vests and a safety razor and five Wilkinson Sword Edge blades and was excessively pleasant to him and fairly cool to me, and packed her little square suitcase and said she would be back in two or three days, depending how she enjoyed Christmas with Mummy and Daddy in their retirement home in Weymouth, and told me, when I carried her case down to the front door, purely to have a word in private, that she wasn't worried about what damage Shand might do to her flat.

"You'll make some woman a fine house-proud husband," she said. "Don't be so neurotic. The whole building's a ruin, for Christ's sake. Just try not to let him set my books and things on fire. Here's a key."

Then she went away, taking most of the warmth with her. I went back up the bare, unswept stairs.

Christmas alone with Ramsay Shand?

Although Shand insisted that being the son of a Dundee haberdasher (who died leaving eight hundred pounds) made him middle-class, he matched in every boring detail the cliché tradition of the self-educated, working-class artist whose spontaneity makes him too much money too soon. His talent was never given time to develop and in consequence he was never very sure if he had any *real* talent.

Not that he was a victim, to be pitied.

In this next few days I learned a lot about him, both from the increasingly sporadic sessions when he talked for the tape-recorder's—and therefore posterity's—benefit, and from his megalomaniacal outpourings while drunk.

Shand was a world-class narcissist. It wasn't the call of Art that had drawn him at the age of nineteen, when he first started writing Doric playlets for local productions by Edinburgh culture fiends.

It was Fame he wanted, right from the start. If he could have got it walking across the Tay Bridge on his hands, naked, in a hailstorm, he would've hired his own floodlights. (It is not necessarily disparagement to say he had only ever shown proof of a small, primitive talent; only geniuses don't require an apprenticeship.)

One of his plays was put on by a fringe company at the Edinburgh Festival and was there seen by the inevitable London producer on the look-out for raw material that might start a new trend.

Two of his other plays were gutted and worked in to form the only kind of Scottish offering acceptable to London's cultural minority—the spirit of the Dundee poet MacGonagall, incompetent clownishness taken to a stage of imbecility where Hampstead Man will proclaim delightedly, "It is *so* grotesquely bad it becomes an Art Form."

Being otherwise sensitive and intelligent Shand knew *why* they were putting on his plays (the hunger for Fame was greater, than his sense of dignity) and he originally took up the clownish drunkard's pose as a satire on the situation. The media took him up after the kind of girlish 'brawl' you expect in pubs next door to theatres and the box-office boomed. Then a famous Hollywood film director saw a way of transforming Shand's domestic Scottish farce into a domestic Deep South farce, white trash hill-billies instead of Aberdeenshire loons and queans.

The big money poured in. From Finland to Japan they found ways of translating Shand's rural Scottish houghmagandie into local peasant terms.

All the time Shand told himself he was made of granite and would still be around at ninety writing *real* drama that would rotate the moldering bones of Ibsen and O'Neill (he saved comparisons with Shakespeare for rare periods of simulated self-mockery).

Then a simple thing happened. One morning he woke up and found that his body chemistry had changed. He had become an alcoholic overnight, none of your soul's black night or artist's crucifixion about it—booze had taken charge.

While the money lasted—and it went on for ten years or more, dribbling in from Swedish radio rights, German TV productions, Canadian stage productions, plus ancillary earnings from personal appearances and TV interviews and the like—he had been kept going by illusions; the next expensive cure would do the trick, the next fame-stimulated woman would be the love of his life, the next stab at writing would produce another effortless winner—most illusory of all, that people still *talked* about him.

I had met him, it seemed, just when the money and the illusions had finally run out.

He sneered at me when he acknowledged me at all but my presence gave him back the illusion of fame and importance. Every time he spoke to me it was like a slap in the face but the moment I looked like abandoning him, even for ten minutes, he threatened to kill himself.

If it had been only the money I would have run away from him before darkness fell that night on Clapham Common.

I stayed, I told myself, because I couldn't do the dirty on Kate. I was also scared he might cut his throat and leave me behind to be publicly branded and exposed—as what I wasn't sure.

The truth was—the only place I could run to was The Rookery and I was sick with fear at the thought of bumping into McMenemy again and of perhaps letting slip, in drink, that I knew he'd murdered The Spoofer. As long as Shand and I were talking I was okay but with every silence my head filled with screaming visions of knives and boots and blood and police cells and broken bodies.

I hated and loathed Shand but it seemed ordained that I was to be dragged into his nightmare.

The night before his execution Jonathan Wild tried the easy way out by swallowing laudanum. The dose wasn't enough. By morning he was able to walk and they took him in the Tyburn cart to the gallows. For some reason the hangman kept delaying the great moment when the crowd would see the turning-off of the hated master criminal and thief-catcher. They began to roar angrily. The hangman put the rope round Wild's neck and shoved him off into eternity. Myth has it that, as he took the last drop, Wild held out his hand, waving a corkscrew he had just picked from the pocket of the unctuous parson who had administered the last blessing. Wild was forty-four.

21

For the next two days we slept in the same room and urinated in the same sink and drank from the same bottles until I could hardly distinguish his voice from mine. Three or four times, when seemingly too drunk to move, he got off the mattress on the floor, in the dark, and climbed into bed, trying to cuddle against me. Each time I hit him off brutally and then lay there paralysed with fear that next time he would be too strong for me. In the mornings he made no reference to these advances; perhaps he was only wanting warmth. On the morning of Christmas Eve I managed to get him to talk into the tape-recorder for an hour and a half; he finished the whisky but sounded like a reasoning human being. Again and again he came back to the obsession he had with the soul of Scotland, which he said lay dormant through the centuries, manifesting itself only in certain individuals and then so rarely that the people did not recognise it, or subconsciously recognised it and felt so threatened by its danger to their mindless complacencies that they would try to destroy it; had they not driven Burns to despair because he represented Life and Art and a golden past when men lived in harmony?

"I have walked the same fields and the same streets that Burns walked and I could feel him walking beside me," he said. He had delirious ideas that he and William Dunbar and Burns and Lewis Grassic Gibbon—and maybe even MacGonagall, although in him the spiritual genes had been mutated by the radioactive poison—and maybe MacDiarmid and others I had never heard of, that all of them were lineal descendants sharing the same genes of Art.

"William Toms, the Aberdeen weaver poet?" he yelled, shrilly, when I revealed my total ignorance of what he called the true Scottish culture, "what a line he wrote—*And grudge the very muck to hap ye.*"

The very look of him was embarrassing to me, with my tenement-Hollywood images of how a grown man should look and act, and my ignorance of most of what he talked about—I had not even read Lewis Grassic Gibbon, although the name was vaguely familiar— meant that I had continually to find new ways of covering up.

To get the necessary facts about the kind of anecdotes I knew would appeal to a newspaper—like the time he flew to New York in his pyjamas—I went over and over the same ground, until I sounded like a moron to myself. He had not, of course, flown to New York drunk in his pyjamas—the hotel switchboard had called him late and he'd merely pulled his clothes on *over* his pyjamas. It was all lies and exaggerations, he kept saying, admitting that his own compulsive desire to impress people had made him invent the untrue or exaggerated incidents.

How about the time he had been arrested in London and had asked the magistrate for time to pay the two-pound fine because all he had in his possession was one pound and a cheque for fifty thousand pounds? "Och aye, that's another yarn—I had five pounds but I wanted that for taxis and whatnot."

But he was carrying a cheque he'd just received for American royalties? "That was a lot of balls as well, I had a letter from the New York impresario saying I had about fifty thousand dollars due to me and how did I want it paid? Just wee stories all these things—just crap." But that was the crap we needed for ten thousand pounds, I said, and we went at it again. He became bored and twitchy. I said I needed something to eat. Kate had left a few odds and ends in her kitchen cupboard and I opened a tin of German frankfurters but Shand didn't even look at them so I ate them all with the last few slices of bread and drank two cups of water. What was success like, I asked, what did it actually feel like when it first hit you?

"At first it was fantastic—like a magic wand had opened up a treasure cave in a big rock. The money started coming in by the bucketload—like a fucking Niagara of money. If only my rotten fucking father had been alive to see it—that would've shown the bastard." Was he a big thing in your life? "Him? That brutal bastard, I can see him now—ach well, that's all in the past, I'm needing a drink—I want to get out of this dump."

He seemed normal enough so I said I would have a shave and that made him bad-tempered, the idea of hanging about, so I didn't bother to shave and we went out and when he said he hated the local pubs I suddenly shook his arm and said, "The hell with it, I'm not scared of the bastards," and we took a taxi up to The Rookery. First off he went to The Hempen Widow, a pub I'd never used before. After a few drinks it bored me. Shand was being charming and I decided it would be perfectly safe to risk The Leafless, hoping I would meet all the familiar faces and cheer myself up by making a joke of it all. I don't know how much I'd been drinking by then but I was full of resentment at my own cowardice and walked along Bishop Henry Street with a terrible aggression on my face, almost hoping to meet McMenemy and ram my forehead into his nose before he knew what had hit him.

There was nobody I knew in The Leafless, Christmas Eve being a Friday and all offices having closed for a long weekend. What was even worse was that Mr and Mrs Wallis did not treat me with the friendliness I expected, considering that my drinking had probably paid for their last Mediterranean cruise. Being neurotically aware of every new face that came through the door—watching both for friends and detectives—I began to feel persecuted and hunted and shunned simultaneously. It was as though they only remembered me vaguely, and that possibly for causing bother. I realised that they had never liked me. Shand directed his flow of jokes and anecdotes at some stall-holders from Pollett Street market, jolly enough men while all was sweetness and light but rapidly hardening their faces when his diction began to slur and his manner became more aggressive.

He had an annoying compulsion to touch people, putting his hands on shoulders, pulling sleeves if their eyes wandered, nudging with his shoulder to encourage their laughter. I did not blame the market men for edging away from us, especially when, having got their attention with genuinely witty chat, he started into long, boring reminiscences. The beard had fooled me into taking his early morning personality as the dominant one— tough, manly, totally in control. I rapidly learned that with an alcoholic booze is dictator. The outer shell is delusory; all inside is rotten.

I intended to stay sober but that only left me feeling embarrassed to be with him so I switched from pints of lager to large brandies, solely to hurry myself into the next stage, where I would not care if he irritated people or not. Eventually, when I was buying a round, Mr Wallis jerked his head for me to lean over the bar and said, "I hope that friend of yours won't make a bloody nuisance of himself."

The pompous way he said it hit me like a slap in the face and before I thought about it I snapped back at him, "Oh yeah? You like a younger type of Scotsman, don't you? Like that wee lad who accommodated you the other day." He knew immediately that I was referring to the Glasgow boy Jackie Brown had sent round from The Rats' Castle. His unhealthy face went red. I took Shand's arm and said we'd better places to go. As we reached the door I heard Wallis shouting something. I gave him a two-fingered salute, shouted Balls to You! and got Shand out on the pavement. We went to The Hum Drum.

It was packed to the door by what appeared to me a crowd of uniformly-dressed, ugly-faced men, none of whom I recognised. The sheer weight of bodies pressed Shand into temporary anonymity and I pushed towards the bar, where Paddy the red-haired Irish barman runt gave me a cheery welcome. I despised myself for having reached a stage where I was desperate to get a smile from a nobody like him—I mean, I found myself being ingratiating, at the top of my voice! "Where is everybody?" I had to shout above the massed voices. "Didn't ye hear—Jim's sold the place—" he leaned forward, eyes flicking left and right to make sure the men crowded along the bar were not listening— "we're gettin' a new element—" he tapped the side of his nose and winked—"if ye know what I mean."

I realised what he meant as I struggled back to Shand with the glasses. The villains had moved in! I saw the faces of ticket touts I'd seen at every big football match in London, and then I saw the faces of a three-card team from Oxford Street, standing a yard away, the big one with the bald head and the hooked nose still with his arm on the shoulders of Chawrlie.

How did I know his name was Chawrlie?

I could see myself walking behind them, listening to a conversation about 'the metal game'. When was that? Fortunately Shand didn't like the crush and we got out of the poisonous atmosphere that assembled villains generate. Shand wanted to go to The Rats' Castle, where he said he knew a decent bunch of Scots lads!

"Fucking murderers," I said.

"I know your trouble—seen too many pictures as a boy," he sneered. "Fantasies for the common herd. An artist has to learn to see things the way they really are, not the way—"

"You patronising bastard, they *are* bloody murderers," I snapped. "Come on and I'll prove it to you. Artists? Lot of self-important wankers!"

Fortunately I lost my nerve at the door of The Rats' Castle and retreated across the street, standing in a doorway a few yards farther down, ready to bolt for it if McMenemy appeared. Shand was back out in two minutes. They had refused to serve him!

"Banned from The Rats' Castle?" I jeered at the top of my voice. "Didn't you tell them you were an important artist?"

He seemed to like me better when I was abusive—it put distance between us and allowed him to act a role rather than be embarrassed by our bogus friendship—and said we would visit some friends of his who were keeping his typewriter and stuff. We bought two bottles of whisky in a cut-price wine shop and drifted about till we got a taxi. He didn't remember the address but it was somewhere north of Regent's Park so the driver took us up to the park and round the outer circle and eventually, after running up one pound ninety on the meter, we stopped outside a terraced house which he recognised and stood on the steps, me carrying the brown paper bag with the two bottles, until he found the right buzzer.

Our mutual sneers and insults made this the easiest time we had spent together and I even began to think he liked me—or at least had started to acknowledge me.

Morag was the woman's name, I fancied her at first glance, tall with frizzy fair hair and red, country girl's cheeks that brought back vague memories of meeting an aunt like that in a farmhouse with hens and dogs, when I was very young. Morag was about forty. She didn't like the look of me from the start and took care, it seemed to me, to mention a lot of their mutual friends, thereby excluding me from the conversation. Her flat was full of middle-class Scots of the quasi-English Edinburgh disposition and I reacted with an abrasive display of Glasgow aggression. I'd never met that kind of Scot much—they were playing Scarlatti on the record-player while telling significant but side-splitting stories about somebody called Goodsir Smith, a poet, it seemed, who farted in high society and said to the Lady Provost, "These reports are false", and once was so bleary and in need of a drink he pushed into the dark brown doors of an Edinburgh pub, rested his forehead on the counter and said, "Give me a pint and a glass for God's sake", whereupon the barman said, "This is the Royal Bank of Scotland, sir."

For fifteen minutes or so these people fawned round Shand but he was deteriorating rapidly. This Morag woman started asking pointed questions, suggesting I was some kind of Glasgow tearaway sponging off Ramsay and wanting to know where Ramsay was staying. He got me to give her Kate's telephone number, which I did with broken glass in my voice. She told Ramsay not to rush into any newspaper deals that might insult his reputation. I took severe offence at this and said it was friends like them, snotty-nosed Edinburgh culture-hawks and parasites, who had seduced him into drinking in the first place, to give their horrible bourgeois lives vicarious drama. Some bank manager type of pan-loaf bastard stuck his nose in and I snarled, "If you're real fucking Scots why aren't you playing Jimmy Shand records, you peely-wally nyaff?" I would have gone then on my own and glad to get shot of Shand but he was already annoying a group of snooty toffee-noses so I went back across the room with the french windows and took his arm and said these people were laughing at him. I felt protective towards him—or maybe possessive—at the time I simply didn't want to leave him at the mercy of these patronising toffs. He wanted to stay but some middle-aged businessman in a waistcoat just happened to say, sarcastically, "The rest of us, of course, have to behave like grown-ups", at that very moment.

Shand took this rightly as a jeer and was near to hitting this man, so I met no resistance in coaxing him out of that flat, not before he'd demanded his typewriter and suitcase, which the frosty-faced Morag woman fetched from another room. We had to walk half way round the outer circle before we got a taxi. I told the driver to take us to Lindehan Crescent.

We were back there about four o'clock on the afternoon of Christmas Eve, with nowhere else to go.

He sat in the armchair and I sat on the bed and we started on the first bottle of Teacher's, out of cups. Shand seemed lucid to me—in fact he insisted on getting the tape-recorder working to tell me vitally important things.

"I want this to be told—success is a mirage!" He nodded emphatically, as if this were enough. I was getting confused over the right button to press. He went on. "You get one good moment, the very first time the news comes. It's a mirage. Success! The day after you get the news you start worrying. Worry! They all hate you, everybody hates you. Friends? You don't have friends any more. When I was writing they used to sneer—aye, all of them, sneer. Why don't you get a proper job? Who told you an ordinary fucker like you could be a writer? The day after you make it they're saying, sneering, See him? I knew him when he was an ordinary fucking labourer, big-headed bastard! It's the loneliness. They all hate you. The good ones — your real friends — they won't come near you because they think you'll think they're after your money. The ones that do hang about you they're the parasites. I tried to play it the right way but they wouldn't let me.

Success! It's a mirage. They all hate you.

They don't want the truth, they want fairy-tales. You think you're writing for the commonality of people? The working class? When do they go to the fucking theatre?

That's your audience, snobs! Make sure you get all this down, I want them to hear the truth!"

I tried to get him back to details about his exploits but every time I opened my mouth I sounded cheap, like a three-card trickster. He fell back and went to sleep and the next time I remember us talking it was dark and he was insisting that he had to get out among noise and people and we saw a taxi and next thing we were back in The Rookery and trying to find friends in all the places I knew and meeting nothing but hostile faces and angry voices and strangers and then finding ourselves in the street, I don't even remember which street it was, the wind was whipping up the rubbish and papers jigged crazily above our heads and eddied in whirlpools until it was like a night-time snowstorm, just the two of us aching to find a place where they'd let us into the warm, this white blizzard of dry rubbish making me think we were the little figures in a glass paperweight, just little figures, and then there was a blessed miracle and a taxi stopped for us, although all the others had raced past after one look at us, and we got back to Lindehan Crescent and switched on the fire and let it heat us up, both so drunk we didn't notice it was burning our trousers till the smoke almost blinded us, and I smothered the smoulders with a blanket and started to tell him about the murder, wanting him to be the big brother who would tell me what to do, but he wouldn't listen, he started crying about his father dying before he knew his son was not a waster but a big success. I was sick in the sink and had to drink more cups of whisky to make myself feel better. Next time I woke up it was light again and I realised we were into Christmas Day.

I was so ill I could hardly move. He walked about the flat for a while saying things I couldn't understand. The electric fire didn't seem to have enough power to heat the room. He said he wanted to go out and find a good pub but I said I would die if I had another drink. His face was shadowed on one side and gradually my eyes cleared enough to see that his cheek and left eye were covered by a big red bruise. The tail of his white shirt was out over his trousers. The shirt was stained brown all down the front, it could have been wine or blood for all I knew. He laughed, standing over the bed, saying I wasn't much of a man if I couldn't take a few drinks without disintegrating. I said I would feel better if I had a wash and a shave. I got off the bed and black waves flooded my eyes. I made it to the kitchen and started to drink the tap dry. The cold water made me throw up again. He laughed a lot and gave me a glass of whisky and water. I took a deep breath and forced myself to swallow, more or less to prove I was as manly as him. I started to shave but for some reason I couldn't get hot water out of the geyser and the razor blade seemed to be dragging the skin off my jaw so I gave up the idea of shaving. I had been sleeping in my clothes and my skin felt cold and sweaty at the same time. I couldn't stop shuddering and my jaw shook uncontrollably. He sat in the armchair with a glass of neat whisky and jeered at me as I tried to go through the motions of dressing. I began to hate him and that, strangely enough, made me feel slightly better. I had a small whisky, gulping it down and holding on until it settled in my stomach. He opened the second bottle of Teacher's and poured himself a cupful. The room was freezing cold. I said I was going to get pneumonia. He said I was a bloody weakling and threw me his black leather jacket, saying he didn't need it. We went out and walked along strange streets, in a direction I was too ill to recognise, until we found a working-class pub where our dirty appearance was not even noticed. From the vestiges of my feeling of responsibility towards him I asked him when he had last eaten and he said beer was the only food he needed, and I realised the very sight of solid food would shatter me. We had a few pints of draught Guinness. He didn't remember how he'd bruised his face. He even managed to make some men and women laugh. My jaw shivered whenever my lips sank into the cold stout but gradually I found myself able to straighten my shoulders and look less like a corpse.

Shand said the pubs would be closed for the rest of the day, it being Christmas. We had to buy enough *to see us through*, he said, making it sound like a party. We went back to Lindehan Crescent—having to ask the way several times—carrying two more bottles of whisky and four big cans of beer, plus packets of cigarettes. The idea that we were spending Christmas Day in that room, in that deserted building, so horrified me I spent half an hour on the phone trying to get directory to give me the phone number of Angela Browne in Marylebone High Street. I had some idea of getting a taxi over there and letting Neville and Angela know I was so delighted to see them I would kiss their cheeks.

Directory enquiries could not find a number for Angela Browne and I realised it must still be under her married name, for she had told Neville she had ejected her husband for being violent. I put down the phone and closed my eyes for a few moments, willing myself to take a grip. I even got the tape-recorder going and we started to talk into it, drinking beer and whisky and smoking until the room was fuggy from ceiling to knee-height. Shand wanted to talk about his childhood, saying he intended to get down to work to write a play about that lost era. The big red bruise down the side of his face made him look like a clown who still had the rest of his make-up to put on. It became dark outside. My stomach was empty but whatever food there was left in the kitchen cupboard I knew I couldn't face it so I went on drinking neat whisky and beer alternately from the same cup. Shand actually started jumping about, acting scenes from his boyhood, putting on different accents. I remember telling him he was a natural performer and he said, ignoring the sneer, yes, he would've been a lot more fulfilled as an artist if he'd only had the guts to go out there on the stage because you only pretended to despise actors because they had been Out There in the light, where the real and only magic was.

Next thing he sat down heavily and stared into the past and started to cry and said he had to tell me what had ruined his life, right from the start, he had been terrified of his father and was still scared to death of him, although his father had been in. the ground for quarter of a century, because his father used to belt him with a razor-strop and beat him with a stick and how his whole life had been pointless because the success could only have meant something if it had proved to his father that he was not a useless person.

"Would you tell me one thing?" I asked, going over to his chair and squatting down. Half-drunk as we both were I was still hesitant about what I was going to reveal about myself. Big tear blotches stained his cheeks, making him look like some monstrous boy. "What does it actually *feel* like—to be successful?

I mean, to be recognised by people—and asked for your autograph? Is it really—well, *fantastic?*"

"It's a fucking bore."

"No, tell me the truth, please." I put my hand on his shoulder. "Isn't it really the greatest thing anybody could imagine? I've been with well-known people and it's always been as though I'm in black and white and they're in colour—or they're in some kind of private sunshine—maybe it's some kind of light inside them—"

He blinked as he looked at me. His eyes were filmed and his head drooped forward.

"It's always in the past," he said, nodding in corroboration, "or in the future. You look forward to it, dream of it and it never seems to be coming. Then one day you realise you've been through it. That *was* it, last year, when you felt just as hellish as you ever did before." He put his hand on my arm and pressed it, as if holding on to a rescuer. "It was always last year. Or next year. You never recognise it while it's happening. It's all a fucking trick—and I know better than anybody. A fucking trick."

His sagging head nodded. "If only you could realise it was here and now when it's actually happening—but you never do. Not until the day you wake up and realise it's all over. You recognise it then." A new tear ran down his damp cheek, changing the outline of a stain. His hand was moving on my arm in little stroking motions.

"It's all over and you never got a chance to enjoy it."

"Yeah but when somebody, like a good-looking woman, asks for your autograph and says—"

"It's all a fucking cheat!"

His head dropped forward and his forehead pressed down on my arm. Suddenly I realised he was trying to put both his arms round me. I shot to my feet and was near to kicking him on the legs. I started walking about, kicking chairs and shouting at him, big-headed, self-loving bastard, always assuming that scribbling a couple of fucking plays made his problems more diabolical than anybody else's and screaming at him that my father had walked out on my mother when I was only eight and that I'd never been able to trust anybody ever since because of my father deserting me when I was a defenceless wee boy and leaving me in the clutches of that bitch my mother and how the more I heard about Ramsay fucking Shand the more I could see he'd been a pampered little middle-class shit while I was being dragged up in that stinking Shettleston tenement and all he did was romanticise a soft bloody life while all us ordinary bastards were struggling to stay alive let alone whine about how nasty our fathers were and why didn't he wake up to himself and stop all this persecuted rubbish and do some work like a grown man, if he was a grown man, which I said he wasn't, not compared to the ordinary Scottish man who had to show *guts* just to get through his ordinary life instead of yelping about how cruel it was to earn a quarter of a million bloody pounds.

"I know," he said, waving me aside with a haughty hand, "it's being an artist, you see, you get it worse because you get frozen in the past. My father's still alive, you know, in my head. He beats me every day of my life."

"You self-absorbed bastard!" I shouted. "Don't you ever listen to a single word? You make me sick to even look at you!"

"Jealousy, is it?" he said, slyly.

I would have gone through the roof if I'd been able to stand up.

"Jealous? Of you?" I screamed. "You pathetic, drunken bum. If I couldn't write better fucking stuff than you . . . What made you an artist, eh? Scared of real life were you? No, scared of your daddy! Jealous of you! Me? I know real murderers I'm jealous of—they're real *men*. Artists? Lot of fucking wankers!"

That is the last I remember of Christmas Day.

During the night he crawled into the bed and I thought he was pissing on me when I felt the cold wetness round my ear so I kicked him off the bed.

In the morning I found the whisky bottle resting against my back and I realised he had not been pissing on me. I remembered how violently I had kicked him and immediately wanted to apologise.

I got off the bed, still wearing his leather jacket. All that booze seemed to have turned my insides to steel and I did not feel too bad.

His head and shoulders were covered by the twisted blanket. His legs were sprawled off the single mattress across the carpet.

"You must be freezing, old son," I said, leaning over him to get hold of the raincoat.

Pulling the blanket down to his shoes I uncovered his head. Another whisky bottle was resting against his nose, a big wet stain running under his head.

I lifted the bottle.

Then I saw that his eyes were wide open and that the rest of his face was as dark as the big bruise.

*In 1784, when the government decided that the crowd
scenes provoked by the journey of condemned men
and women from Newgate to Tyburn were no longer
tolerable in a civilised society, Dr Samuel Johnson, often
claimed to be the greatest Englishman, said:*

*"Sir, Executions are designed to draw spectators. If they
do not draw spectators they do not answer their
purpose. The old method was most satisfactory to all
parties; the public was gratified by a procession; the
criminal is supported by it. Why is all this to be swept
away?"*

Ambrose Foggo, Esq,
Managing Editor,
Hodder and Stoughton,
London E.C.4.

Dear Mr Foggo,

Don't you ever read my letters? I will say it again—no
interviews. If the damned book is causing so much excitement
this late in the day why aren't my royalty cheques bigger? It
always causes me a modicum of bitter amusement when I hear
people like yourself describing writers as difficult people—
perhaps if you gave up your comfortable salary and lived each
day with the fear of poverty gnawing into your guts you, too,
might develop a less than equable temperament.

However, just to prove that I am not ungrateful for your part
in the book's success—a success, I must say, that owes little to
the awful jackets which have adorned each successive edition—I
have decided, reluctantly, to answer some of the questions which
seem to agitate you so much.

Yes, I have been back to London—once—during the last few
years. It was to see a fringe theatre production of *Tinkers'*

244

Welcome. Physically turning up is the author's best chance of getting the money.

Being unable to stay in the United Kingdom for more than a few days, in case the Inland Revenue, got on my trail, I only managed a quick look at The Rookery on my last afternoon. In that quick walk I did not see one face from the past—just as well, probably, for I've never heard of anyone being arrested for the murder of the man I called The Spoofer in the book.

For all I know the police may still looking for me under the name of John Thompson—another reason I don't want any personal publicity.

The Rookery was not the place I remembered—multistorey car-parks for the rich, government offices, entertainment 'complexes' and miniature freeways have crushed to oblivion most of the old rat-holes. Insurance offices stand where The Hum Drum was; what used to be The Rats' Castle is now a brewers' idea of a young persons' discotheque. All this delighted me—The Rookery was an evil, poisonous contagion; only those who didn't know it could ever be sentimental about its disappearance.

If only the memories could be obliterated as easily as the buildings.

In the book I tried to tell the truth. I realised that it did not portray me as sympathetically as I might have wanted but unlike the used-car salesmen of culture now exercising a ponce-like grip on what passes for British 'letters' (in the old days I knew a couple of ponces and would never underestimate their brutal virility), unlike these self-rewarding jackanapes the serious artist knows his first duty is to honesty.

You say it's often occurred to you that some of the people I put into the book might sue for libel. To identify themselves they would have to admit that I told the truth about them!

In fact, the one person I would seriously have liked to crucify got off very lightly—that middle-class bitch Morag Sutherland. She tried to brand me as a manipulative parasite who encouraged

Shand into his last alcoholic bout. (I know that you cannot find much newspaper coverage of the inquest in the cuttings library—what was Shand anyway but a largely forgotten minor Scottish dialogue writer?)

At the inquest the coroner pointed out that he would have died soon anyway, suffering as he was from degenerated heart, cirrhosis of the liver, malnutrition and cancer of the throat. The fact that he died by choking on his own vomit was possibly another reason for lack of newspaper interest.

In my evidence I said I'd met him alone and broke in The Rookery and merely tried to help him. The name I gave at the coroner's court was John Thompson. Nobody asked me for a birth certificate and that same afternoon I got a train from Euston to Holyhead and then a boat to Dublin. I had just over two hundred and fifty pounds and as I managed to give up drinking I was able to live on this for three months or so. During that time I applied for Irish nationality under my own name, Ian Mintlaw McGraw, having to send off to Edinburgh for a copy of my birth certificate. That was when I found out that I was born a year before my parents married.

Paradoxically, it was my obsession for revenge on that brute McMenemy which turned me into a professional writer. I had started to write a play, feeling that I could probably write at least as well as a bum like Shand, but each day I woke with a burning desire to crucify McMenemy. In those few moments in The Rats' Castle he had, I imagined, robbed me of my manhood. I started composing anonymous letters to Scotland Yard, telling them how Whately the Spoofer had conned seventy or eighty pounds from Terry Pilbeam the disc jockey, and how a man called Stan Callaghan had beaten him to recover the money. I had never forgiven *him* for holding my wrist in The Holy Land.

It was obvious that he had taken different bank-notes from Whately; what obviously happened then was that another person or persons came along while Whately was recovering from Callaghan's attentions and stabbed him to death. I suggested that

246

this person was Joseph McMenemy, a Glaswegian in his twenties, generally to be found in the pub known as The Rats' Castle. I said that I, the anonymous letter-writer, had been in the company of McMenemy and his accomplices a day or so later when they were spending ten-pound notes. I had even seen McMenemy with a knife, which they might search for at the bottom of the drain outside the pub.

Two things stopped me from posting this tip-off letter; one was the obvious fact that it hardly amounted to a watertight case against McMenemy, from whom I could never be safe unless he were locked up for life, and the other was that I might just conceivably be traced, either by the police or The Scots Team.

One morning I put two sheets and a carbon into Shand's portable Olympia and instead of a letter to the Murder Squad typed *Chapter One*. I had made no conscious decision to write a book and felt that I was only a medium *chosen by the book itself.*

In nine days, typing twelve hours a day in my disgusting Dublin lodgings, I finished an extremely violent chunk of ostensible fiction, having changed The Scots Team into West Indians and The Spoofer into a pickpocket. Remembering Neville talking about a woman literary agent he had met and failed to seduce at a party, I looked her up in the London directory in the O'Connell Street post office and posted the manuscript to her, humbly announcing myself as Jack Lang, a Scotsman living in the Republic, and wondering if the enclosed was worthy of her professional attentions.

She got me an advance of fifteen hundred pounds. The paperback still brings me in around two hundred a year.

How easy it all seemed then . . .

Fired by this success I tore into the play. Of course I stole the idea from Shand's rough draft. I deserved something from that nightmare, didn't I? And I couldn't write his story for the newspapers without revealing myself to all the people who were after me. In any case I didn't have the tapes—I threw them into the dustbin before the police arrived that morning. Those bloody policemen! I can still see the contempt on their faces. To them we were just Scotch derelicts dying in our own shit.

Anyway, I made a much better job of the play than Shand could have done. I am still hopeful of a commercial production—is there any chance you could pull a few strings? The money would solve most of my problems. With a little security I know I could easily cut down my drinking and get out of this rat-hole. A few thousand in the bank would probably persuade my wife to consider a reconciliation, ignorant Irish bitch that she is; I miss the child dreadfully. I only married her out of loneliness in Dublin—right from the start I could only make love to her by thinking desperately of Angela Browne in high boots.

I think of Angela Browne every day. My whole life is a lonely mess because I was too stupid to realise that she was the one woman in the world I could have loved.

Lonely? Nobody else knows what it means.

If only I could get a few thousand in the bank I could stop knocking out these dreadful Jack Lang paperbacks and write my Scottish novel. Scotland! Its memories are a deadweight on my back. I have taken a vow never to see the place again but it haunts me to despair.

Why won't the damned past leave me alone?

Hardly a day passes but I don't go to the cupboard and get out Ramsay Shand's black leather jacket and look at the dirty foolscap pages of his last pathetic stab at writing a play. I keep these pages folded in the inside pocket, just as he had them when I first met him. Every time I touch them I tell myself to burn them with the jacket.

Then, perhaps, the nightmare would be exorcised.

I go through it every bloody day.

I am in that stuffy little room. I am cold. My teeth are rattling against my upper denture plate. I am moaning little snatches of prayers, imploring God to help me. I know I should get up and phone for outside help but I am paralysed by guilt and fear. I pull the blanket over my head to blot out the dark face on the floor. Each time I try to move I hear angry voices calling for my punishment. I have helped to kill him.

I lie there for two or three hours; they are as long as a lifetime in Hell. Is he actually dead? Could he be revived, with expert attention? The kiss of life? I visualise myself crouching down to kiss his cold, dark sightless face, pressing my lips on his. I want to scream.

That is where I am perpetually trapped, in the longest of all the mornings. Am I being punished for having been born?

Yours sincerely,

Ian Mintlaw McGraw

PS. You can use this letter any way you want. Writing it has been extremely painful but perhaps therapeutic. Do I have any money to come? If not could you possibly see your way to letting me have a thousand in advance? I should be eternally grateful.